BEFORE ELEVATION

ARZIKI PHENYO

To order additional copies of this book, contact:
Bookwhip
1-855-339-3589
www.bookwhip.com

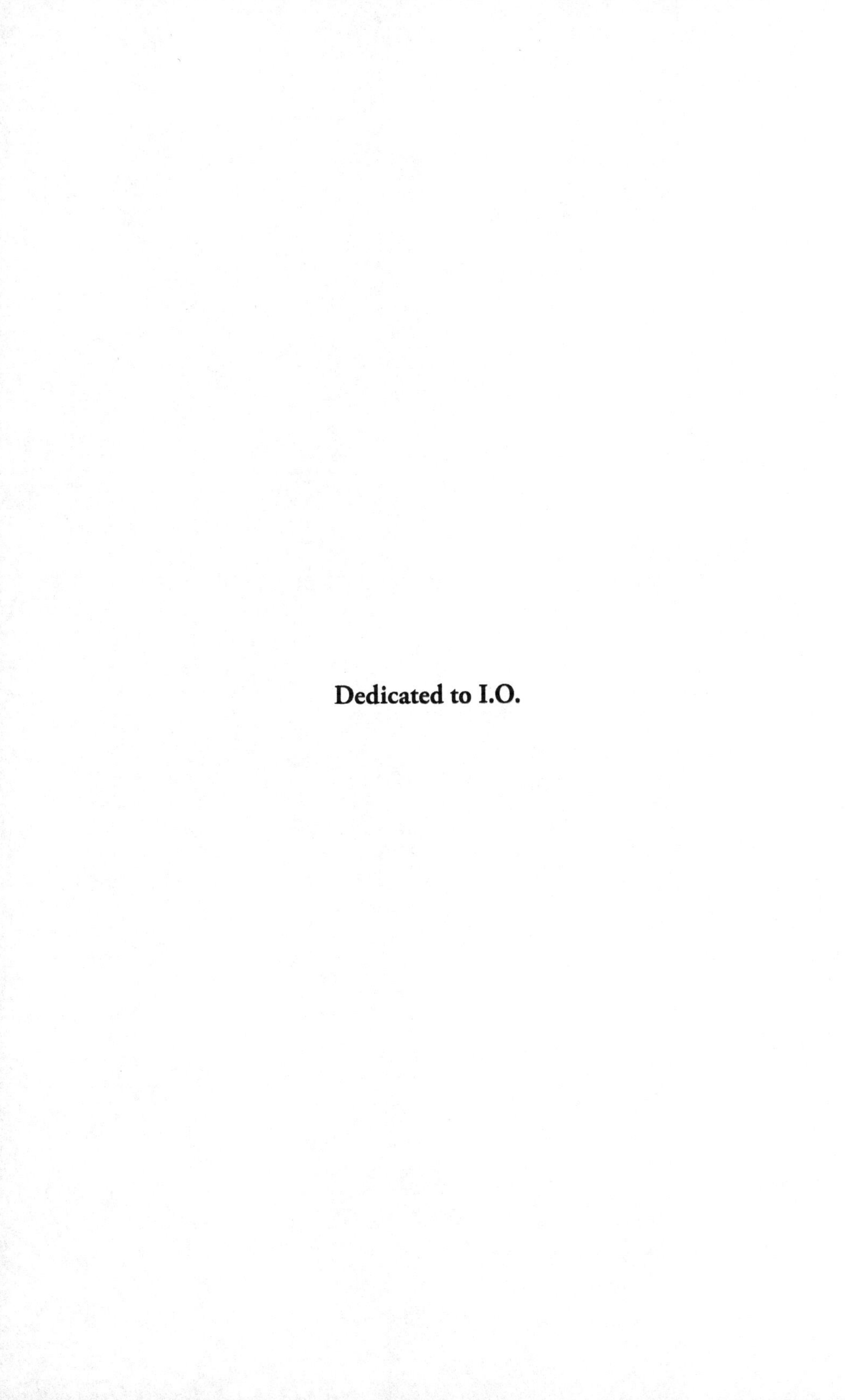

Dedicated to I.O.

TABLE OF CONTENTS

I

The home should be a seat of calm, serenity and peace of mind. It should stand as a convenient, if at times mundane, haven in which our worth is not measured by our paycheck, the model of our car, or the clothes we wear. Essentially, it should be the base from which we reconnect with our core, constituted of self, spirituality, and awareness.

"WHAT?" Rebecca Lewis screams to her husband upstairs. "WHAT DID YOU SAY? I'M DOWNSTAIRS ON THE PHONE… I HAVE THE DOCTOR'S APPOINTMENT AT 9, THE SALON APPOINTMENT AT 12, AND THE IPO MEETING AT 3. AND ALL THAT OTHER SHIT. I CAN'T DO IT."

The operative word is "should."

This morning—as it is most other mornings—the Lewis home is an ocean of deafening telephone rings, futile calls, and plaintive cries. It is overwhelmed by the excruciating clamor of Corporate America, and Rebecca Lewis is the one screaming. The kids are noisily pounding down the stairs and storming into the family room. Nevertheless, Rebecca is oblivious as she strains frantically to put her representative on hold. She places the phone back on her ear.

"Hey Laura… yeah I'm going to put you on hold, OK? You know how it is in the mornings. Yeah, so busy… I'm trying to get out; my husband getting ready for work; my kids going to school... It's just frantic... Uh huh, OK, all right, just one second."

She presses the "hold" button repeatedly. She checks to see if Laura is still there.

"OK," she says to herself as she lifts her phone up again. "All right, I think I actually got it right this time. Hello? What? Oh no. SHIT!"

To her dismay, Rebecca only hears silence.

"Shit, shit, shit", she says to herself. "I lost her. I knew I should have gotten a Galaxy. This is just fuckin' beautiful, *beautiful...*"

She hears her husband again.

"WHAT, YOU DIDN'T HEAR ME?" Rebecca yells toward the stairs. "I thought yelling maniacally at you for the last ten minutes would have accomplished something." She murmurs some more barely intelligible (but presumably colorful) phrases and takes a few deep breaths. "OK, I SAID—" Before she can complete the sentence, she hears her husband trudging down the circular staircase. This is the only sound, save for the phone and Laura's voice, which she has consciously heard all morning. Peter Lewis begins to form a friendly smile as he approaches his wife.

"I figured yelling down to you wasn't that good of an idea," he says while straightening his tie. Dr. Lewis shares his wife's snide matter-of-factness.

Rebecca lets out a sneering grin.

"What I was *saying* is—"

Angelina-Skye, the couple's 14-year-old daughter, rushes up to her mother.

"Mom, mom," she blurts out furiously.

"Yes honey," Rebecca replies with a sweet, affectionate smile as she gently strokes her hair.

"Can I take those last two Rice Krispies treats for lunch?"

"Sure can hon. And, it's, '*May I, may I,*'" she says exasperatingly. "How many times do we have to go through that?"

"Thanks mom," Angelina says and scampers off.

"Who's going to take Denver to his soccer game at 4?" her husband asks calmly.

"I thought Cindy was available? Well, I told you that I have the doctor's appointment at 9, the salon appointment at 12," she explains while pouring the orange juice. She is also meticulously arranging her coffee mugs. "The—"

"IPO meeting at 3 and all this other shit," Peter finishes.

"Oh, so you heard that part?" she says with a grin.

"Not really. I filled that in myself. But, you know we have that conference today; and, I'm the keynote speaker," he replies.

"Oh yeah, that's right. Well, good luck with that. I'll check again with Cindy (aren't we paying her for something?). If she can't, I'll see if I can get out of the meeting early or reschedule." Rebecca picks up the phone.

"Hey Laura," she says.

"Um, honey," starts Peter.

Rebecca turns to Peter with slight irritation.

"Babe, I'm on the phone."

"I don't think you are. Didn't you lose her?"

"Fuck. Right."

"Shhh, shhh," Peter says motioning "quiet down" with his hand.

"Oh whatever. They know it's bad to curse. I have to get her back on."

"You know what, forget it; I'll drop off Denver. I'll just make sure I get out of the conference right after I deliver the speech. Besides, I've missed the last three games. I should stay for this one."

"Thanks babe. Damn, Laura probably hopped on the train. I'll try to catch her later."

Rebecca is finally calming down.

"By the way, you think that soccer is helping him out? He's been so withdrawn for a while. I really want to get him out of his shell."

"Yeah I think so. He's talking more now. Oh, I've been meaning to tell you something." Peter slithers toward his wife. He hugs her from the back, snuggling her against his lower torso. Rebecca quietly purrs as his hands massage her waist.

"What?" Rebecca whispers.

"You know we haven't—"

"Why did you stop? I didn't hear anything?"

"I just wanted to make sure one of the kids wasn't around," he says as he perks up his ears.

"Oh," Rebecca says with a chuckle.

"You know we haven't had that much real time together in like the last *year* and I think I've got the solution." Peter whips out a brochure with "Summer Delights" emblazoned on the top. It features a couple in a contrived pose of delight and affection at the center.

"Are you serious?"

"A guy had a stand in Union Square and I figured I'd pick one up. Come on; just look at it for a little bit. It's this spa/resort facility down in Baja where couples go, and you know, have a little fun." He embraces Rebecca again and begins to run his hands around her hips. "I mean, we're both in dire need of that."

Rebecca rolls her eyes.

"Bec, just hear me out for once all right," Peter says with his voice raised.

"You sound like one of those couples who come on Dr. Phil," she begins mockingly and affects wiping tears. "Oh, we don't make love anymore. Oh, we're growing apart. Wa, wa—"

"Oh grow up," Peter rebuts. "You know it's true. I mean we've averaged, what, once every three weeks if we're lucky. You're OK with that?"

"Look, we're not like everyone else. We're both busy, driven people with very demanding careers. On top of that, we have two kids. And, besides, that's not the most important part of a relationship."

Rebecca Lewis is CEO of Windows to the Soul. It is a web-based company (www.windowstothesoul.com) that sells sunglasses and prescription lenses engraved with spiritual words of wisdom (their slogan is, "We'll help you see the light"). When the company began in 2008, it focused solely on sunglasses. But, with several years of strong performance, Windows to the Soul expanded to headbands, watches, and other accessories. Some media buzz has also helped with growth. Its fun and sophisticated image has really caught on with the public—namely, Hollywood stars—who regularly sport the latest models. Windows to the Soul's marketability has not been lost on Wall Street insiders; the company is gearing up to go public in six months.

Peter Lewis is a distinguished neurosurgeon. Though he still performs surgeries (about 20 per year), much of Peter's time is now devoted to research. Currently, he and his team are examining genetic contributors to Alzheimer's disease, Parkinson's disease, and other cognitive disorders. He was appointed chair of the New York State Neurosurgical Society after a series of leading-edge dementia studies by his research team. For the last five years, he also has been contracting as a consultant with some of the country's leading facilities. Additionally, he serves as a visiting professor at Columbia University, and is a frequent contributor to JAMA.

Actually, his and Rebecca's work have made them celebrities of sorts. They have made a variety of TV appearances and have recently been featured in *People* magazine. Not surprisingly, they are asked frequently to participate in community and charity events, and they usually respectfully decline (preferring to donate money rather than their time).

"Yeah, maybe too driven," Peter mutters.

"Fine, we'll talk about this later." She grabs the brochure out of her husband's hand. She starts moving her pointer finger across the title as she reads it.

"*Summer Delights*," Rebecca says to Peter derisively. "I guess it's better than the 'Wet Dreams' one you picked up before."

"Oh admit it; you liked that. It had a *touch* of subtlety."

"Yeah, as subtle as a cock up my—"

"Why is it always like that with you?" Peter intrudes. "Everyone else is stupid, and you're the sole voice of reason right?"

"Yeah, I thought we've already established that."

Peter lets out an exasperated sigh.

"*No*, just kidding," Rebecca says as she lovingly strokes her husband's back. Peter is hunched over the kitchen counter with his arms crossed. An annoyed grimace waxes on Rebecca's face.

"What's wrong?" Peter asks.

"Angelina put the plates in the wrong place again. I'm always telling her about that. She knows my system… Anyway, I'm sorry honey, and I'm not trying to be difficult. I just don't think we need the resort. But on second thought, that 'Wet Dreams' one may not have been such a bad idea. That S and M class did sound interesting."

Peter gives her a quizzical glance, as Denver, their 10-year-old son, is walking down from his room. He is scrolling through Snapchat, as he does every day before school, to see new comments from his schoolmates. "Why is Denver still alive?"; "Denver's a fag"; and "If he's so smart, why is his hair rekt?" are some of the messages this morning. He spotted a picture of Tyrion Lannister with the words,

"The difference is Denver never gets out" on Instagram. He turns to his parents without any hesitation.

"What's S and M?" Denver asks curiously from the stairs. He is waiting for his parents to finish their conversation.

"Oh, hey Denver. Are you almost ready?" Rebecca says within a millisecond.

Rebecca quickly files the brochure under her robe. Denver nods his head while making his way toward the kitchen. His golden blond hair rhythmically bobs as he walks. He grabs an apple from the fridge and places it gingerly in his lunch bag. His mother stops him as he heads toward the stairs.

"Why didn't you comb your hair?" Rebecca says as Denver restlessly fidgets. "You should take extra care of those beautiful blond locks." Denver's hair is just like hers. "You know how they bring out those sparkling green eyes of yours." They are also just like hers. "And, your shirt's all wrinkled." Ms. Lewis affectionately smooths out the oversized "Nike" shirt hanging from his thin frame. "I think it's time for the live-in nanny again."

"Mom," Denver starts.

"Yes dear?"

"I don't feel like going to school today. I don't want to go to my soccer game either."

"Oh honey, we all feel like that sometimes. Honestly, I haven't been feeling that well lately either; but, I still do what I need to do. Don't worry, the soccer game'll be fun. You'll have a great time."

"But, I really don't want to go," he says as he gives his mother a weary stare.

"Denver... Denver..." he wasn't responding. "Oh stop. You'll be all right. Go upstairs and get your books OK. You're gonna be late."

Denver takes a labored breath and lumbers up the stairs.

Peter comes out from the bathroom. "What happened?"

"Nothing. It was just Denver."

"Is he all right?"

"Yeah. He seemed OK. Just a little tired."

"Hey babe, you better start getting ready. It's almost 7:30. Only if you want to go to the meeting like that."

Rebecca is in a pink bathrobe with disheveled hair and sloppy makeup. Peter rubs a lock of his wife's hair between his fingers, inspecting it.

"That's why you're going to the salon right?"

She looks at herself through the refrigerator door and recoils in terror.

"Well, I have one look down…new client at the Seaside Substance Abuse Clinic."

"No, it's more like 'fringe couture' to me. Just hurry upstairs and get ready."

Rebecca rushes up to the bedroom to throw on her clothes. She misses the interaction her daughter is having in the neighboring room.

"Hey Chris. Thanks for making time to talk this morning," Angelina-Skye chirps through the Duo app.

"I always have a little time for you," Chris returns with a warm smile. "You had an idea for this year's outreach event right?"

"I did. Oh, congratulations on the official promotion to Northeast Youth Director for UN Ambassadors. You've put so much into the organization. Nobody deserves it more than you do."

"I'm really excited Angelina. And, I'm even happier to be able to work more with motivated kids like you."

Angelina lowers her head as she blushes, and a humble smile sneaks on her face.

"Right, I still have to tell you about the outreach idea. The focus of the relief work in Africa has been distributing food and supplies to families, which is totally needed. I was thinking we could put a little more focus on the kids, especially with helping schools acquire needed resources, and setting up computer labs that could be used across different sites. Me and the other ambassadors (but, honestly, it'll probably end up being me) can research practical areas in Congo, Mozambique, and South Africa."

"That's a great idea Ange. We have to start looking at sponsors, and also consider how to make up for infrastructural shortfalls (think about coordinating with Project Loon). After the team meeting on Wednesday, we'll talk more."

"Thanks Chris. I know you have to go. Wow, I gotta head off to school."

"Sure, see you Wednesday."

"One more thing Chris," Angelina blurts out as she quickly curls up her shirt.

"What—?"

Angelina is already bouncing in her chair, her full, bare breasts bobbing as her curled up shirt rests just above her chest.

"I've been planning that since last week," Angelina says coquettishly.

"I thought we weren't doing that anymore? But, my deepest, heartfelt thanks."

"I knew you'd appreciate it. See you Wednesday babe. Gotta go."

"That's a great place to end. See you Wednesday."

Angelina is making her way out of the room.

Rebecca quickly gulps down three more Oxycontin pills, and stuffs the container into her Versace handbag. She is still relieved that the alias slipped through for the other Vicodin prescription. As Rebecca closes the bedroom door, Angelina bumps into her mother.

"Oh sorry."

"That's OK dear."

"You like this new outfit?" Angelina-Skye begins to turn around, putting her lustrous red hair and long body in a flirty whirl. She models a pair of black, metallic, low-rise jeans topped with a red and black polyester shirt clinging to her precociously developed 14-year-old body. "Will put out for $15" is printed in red across her chest. The ensemble is completed with black, five-inch platform boots.

"Isn't the rate higher now," Rebecca responds. "Why the hell are you wearing that?'"

"Oh this?" Angelina says pointing to her tee shirt. "It's just a shirt."

Angelina catches a picture featuring Rebecca, Rebecca's mother, and Rebecca's stepfather near the kitchen.

"Hey, how come your dad never gets us stuff, needless to say come over. I mean, when's the last time we saw 'im?"

"*Him, him.* There's a lot of reasons honey. It gets complicated. When you have a family, you'll understand what I mean. Besides, he keeps in touch. He sends you and Denver money a couple of times a year."

"Yeah OK, 20 bucks."

Rebecca shrugs her shoulders.

"Are you and your parents cool?"

"Yes, everything is fine Angel. What you need to worry about is getting ready for school. Tell your brother to get his stuff and come down here."

"Denver? He just stormed up to his room and shut the door a couple of minutes ago. I'll see if I could get 'im down."

Rebecca is already out of the kitchen. The kids come down after a few minutes.

"Come on! Let's go! Sam's mom is outside!" Rebecca cries.

"Hurry up," Peter echoes.

"We're coming! We're coming!" Skye yells.

Angelina is playfully caressing the family's Yorkshire terrier, Annie Hall (Peter and the kids deferred to mom for that one) and goes toward the backyard. Skye opens up the screen door and lets her into the doghouse (Doghouse is really an understatement; it is actually a miniature, loosely adapted version of Frank Lloyd Wright's *Falling Waterhouse*, enveloped by soaring sunflowers. "Animals also appreciate aesthetics," Rebecca frequently says).

"Hey mom, you look a lot better now," Angelina says. Denver and his mom release a little smirk. Now, Rebecca is wearing a long, lime green jacket over a matching top, and flared pants. A pair of emerald heals complement the outfit. "Thanks, honey. OK, go on now."

"Oh mom I wanted to ask you, when can we start working on the volcano for my science project?"

"Volcano? No honey, you have to do something more creative."

"Like what?"

"Oh, like if surplus sodium compounds disrupt the process of reuptake in synapses. Your father can help you with that," Rebecca Lewis says nonchalantly.

"Yeah, you're right. Maybe we can do that."

"We'll play around with some ideas. You've won the science fair the last three years. We wouldn't want to break that streak now would we?"

"Nope, not at all," Angelina smiles back. "When are we going to start preparing for the National Merit Tournament? It's coming up in October."

"We'll start before the end of the month, in two weeks. Don't worry we'll get you in prime shape for that. Maybe we could get to the Nationals this time," Rebecca says sweetly. "Sam's mom has been honking the last five minutes. Have a great day guys. LOVE YOU!"

Rebecca hears Peter get off the phone.

"Who were you talking to babe?"

"I was just talking to Dr. Schleindman about leaving the conference a little earlier. I'll be at the game."

"Great. Well, I should start going."

"Yeah, me too. Let me grab my files. I should make sure the presentation saved on the flash."

"They're right over there." Rebecca points to the dining room table. She feels a migraine coming on. She painfully closes her eyes and furrows her brows as she rubs her temples.

"Is everything all right Bec?" Peter asks his wife with a concerned look.

"Yeah, I'm OK. I think I left my tablet upstairs." She fumbles through her bag. "Damn. Now I have to go back up."

"Are you sure because I remember you putting it in this morning, about a half hour ago."

"Yeah, I thought so, but I think I took it out. You don't see it here do you?"

Peter looks around and shakes his head.

Rebecca starts up the stairs.

"Well, I really have to go hon. I love you babe."

"Love you too." Rebecca almost whispers from the top of the stairs.

"Hey Bec. Come down here for a second."

She rushes downstairs. "What?"

He quickly snatches her, embracing her in a passionate, wet kiss. He releases her.

"You always knew how to use that tongue of yours."

"You remember?" Peter responds. She whacks him on his arm. "Ouch! Hey, how about over here?" Peter then bends over with his behind protruding, awaiting his wife.

"Maybe we should go to that spa. KIDDING, KIDDING."

"All right. Love you."

"Love you. Bye honey."

Rebecca lumbers up the stairs as she watches the red BMW pull out from behind the fence. She let him take it today. He spots her and gives her another wave as he pulls out of the driveway.

Peter docks his iPhone as he arrives at the next block.

"Right, I was supposed to FaceTime Amber at 7:15. I hope I can still get her."

The phone dials the promising neuroscience student. Amber Crenshaw answers after one ring.

"Hi Dr. Lewis."

"Hi Amber. Thanks for answering. So sorry about missing our 7:15. It's always at least a little hectic in the mornings."

"No, I understand. And, I didn't want to intrude and call you, in case something happened."

"Oh, not at all. My line is always open for you. You can get in touch any time," Peter reassures warmly.

Amber returns a bright smile.

"I remembered the presentation about ultrasound therapy, for relieving Parkinson's tremors, the University of Virginia team gave last month at the conference. It made me think about how other treatments should be further explored or modified, including deep brain stimulation. As we know, the areas that have been conventionally targeted by DBS are the thalamus, subthalamic nucleus, and the globus pallidus interna; but, perhaps, stimulation—and increased activation—of the posterior precentral gyrus, the central sulcus, and the vermis, directly, toward improving movement through enhanced motor relay, may be even more promising. Furthermore, we could investigate the effects of using staggered pulsation rates—namely, varying durations of longer pulses, that may have more resonance and a more enduring impact on the brain, versus a rapid succession of pulses that can get the brain "amped" and raise activation levels more quickly—on movement and the frequency of tremors. You think that research should be pursued?"

"I think that could be quite promising Amber. We can start with a 3 x 2 design to assess the impact of DBS on the precentral gyrus, the central sulcus, and the vermis, and the effect of protracted pulses and rapid-fire pulses concurrently. Thanks, especially, for highlighting the vermis, along with the sulcus and gyrus. I think cerebellar and cerebral cortex activity can be overlooked, even among leading-edge treatments. Have you started on a proposal?"

"Thanks for the encouragement Dr. Lewis. No, I haven't. I've been flirting with it in my head; but, I wanted to discuss it with an experienced researcher in the field, and get the imprimatur, so to speak, before moving forward. Thanks for taking the time to listen, and for the feedback."

"No, thank you Amber. I knew you were a woman of incisive ideas when we met at the conference last month. The work to which you contributed, even as an undergrad at Cambridge, is impressive. What you have this morning are just more examples.

We don't want to lose sight of the neurotransmitter aspect though. Stimulation of those areas could, potentially, raise dopamine levels for instance. Oh, an Australian research group has been studying how Parkin helps maintain cells and prevent cell death by inhibiting BAK while also reducing inflammation by restoring mitochondria. Findings should be published in the December *EMBO Journal*, a little less than three months from now. Fruitful studies can come from centering on approaches for preventing, or stemming, Parkin attenuation. There is also a case for delving into protein clumps and PD onset, and how misfolded proteins, that can trigger Parkinson's, are rooted in the gut or parts of the digestive system. We have to attack from all sides, and stay vigilant of threats no matter—"

"From where they arise. You are so right Dr. Lewis. I don't know how much longer I have at the lab though. Their budget is being cut; and, I'm afraid I'll be among the first ones to go. I hope I can continue to pursue my research."

"Sorry to hear that Amber. A lot of labs have been suffering that fate. But, with the work you've done in such a short period of time, I know you'll get snapped up quickly."

"I hope you're right Dr. Lewis. I just need a team who thinks that these ideas are worthwhile."

"These could not only open new areas of inquiry; they could lead to improved, if not new, treatments. Indisputably, these are excellent ideas."

Peter reflects for a moment.

"You know, we could use another hand in our lab. You can work with us."

Amber speaks through tears.

"Thank you so much Dr. Lewis. You sure? Only if there's space for me."

"There is. And, even if there weren't, I'd make space for someone as talented as you. There's always opportunity for brilliance."

Amber wipes away burgeoning tears.

"I am so touched Dr. Lewis. It would be an *indisputable* honor to work alongside you. When do you think I can start?"

"I have some surgeries next week; and, we need to talk to the Foundation to raise the allocation for salaries and benefits first…we should be ready by October 10th."

"I'm really looking forward to this Dr. Lewis. I promise I won't let you down."

"I trust that Amber. We're lucky to have you as part of the team. I think you'll help us pursue promising new directions."

"Well, you'll be in firm control of that direction Dr. Lewis."

"In several years, you'll be captaining your own ship."

"That's the goal. But, I'll never mind being under you."

Rebecca rises from the bed.

"I think that kiss helped a little. Maybe we *should* have more sex," she says to herself.

She makes her way up the stairway. It is decorated with posters displaying words of spiritual wellness. Many of them are used on her products. "Even in the darkness we can find light," the first one reads. "Serenity is the broom that will sweep up the disquietude and unrest that clutter your soul," reads another. Rebecca has never been fond of that one. However, the scene with the Colorado Rockies in the background featuring a woman sitting serenely in a meditative position always beckons at her.

Rebecca is tempted to begin rearranging her shoes into color-coded rows, but stops herself. She takes her tablet from her pillow and plops down on the center of the luxuriant, canopy bed.

"I'm glad we got rid of that revolving, heart-shaped one a couple of years ago," she says smiling to herself. "Whoa, those were different times."

Rebecca starts to look around. Mementos and golden-lined photo frames adorn the peach bedroom wall. She sets her eyes on the enlarged version of her and Peter's first vacation picture hanging above her bureau. "It was '99. That's my excuse," she remarks as she sees herself doing her best "Rachel."

At the side of the bed are the Mickey Mouse hats they bought at Disney World lying on three-legged stands. Rebecca smiles contently. Right below is a photo taken during Denver's delivery.

"I gained so much weight with him," she says to herself.

The photo of Angelina's delivery is to the left of it.

"That's the first time it wasn't a mistake," she says.

Rebecca rises from the bed and walks across the Persian rug. She takes a few moments and gazes at the copy of *The False Mirror* by Magritte on the wall. She then walks to the dressing table and hurriedly tidies up the bottom drawer. At the right is a tattered, brunette doll. It has grown yellow with age; but, its faded, childlike face still proves affecting. She cuddles it for a moment and neatly places it back in the drawer.

"Breaking Bad," "Game of Thrones," and John Legend posters surround her as she enters Angelina's room ("I like older men," Rebecca recalls Angelina saying). Six of Angelina's paintings also line the wall ("My little cubist," Rebecca would frequently call her), along with pictures from the Christmas dinner she helped to organize in the Mott Haven section of the Bronx last year.

Lying beside the display of her daughter's awards is her lace diary. Rebecca runs her fingers over the cover, and manages to restrain herself from opening it. On the table near the computer is the story Angelina is working on for creative writing: "Little Lara: The Girl Who Conquered Silicon Valley." Rebecca promised she would give her some ideas. A "24" magnet is on the bottom left of the monitor, right next to a banner from the "Inspi(red)" campaign. She actually left her computer on today; it is on the "Democracy Now" website. A vintage "Austin Powers" doll is perched on the top of the system. Angelina stuck a pin in the middle, so it would incessantly say, "Do I make you horny baby? Well, do I?" Rebecca rips it out.

On Angelina's lamp stand is a notebook featuring an emaciated, peaked young woman. A cigarette dangles between the middle and pointer fingers of her right hand. It reads, "If I were 5'10" I could be a supermodel," at the bottom. "Yeah me too," Rebecca says forlornly. "I was screwed three inches. At least I'm a 40C." Hanging from Angelina's door is a tee shirt with the message "#1 Bitch." Angelina would probably wear it tomorrow. Rebecca shakes her head.

Rebecca catches the time on the clock. "Damn, I really have to go."

Before making her way downstairs, Rebecca checks herself out in the bathroom. She looks at the "With the Spirit, I can do it all" bumper sticker pasted next to her bathroom mirror before walking out. She passes by Denver's room and sees his iPad.

"He left it?" Rebecca says as she walks into her son's room. There is a towering bookshelf on the right side where Peter keeps some of his favorite books along with Denver's. There are some copies of neuroscience texts at the left, with the "Divine Comedy," "Merchant of Venice," "Hamlet," and "Romeo and Juliet" standing prominently in the center. Rebecca recalls how the walls boom during the "shows" Dr. Lewis often puts on for Denver, in which he trumpets lines from the famous plays. The ice blue space is basically bare save for some pictures on the wall, all featuring variations of a drawing of a young boy. The boy's face is always rendered with great detail, down to the ridges on his nose and the lines around his cheek. They are done in different colors, as if to indicate mood. An incomplete poem, entitled "Only a Single Tear Falls," lies on his desk. Rebecca quickly glances at it. After checking one last time on all the doors, she makes her way down the staircase. Rebecca tip-toes through the spectral array of flowers and the orange gravel to the Pathfinder. The CEO of Windows to the Soul takes a deep breath and pulls out of the driveway.

II

"My kids never acted like that," Rebecca says smugly. Two little boys are horsing around wildly in the back of the blue Honda Accord to the right of her. Rebecca is on I-87 making her way to New York. It is jammed as usual. She fiddles with a deodorizer branded with the words, "The mind is my tool; the Spirit is my guide" that hangs from her car mirror. She is scrolling through the library of spiritual wellness, Joni Mitchell, and Simon and Garfunkel songs on her iPod. "The Sound of Silence" now fills the black SUV.

"Finally, we're moving. Maybe we can surpass the 15 miles-per-hour rate today," she mutters snidely.

Just as the traffic begins to move, a white Chevy Blazer sidles up to cut Rebecca off. Rebecca applies slight pressure on the accelerator and pummels the horn. Indignantly, she opens the window and yells out.

"NOT GONNA HAPPEN ASSHOLE!" she yells. "FUCKIN' BASTARD!"

Rebecca settles down and begins taking deep breaths. "Once they get a 4x4 they think they own the road." She stops herself. "Hey, that's me." She leans forward, raising her head to the left and peaks at the license plate. "Oh, Jersey. Figures."

Rebecca turns to her right and catches a friendly-looking man in his late-30s with curly, auburn hair and warm, olive skin in a black Audi. He gives her an inviting, tenderly flirtatious smile. She offers a shy but coquettish grin. Rebecca quickly turns into the exit.

∞◦◦ ▶◀ ◦◦∞

Pink Floyd's "Us and Them" drifted atop the din of the television, phone rings, and small talk at Dr. Grossberg's office.

"You know Jeff, I can never get tired of listening to *Dark Side of the Moon*. I just drift into this enchanting state of poignant rumination and pensive reflection."

Dr. Grossberg laughs wryly. "I couldn't have said it better myself. You want to get on the scale."

"Oh sure."

Dr. Grossberg walks over. He jots down the number. "Hmm," he says to himself.

"*Hmm*? That doesn't sound good. I knew I shouldn't have had two pieces of that chocolate chip double cheesecake last night. I gained weight didn't I?"

"No, actually you lost a lot. You're down about 17 pounds from last year."

"Really? Well, it's not that big of a deal."

"Well, it can turn into one. Have you been under a lot of stress, any discomfort?"

"Not any more than I'm used to. Just the occasional headache. Well, sometimes I do have a little shortness of breath and chest pains, but not often."

"Really? Well, just to make sure everything is OK, I'll set up an appointment with the radiology clinic."

"I'm sure it's nothing. I'm very healthy."

"No, those symptoms are a little concerning. I also want you to come by in a month or so. How about October 13?"

Rebecca takes out her phone and looks at the calendar.

"That should be fine. I'll let you know by next week if it isn't."

"By the way, how's Peter doing?"

"Oh great. They have a big neurosurgeons' conference today; and, he's the keynote speaker. He's going to leave early though to catch Denver's soccer game."

"Well, family comes first. The nurse will give you a call later this afternoon to confirm the appointment."

"All right Jeff. Take care."

Rebecca Lewis quietly enters the Windows to the Soul office on 46th and 9th. Windows to the Soul's 25th floor offices are a little more than a proverbial stone's throw from the craziness (or energy, as some might call it) of the too-much-is-never-enough embodiment of corporate excess that is the detoxified Times Square. Peter would always ask his wife when he could stop by and see her office. He has dropped her off and picked her up here; but, he has yet to actually go inside. Rebecca has never been very comfortable bringing her husband around.

Windows to the Soul's office is right across from the elevator. The company's shimmering blue and white logo beckons. Four offices comprise the company's central suite, inhabited by members who have been with the company since its beginning.

The first office belongs to Alexander Cortés, Windows to the Soul's CIO. His cotton, pale-green shirt rests casually on his khakis, and his Converse sneakers are crossed on the table. Alexander is 5'10"; but, his lengthy, almost awkward, legs make him look more like 6'2". His square hands fumble through his curly, chestnut fade. There is not much on his desk except for his laptop, the haphazardly arranged Windows to the Soul notepads and papers, a calendar (he has been marking off the days till his 29th birthday) and a Halle Berry picture ("The only reason I saw the Flintstones movie," he once told Rebecca).

Some books containing the works of Descartes, Nietzsche, and Rousseau also decorate the desk. But, his walls are replete with glossies and posters of the world's most desired women—Giselle Bundchen, Angelina Jolie, Jessica Alba, Tyra Banks, and Marilyn Monroe among them. A deflated blowup doll of a model in the nude is cleverly hidden in his desk (Alexander only exhibits it when she is away).

To the left is Mimi Scott's office, Windows to the Soul's Artistic Coordinator (the staff is still trying to determine exactly what that means). Mimi had on a snug, pink, fuzzy Cardigan sweater that wore tightly around her bosom. It truncates at her bold yellow, latex miniskirt. Naturally, black-striped stockings peak out from behind her towering, green platform boots.

Trolls on homemade stages dot the desk. One is actually hanging on the side of her rolling, strawberry-auburn hair. Her metallic blue fingernails are tapping on the "Legalize Marijuana!" sticker on her table (the country finally caught up to her). A "Pisces/Gemini rising" sticker is on the bottom of her drawer. "Free Tibet!" and "Mr. Owl, how many licks does it take to get to the Tootsie Roll center of a Tootsie Pop?" are the screensavers on her phone (everyone in the office took the latter as a double entendre). Assorted Barbie dolls in Native American or East-Asian outfits, standing on painted rainbow doilies, circle her desk. A picture of her and her boyfriend, Max, in a sensual hug is in the middle. She would give it a little kiss numerous times a day. Right now, Mimi is reviewing designs for upcoming Windows to the Soul products, preparing for the Zoom conference with her San Francisco colleagues at 1:30pm (she would put on the navy-blue cardigan for that one).

Xavier Marx (affectionately called "commi" on some days), Windows to the Soul's COO, is right next to Lisa's office. Xavier is wearing a black fisherman's hat on top of his clean-shaven head. A fine, neat goatee encompasses his full, round lips. An understated gem gleams from his right ear. Flowing over his charcoal pants is a red, silk shirt, thinly masquerading his toned body. The leather jacket, which matches the rest of the outfit, cushioned the back of his chair. His black, leather boots add about two inches to his 6'3" person.

There are several issues of *Vanity Fair*, *The Source,* and *The Atlantic* on his desk. He is scrolling through The Washington Post site now. A charm with "Marx 9-28-79" hangs from his jacket, draping the back of his chair. He switches between an Access file, detailing the performance of Window to the Soul's summer issues, and a video of Bob Dylan's "Blowing in the Wind" on YouTube. A picture of his gorgeous girlfriend, Adaora, is placed on the right side ("My heavenly Nigerian chocolate," he would always call her). He is smiling and laughing on the phone with her now, pleasantly distracted from his analysis as he twists the ring (not engagement yet, "commitment") on his long, sturdy right finger. George Carlin and Albert Einstein quotes now run across his computer's screen ("My two favorite White guys," Xavier would always say), with a Stanford sticker posted on top. Shrunken works of Kandinsky, Rubens, Rembrandt, and Vermeer punctuate the left end of his desk.

Rebecca walks toward the central server in the back of the room. Mimi looks up from her tablet and realizes Rebecca came in. She bolts from her chair and darts toward the CEO. "HEY REBECCA!" Mimi exclaims while embracing her in a big hug and kissing her on the cheek.

This has been a ritual since 2008. "Hey Mimi," Rebecca reciprocates with a friendly smile.

"You did something with your hair?" Alexander remarks.

"Yeah, you like it?" Rebecca coquettishly runs her hands through it. She has a layered look with flipped ends.

"It looks hot. It really brings out those green eyes," Alexander says.

"Thanks," Rebecca replies with a bright smile.

Rebecca sits down at the swivel chair right in front of the server.

"Up to a lot of hard work here huh? Espn.com, hipsternation.com, oh even bustybabes.com… I prefer comelycocks.com myself." Rebecca heads to her desk. She passes by Rhonda Byrne's *The Secret*, Gary Zukov's *Seat of the Soul*, and James Redfield's *The Celestine Prophecy*. She's slightly into Abd-Ru-Shin's *In the Light of Truth* lying at the top left of her desk. Rebecca quickly checks her stocks and scrolls through her e-mail.

"Hello Ms. Lewis," Xavier says in a faux British accent.

"Hey Xavier, nice accent," Rebecca says without taking her eyes away from the computer. "Wassup!" she says after looking up at him in an affected urban accent.

"We're still doing that?" Xavier asks.

Rebecca gives a resigned shrug. "I'm still White."

Xavier sidles up to Rebecca's desk. One of the pictures strikes him.

"I've seen this picture for three years, and I've been meaning to ask you who this is." Xavier holds up a picture of a tall, tanned man with shoulder-length hair. He is wearing a Nirvana shirt, boot-cut jeans, and Doc Martens. "Is this Peter?"

"Oh no," Rebecca says bursting out laughing. "That's a guy from high school. His name was Anthony D'Anino; but, we called him 'Shaft.'"

"Shaft? He's Italian," Xavier says with a laugh.

"Well he had a long, you know..."

"Oh OK," Xavier says nodding his head. "You guys went out?"

"Yeah, the whole of senior year."

"Cool. He's a good-looking guy. How was he?"

"You mean like that?"

"No, I meant like personality-wise. But if you want to share details..." Xavier says playfully.

"Oh, he was very sweet. Really thoughtful and intelligent," Rebecca says wistfully as she reminisces. "We would always have the greatest conversations. I think he's a big real-estate lawyer now. We really loved each other. You know, he was my first time."

"Really? That's always special."

"But, he went off to Berkeley and I stayed back East. We still kept in touch and talked to each other; but, we just realized that it wouldn't work out."

"It doesn't make it any easier though."

"There was a lot of tension created in my house by the whole relationship. My mom thought we were getting too serious, and my stepfather didn't like him very much. Well come to think about it, he wasn't too thrilled about anything I did. We were never close. I guess I just grew tired of all the aggravation."

"Well, you met a great guy anyway. It all worked out."

"Yeah I guess you're right. It's just that I've always had these problems with my family and—"

Rebecca hears the e-mail alert on her phone.

"It's an invitation from the Seavers. It looks like a party at the Westchester Supper Club."

Xavier takes a look at the invitation.

"You go to that crap?"

"What do you mean?"

"It sounds like one of those bourgeois, self-congratulatory parties."

"Hold up!" Rebecca says with her hands up in the air.

"Huh? What was that?"

"Just a weird reaction. I was just trying to be Black again."

"Oh OK," Xavier replies.

"Look, I'll be the first one to tell you that Westchester is full of snobby White people; but, the Seavers are very nice. Anyway, I don't think I'm going. I'll probably be in Chicago that week anyway. You know, I dated a Black guy once," Rebecca adds with a smug whisper.

"Oh, you wanted to find out if our dicks were really that huge?"

"Xavier!"

"Just kidding. Was he Obama Black or *really* Black?

"Are you kidding? He was a 100%, dark chocolate brotha. Straight up…" Rebecca extends her hand to Xavier as if to signal a cue.

"Nigga?" he finishes. "Whoa. Straight outta Rochester, right?"

"Shut up," Rebecca says laughing. "Oh, why is she texting me now?"

"Who?"

"Angelina-Skye."

"How did you and Peter come up with these names? Were you guys raised on one of those hippy communes?"

"Nope, close though—the mean streets of Rochester, New York."

Xavier starts laughing.

"No, it was the 2000s, new-age resurgence…She wants to hang out with her friend after school."

"Did you get anything from Peter?"

"Yeah, I'm reading it right now. I thought he was too busy today. I guess not."

"He probably missed you."

"He's just talking about his day."

"Could I ask you something?"

"You know, why do people even ask that question? I mean, you'll look like an ass if you say no. What is it?" Rebecca says as she is reviewing the compliance report for the IPO meeting.

"When's the last time you've been through the turnstile?"

"Wow, I guess I am old. Is that what they call it now?"

"I'm asking seriously. It just seems like you've been really worked up lately. I'm sure you and Peter don't have that much quality time together."

"*I know. I know,*" Rebecca groans. "Truthfully, it has been a while. It's just that now both of us are so busy and there's *so much* going on. It took some years to get this company off the ground, and I want to maintain the momentum. He and the research team are making great strides; and, he has so many consulting projects lined up. Added to all that, we have the kids. Most days I'm exhausted by the time I get home. We'll get back on track once things settle down."

"Everybody says that; but, they never do. You need to make time."

"I understand, and we do. Just not as much time as we would like."

Rebecca turns back to her laptop and goes through the presentation she will show the H&M executive in the afternoon. She then looks back at Xavier.

"I've always promised myself that no matter what, I'd make my life a success; and, maybe that takes away from other parts of my life. But honestly, I wouldn't trade it."

"I can't say you haven't done that," Xavier responds. "How did you guys meet anyway?"

"Well, I went to business school at NYU. I was coming out of a bar in Chelsea and I accidentally bumped into him. I was scared at first, since he had this really angry look on his face, like he wanted to kick my ass (I didn't know his sense of humor yet). Then he assured me that he was just kidding; it was all right. Peter said he liked my shirt (it was this tight V-neck) and I said, 'thanks.' I know he was checking out my chest; but, I really didn't care. He was cute anyway. We started talking and I asked him what he did. He said he's a doctor at Columbia Presbyterian. I asked him where he went to school, Columbia and Cornell, and we started talking about college. We just hit it off immediately."

"Was it love at first sight?"

"In retrospect yes. But, at the time I just thought of it as instant friendship, and lust. I thought he was really hot. I hadn't felt that strongly about a guy in a long time. He's just one of those people, and anybody who knows him will tell you the same thing, that you feel so comfortable with instantly. He has this acerbic wit and cutting sarcasm, but can be so understanding when you need it. Some people say we share the sarcasm thing. I don't see it."

"I wonder myself."

"You just feel like you can tell him anything. There are times when I'm a little guarded, but not with him. I just started to tell him everything and he reciprocated it. We must have spent hours talking. I think I had a report due the next day, and he surgery the next morning; but, we didn't care. I even told him about my relationships. You know what he said to me?"

"What?"

"'That's OK. The slutty girls are better anyway,'" Rebecca and Xavier laugh. "I wasn't even offended you know? It was like the first time I really laughed—in a long time. He was teasing, but it was in a really chummy way. He was the sweetest and most charming guy. He even bought me a birthday present a couple of days after. We met two days before my birthday, January 23. It was a red vase filled with a dozen red and white roses, six of each. I *melted*. He had me ever since that moment. We got engaged five months later. He really saved me in a lot of ways."

"So few people ever get that."

Rebecca's phone rings.

"Hello? Rebecca Lewis speaking."

"Hello Ms. Lewis. This is Shannon Waters from ABC. I'm sorry if I'm bothering you; but, your assistant said that this would be a good time to reach you."

"No, that's fine."

"Great. Well, in the coming months, 'Good Morning America' is planning a special week-long series called 'Cracks in the Ceiling.' During the special, an accomplished female entrepreneur will be profiled each day. We've watched Windows to the Soul take off over these last few years; and, the show would love for you to be one of the profiles. I'd like to set up an interview. How does that sound?"

At this point Rebecca is silently mouthing an ecstatic "Yes!" and violently pumping her fist. "Yes, that would be lovely," she says quietly in the receiver.

"Wonderful. We would like to film you at home and at work; so, it would basically be a kind of 'day-in-the-life' piece. It'll end with an interview at your office. What day over the next month would work?"

Rebecca scrolled through her Google calendars. "Let's see...How about October 4?"

"Good, now that we got that set, I would like to ask you a few pre-interview questions. I heard you're a very busy woman; so, if this isn't the best time, I'd be glad to call you back later on."

"No, this is a good time," Rebecca says as she was registering for the Vision Expo West trade show.

"Great."

"What's your full name?"

"Rebecca Annabelle Bridget Slavin Lewis."

"Wow, that's a good one."

Not certain if Shannon meant it sarcastically or sincerely, Rebecca just stays silent.

"What's your birth date?"

"January 25, 1974."

"And birthplace?"

"Boston, Massachusetts."

"Really? Mine too!"

"Wow, what a coincidence!"

"Yeah it is. Is that where you grew up?"

"No, actually I was mostly raised in Rochester, New York."

"What did your parents do?"

"Well my biological father, Charles, was a pilot. My stepfather, Jake, was an actor; and, now he's in sales. My mother, Dawn Lillian, was a secretary, waitress, and sometime actress at any given time in my life."

"We'll figure that out later. Which high school did you graduate from?"

"Rochester High School."

"Did you graduate with honors?"

"Yes, I was salutatorian."

"With the way you turned out, you should have been number one."

"Thanks," Rebecca says with a laugh.

"Were you in a lot of extracurricular activities?"

"Oh yeah. I was editor of my school newspaper. I was on the debate team. I was pretty good in track. I was also in the student government. I was a trumpet player in marching band, sadly. You know what, don't put that in.

Ms. Waters starts laughing.

"Oh whatever, just mention it briefly. I was a tutor for a local elementary school. I was a cheerleader for a little while; but; I soon realized that it really wasn't for me. I participated in many activities in college as well."

"Wow, we have quite enough there."

Again, not sure if she meant it sarcastically or sincerely, Rebecca stays silent.

"You live in White Plains, New York right?"

"Yes."

"OK, where did you go to college?'

"I did my undergraduate at Brown and got my MBA at NYU."

"You're married, correct?"

"Yes, I'm married to Dr. Peter Lewis. He's a neurosurgeon and neuroscientist."

"Fabulous. Do you have children?"

"Yes. My daughter Angelina-Skye is 14 and my son Denver is 11."

"Uh huh. Angelina, with a 'g'?"

"Yep."

"And Sky is with an 'e' at the end?"

"Yeah, how did you know?"

"I just figured. Denver is d-e-n-v-e-r?"

"Right."

"Would you like them to be on TV?"

Rebecca thinks about Angelina and figures she would be fine. Then, she thinks about Denver.

"Um, just a few words. That would be fine with me."

"Sure. Your husband would have no problem being interviewed, would he?"

"Not at all."

"How many people do you have in your company?"

"We're a virtual organization. We have an over 300-person team across our New York, LA, and Miami offices. We have alliances with firms here in the States, Europe, and Asia, and production centers in Scranton, Pennsylvania; Peoria, Illinois; and Chattanooga, Tennessee. We also have 25 individuals on our board of directors."

"Would you like to have a few of your co-workers featured in the segment?"

"Of course. We're all important parts of the team."

Rebecca looks over to her associates with a warm smile.

"I understand. I just have one last question."

"Sure?"

"Why did you launch Windows to the Soul?"

"You know, we're all living in a really incredible, yet dizzying time. We all want to live, and be, our best, and achieve balance. Yet, the frenzied pace of our lives has made so many of us lose touch with our essence—spirituality. Windows to the Soul strives to give people a convenient way to keep connected to that on a daily basis."

At that moment, Farrah, Window to the Soul's receptionist, comes in.

"Please hold on a second Shannon." Rebecca puts Shannon on hold. "Yes Farrah?"

"Hi, it's a rep from Verizon. He said that you put a rush order on your new cell, and he needs to confirm the color before noon. He wants to know if you want the phone with the red and white stripes, or the one in blue and green dots."

"Oh, uh, tell him in white and red stripes. Blue and green dots may be a little loud."

Rebecca gets back to Shannon.

"Sorry about that… Oh nothing, just some personal business. As I was saying, we at Windows to the Soul would like to think that we haven't lost our spiritual connection. We strived to give people a stylish, practical yet imaginative way to keep it alive."

"That's beautiful. I really mean that."

"Thank you Shannon."

"Well, we'll leave the rest for the interview. Thank you so much Rebecca. I can't wait to see you on the show."

"Thank *you* Shannon. Bye now."

Rebecca hangs up the phone.

"WE'RE GOING TO BE ON GOOD MORNING AMERICA!" Rebecca exclaims to her team.

"This is awesome! Like Coachella, Bonnaroo, and Sasquatch all rolled into one," Mimi squeals.

Xavier and Alexander shoot perplexed glances at each other.

"You can throw Electric Zoo in there," Rebecca says casually.

Xavier and Alexander share another pair of puzzled glances.

Denver is making his way to second period. He gets a news alert on his phone.

"Windows to the Soul Lands a Super Bowl Spot," reads the headline.

"Wow, mom's slayin' it."

"Yeah, you never will," Rob snidely remarks.

Denver rebuffs the comment, and continues to make his way to class.

"I was talking to you bitch."

Denver continues to ignore him. The classroom is just around the corner.

I said, "I'm talking to you cunt."

That one irks Denver just a little more.

"There aren't any cunts, nor are there any bitches, in this school Rob. I'm definitely not one. But, I'm looking at an asshole."

"That was weak. No, you're the cuntiest bitch here. I thought you were changing into a girl this week."

Denver has one minute before he is late for class.

"You think you're getting to class turd?"

Denver is right outside the door.

"Just did fucker." He brazenly bends his right middle finger, up-and-down, at Rob, effecting a sarcastically derisive wave. Denver slid into his seat with five seconds to spare.

"This has made my day. No my week, my month, my... well you know what I mean. This is absolutely fabulous!" Rebecca exclaims. She surreptitiously pops another Vicodin.

"Even more reason why we should finalize next quarter's frame ideas (just got some more files from the design team). We should be making headway on the headbands too," Xavier says.

"Always focused. I'm going to give Peter a quick call."

The phone starts ringing.

"Hello, Windows to the Soul."

"Hi Rebecca."

"Laura! I'm so sorry about this morning," Rebecca says laughingly. "I didn't mean to hang up on you."

"That's all right dear. Remember how I was trying to land a commercial spot for Windows to the Soul?"

"Yeah, yeah I remember that."

"You're getting it!" Laura says in an excited whisper.

"WHAT!!! Are you serious? Getouttahere!" Rebecca exclaims. "This day is incredible!"

"I learned that you're going to be on 'Good Morning America,' so that really upped your profile. The network seems very enthusiastic."

"Thank you *so* much Laura. This has to be a dream."

"Well, I make them come true. So, are you excited?"

"Laura, I can't even begin to tell you."

"Great. Channel that excitement into some great ideas for the ad. Call me up as soon as you, and your wizards, think of something."

"Sure Laura. We'll start brainstorming tomorrow."

"I can't wait. I'll talk to you later Becky. Congratulations!"

"Thanks Laura. Love ya! Bye!"

Rebecca sneaks another Vicodin pill. She turns to her co-workers.

"Just when you thought this day couldn't get any better—"

"Oh, oh, let me guess!" Mimi yells as she jumps up and down.

Rebecca sighs. "OK Mimi, take a shot."

"They're bringing 'Enlightened' back?"

"That is a good one; but, I think this is just as good. Here it is: WE'RE GOING TO THE SUPER BOWL!"

"We got tickets?!" Alexander asks.

"Not quite. We got a Super Bowl spot!"

Mimi and Xavier start cheering and hollering.

"That's pretty cool too." Alexander says.

"It definitely is. I'll get in touch with the ad team this afternoon."

Rebecca remembers some little things.

"That's right; I was supposed to follow up about the watch idea. The H&M exec drops by in about an hour, and there's the IPO meeting at 3..."

"I'll forward the new sketches for the design, and the link to the Vision Board for the new message ideas. The Slack channels have really boosted our efficiency. It's helped so much in syncing with the Tokyo team especially," Xavier says.

"I thought this was going to be a slower day Becky," Xavier says with a smile.

"Didn't I say there's always too much going on."

III

Rebecca whistles happily as she skips to the front door. Peter opens it before she rings the bell.

"WE'RE GOING TO THE SUPER BOWL!" he exclaims. He lays a big kiss on her lips.

"I said the same thing at work; but, it didn't go over quite as well." Rebecca says with disappointment. "Did you tell the kids?'

"No. I wanted to leave that to you."

"Thanks babe."

"You got a letter from Jake."

"Really? The holidays aren't for a few months. Did he send the kids money?" Rebecca says sardonically.

"Of course. It's his routine $10 each. I'll get it."

Rebecca walks through her front door as Peter brings the letter from the dining-room table. She skims through it.

"This must be urgent. He wants me to reply immediately."

"Maybe he wants to finally patch things up. You should take him up on it."

"Peter, it's the same garbage all the time. Put it back on the table for me. Oh, how was Denver's soccer game?"

"Fantastic. They blew them out—five zip. He scored *two* goals."

"Awesome! Is he upstairs?"

"No, the coach took them out for pizza after the game. I have to pick him up soon."

"OK, I'll wait till he gets back. Where's Angelina?"

Angelina bounds down the stairs.

"Mom, mom. You guys are gonna be like that Apple commercial back in '84! It's gonna be *awesome*!"

A disappointed look overcomes Rebecca's face.

"Wait a minute? How did you find out?"

"Oh, it was online. Plus, I was getting like 30 posts per second."

"There goes my big surprise announcement."

"No. You didn't tell Denver yet. Well, he probably knows too. But, you can tell me again. Wait, hold on. I'll pretend like I'm hearing it for the first time. I'll go up to my room and come down the stairs again."

Angelina-Skye rushes back up the stairs. She scurries back down.

"Hey mom!"

"Hey hon! I have the biggest news!"

"Oh really? What is it?"

Rebecca delivers the news in a crescendo. "There's going to be a Windows to the Soul spot DURING THE SUPERBOWL!"

Skye and Rebecca immediately squeal loudly.

"Girls," Peter says contemptuously.

"See mom, didn't that feel better?" Angelina asks sweetly.

"You know what honey, somehow it did. Wait, you don't know about—"

"The 'GMA' thing? Oh yeah I do," Skye casually interjects.

"Damn," Rebecca says.

"All that stuff is awesome mom; but, we have to work on my story."

"Oh yeah. Where are you up to now?"

"The part when she is blessed, no there was a better word than that, with 'bitch powers.'"

Peter begins shaking his head.

"Bestowed Angel. And remember, we said we couldn't use those words?"

"Oh yeah. We substituted it with *strong, confident, smart-women powers*," Angelina says proudly.

Peter could not choke back scornful laughter. Rebecca scowls at him. He begins to chuckle silently.

"But, why did that happen again?" Angelina asks.

"Oh, because she had to be equipped with the weapons that would allow her to effectively battle the sexism and antediluvian attitudes that continue to blight modern corporate America. And, the Me-Too movement has given her even more lift."

Rebecca turns to Peter. He puts up his hands as if to recuse himself.

"Oh all right. Hey, could you come to my play next week?"

"Oh baby, you know next week will be so hectic. I don't think so."

"But mom—"

Peter's phone rings.

"It's Denver," Peter says to Angelina and Rebecca. "Congratulations again sport! You *are* the man. Soon, MLS will be scouting for you buddy. All right, I'll stop. You're all done? OK, I'm coming. What's that? Oh OK, I'll tell her. See you soon. Oh, one more thing D. What are you again? That's right. See ya in a few."

Dr. Lewis hangs up.

"Denver told me to tell you congratulations about 'GMA' and the Super Bowl commercial."

"Sorry," Skye tells her mother sympathetically.

Rebecca shakes her head and throws her arms up in defeat.

"You know, I think delaying it is prudent. Next time we talk, I also want to look at different scenarios for buy-backs and options (I was thinking those projections were optimistic, but it looks like we may even exceed them). Oh, and did you have a chance to examine the Malaysia outlook?

"Yeah, Kuala Lumpur looks promising. It has a large young population, rising middle class, and Malaysia's FDI has increased significantly, I believe about 700% since 2009. And, fashion is among the most prominent industries, with high demand. There have been improvements; but, there's still a significant amount of red tape. We can look at that and other areas for international expansion," relays Windows to the Soul CFO, Ed Stancik.

"Thanks a lot Ed. I always value your insights. Talk to you on Thursday."

"We're pushing back the IPO?" Xavier asks as he walks by.

"Yeah, late spring seems like a more practical time. It's set for May 19th."

The Windows to the Soul team is already hard at work getting some preliminary ideas together for the Super Bowl commercial, in preparation for the meeting with the ad team.

"Guys we really need something that will make us break out, put us in the stratosphere. After this, we want Windows to the Soul to truly be a household name," Rebecca says.

"You're right, we have to be different. Why don't we make it a cartoon?" Alexander suggests.

"OK you *might* have something with that. What's your idea?" Rebecca asks with polite reservation.

"Well we can have a superhero theme. We take some of our most popular frames and make them each superheroes. One could be like Mr. Wisdom and another could be like Wellness Woman and they're saving the world from shallowness and superficiality, leading it to the refuge of spiritual wellness. The tag line could be 'Windows to the Soul: Making the world safe for you,'" Alexander explains proudly.

"That last part kind of killed it," Rebecca responds with a pained smirk.

"Well, I'm just going to throw my idea out," Xavier says.

"Sure, go ahead." Rebecca encourages.

"I think it should take place in an art museum. There's a crowd of people in front of a painting, with their heads tilted and cogitative glances, trying to decipher what the piece's message is. The painting features one of our frames, maybe painted in a kind of surrealistic, abstract style. Every time somebody passes by, it morphs into something different, each image being representative of the company culture. And on the bottom of the screen it reads: 'Reveal your spirit,' or something like that."

Alexander turns to Rebecca awaiting her reaction.

"Yes, but is it art?" Rebecca replies.

The other three chuckle.

"That's not bad; we could keep in line with that vein. Well Mimi, you haven't said much. Do you have any ideas?" Rebecca asks the redhead cautiously.

"Um, yeah, something popped into head."

"Let's hear it," Rebecca asks apprehensively.

"I think it should be a continuous shot of one of our frames," Mimi begins sitting up. "The camera concentrates on the frame, follows it and travels it, revealing its message. The camera is zooming in on the frame, extreme close-up. The message will be, uh, let's see... All right I got it: 'True greatness doesn't lie without, it lies within.' Then you pull out and you reveal the frame and the logo. Then you have something like, 'Let your eyes be the windows to your spiritual soul' written on the bottom of the screen along with our URL. Don't yell at me Rebecca," Mimi ends timorously.

"No, I won't," Rebecca says with encouragement. "As a matter of fact, that's another good idea. We just want to keep our slogan in there. Let's get some more concepts out and set up with the ad team."

Mimi skips out of the room to call Max. Alexander scrolls through the *Variety* app as he walks toward Xavier.

"Tony Jaa just signed for his next movie. I'm happy he got back in it," Alexander says.

"Yeah, he's all right, but Jet Li is still in a class by itself. He can do the 'high-octane' stuff with elegance. Plus, he's stronger."

"Fuck that. Tony Jaa established the new guard. All those other guys are washed up compared to him."

"Really? Jet Li is like a virtuoso. And, Jackie Chan was, is, a pioneer..."

The boys go on and on, becoming louder and louder as Rebecca Lewis grows increasingly annoyed. She lets out a pained moan.

"What's wrong Rebecca?" Xavier asks concerned.

"Oh nothing serious...I think I'm ovulating."

"See ya," Alexander says. And with that, the two rush back in their offices.

Mimi comes in.

"Wow, they were out of here in a flash," Mimi remarks.

"Yeah, I wonder why. It was like I said I was ovulating or something."

"Right," Mimi says with a laugh.

Rebecca notices that Mimi has a very satisfied look on her face.

"What did you and Max do on the phone there?"

"Nothing. We could only say hi 'cause he had to get back to work."

"You guys still do it a lot don't you?" Rebecca says with a smirk.

"Nope, just four times a day. Once when we get up, then after I take a shower…"

"That's quite all right. But really, where do you get all that energy? Wait, who am I kidding?"

"What's more important than love? I mean here we're all about spirituality. Intimacy is a big part of that."

"Yeah I guess," Rebecca concedes. "You never say no."

"Of course not."

"Slut," Rebecca jokes.

"I mean, I know he wants to show his love for me. Why would I want to reject that?"

"Yeah I get that, but you don't need to feel pressured…"

"I don't at all. I'm just grateful to have someone who feels that strongly about me."

"You should…So when are you and Max getting hitched?" Rebecca asks cheekily.

"Soon."

"Good."

"We're going to start shopping for rings. We're waiting for things to settle down for him after the gallery show, and some of the other exhibitions. We love each other; there's no rush to make things legal."

Rebecca snickers.

"I hear ya."

Mimi was about to start on her way out when she turns back to Rebecca.

"Hey Rebecca, there's always something I wanted to tell you?"

"What is it?"

"If I had Peter, I'd be on him like a spring breaker on tequila."

"Really?" Rebecca says uncomfortably. "Let me show you the new frame design from the SF team."

—◦◦◦▸◉◂◦◦◦—

Alexander is busily working on his tablet. Rebecca is coming from Mimi's office.

"So, who won?" Rebecca asks while passing his office.

"Who won what?"

"The Great Tony Jaa/Jet Li Debate."

"Oh that. I let Xavier take it. Jet Li's still kickass."

"Great job on the new site design by the way."

"Thanks. I felt we really need to up the ante. Working on expanding the bandwidth too. Narrowing down options for servers with the team."

Rebecca gets an e-mail alert on her cell.

"Angelina? Aren't they supposed to be having art now or something? Yeah, they are. They're doing sculptures this week. I thought she was looking forward to it."

"Is she OK?"

"No, she's fine; she's just being a kid."

"She probably wanted to talk to you though. Text her back."

"I'm sure everything is fine. I'll just talk to her when I get home."

"You can't always be that busy Becky."

"You should be happy I am; that's how you have a job," Rebecca retorts. "Just kidding."

"Yep, that's how I can afford Le Bernardin now."

"You, date? That's a snazzy place."

"Yep, no lonely night on the couch for me."

Rebecca guffaws.

"I'll tell you tomorrow."

"Please. Have a great time."

"You know, I'm already having one. Good Morning America, this Super Bowl commercial, we're going public in May… we're gonna blow up. I mean *huge*," Alexander is walking out the door. "Have a great weekend Becky."

Rebecca waves good-bye as Alexander skips out the door.

"Yeah, huge," Rebecca whispers.

Rebecca is nearing the exit on I-87. The radio is set on 1010 WINS. An ad for a book comes on the air.

"You have the great job. The perfect family," a sonorous voice says compellingly. "The beautiful house. Nonetheless, something is missing. Buy Gary Gray's new book *Finding the Essence*. He'll let you know what really matters. Available on Kindle and Random House hardcover."

Rebecca turns the radio back down.

IV

"Hey honey. How's it going?" Peter asks.

"I'm all right. How was your day?"

"Your mom called me. She said it was very important. A letter came in the mail too, in case she couldn't reach anyone on the phone."

Rebecca races toward the couch. She pulls the letter out of the package. Her eyes race across the page:

My precious Rebecca,

It's been ages since we've spoke. How are you doing sweetie? Well, I know very well—my baby is going to be on TV! Congratulations on Good Morning America and nabbing the Super Bowl spot! I heard you're going public soon too. Peter called me. Things are going so great for you. But it doesn't surprise me. I always knew you would be famous. You always made me so proud. Now you'll be working even harder. I hope you aren't wasting away. You always were so thin.

Your father had been trying to get in touch with you too. Did you get his letter? There was something for the kids. How are they? They were always so brilliant. Denver is a future Pulitzer Prize winning poet and Angelina is the next Picasso. I know they inherited it from my side of the family. Ha ha. And they are so well-behaved to boot. You and Peter really did an outstanding job. They can message me on Facebook.

How am I doing? Oh I'm hanging in there as always. I'm just living from day to day, you know how it is. I'm always missing my beautiful Rebecca, especially at a tragic time like this. Yesterday, Jake passed away after a heart attack. He had been in and out of the hospital for the last few months but nonetheless it was…

The letter drops out of Rebecca's hands. She tries to gain her balance as she feels her heart dropping to her feet. She quickly clings to Peter. He embraces her and begins stroking her tenderly.

"She told me the funeral is on Saturday in Fresno. The address is in the letter."

"I'll be on a plane tomorrow."

The Slavin family and their friends are gathered in the Jacob funeral home. The abundant bouquets of flowers and gentle music overlay the somber ambience.

Rebecca trudges toward the funeral home. Her heart beats rapidly as her mind races. She surveys the lush, green compound. Stealthily, she walks through the front door, so nobody would approach her. Most of the gatherers are engaged in conversation; but, her brothers spot her, and begin rushing toward her. Rebecca signals for them to wait a moment as she walks to the coffin. She gazes at the brown-haired man with the broad lower lip and prominent nose lying peacefully. She begins sobbing. Rebecca rips tissues from her handbag and wipes her face.

She turns for a moment and spots her mother. The two women engage in a long, warm hug. It is the first time that Rebecca has seen her mother, let alone touched her, in so long. Both women are transfixed, reminded again of how much they resemble each other.

"It's like looking at myself 20 years later," sounds in Rebecca's mind.

"I know," her mother whispers.

The golden blonde hair, the nose, the angular face, the lips… the only thing Rebecca does not have is her mother's blue eyes. She had inherited the green eyes from Charles.

Rebecca and Dawn somberly walk away from the casket. Rebecca affectionately caresses her daughter's face.

"I still can't believe he's gone," Dawn says reflectively, staring at the ground. "He loved you so much."

Rebecca pauses for a moment. "He never showed that to me," she murmurs.

"If you only knew. He would be boasting about you all the time. Every time he heard about the company, his eyes would just light up."

"So, after I became something he loved me. I understand."

"You were always something honey, and he always loved you. You were his pride and joy."

Rebecca's eyes begin to burn.

"That's a load of bullshit!" Rebecca roars in a loud whisper. "If Tom, Greg, or Michael won a baseball game, it was a big event. I got a 1570 on my SATs, got accepted into an Ivy, and he shrugged his shoulders. He. Didn't. Care."

"How *dare* you Rebecca! Right near his dead body. He *adored* you. Have respect for your father," Dawn Slavin says to her daughter. Her voice is beginning to rise.

"He's not my father," Rebecca replies sternly.

"Rebecca, stop it," Dawn scolds through a simmering whisper.

"No. He wasn't. No part of me came from him, and no part of him is in me. He was never there for me, he never comforted me, he never showed me any affection… You call that a father?"

"Quiet. They can hear you," she whispers to her daughter.

"I DON'T GIVE A SHIT IF THEY HEAR ME!" Rebecca yells. "Fuck, I hope he hears me too!" Tears begin to form in her eyes. "He treated me like shit. He treated *you* like shit."

"Watch your mouth Rebecca," the elder Slavin says firmly. Now, virtually all the gatherers are looking at the women. "He treated me very well."

"He treated you very well huh? He treated you very well. All those times that he cheated on you, beat you… I still remember that Saturday night when I was 12-years-old, after he came back from Miami. You came into the room covered with bruises wishing me good night. Have you forgotten those times?"

"That's in the past. Now please, behave yourself," Dawn pleads with her daughter. "I know there were times that he was very harsh with you; but, he regarded you as his very own daughter."

"WHAT? This man *violated* me."

Rebecca is sobbing at this point, her body quaking with anger. She begins again quietly.

"He would fucking rape me. When he was fucking me, that's the only time I would hear I love you."

Dawn is seething. She struggles to calm herself down.

"He got help for that!"

"Oh sure, that makes everything better. Has that taken away my pain?"

"Calm down honey, calm down," Dawn whispers desperately.

"This jerk is fucking your daughter and you didn't leave him? What's wrong with you?"

"You know when I married Jake it was a very difficult time for me. I had a lot of issues and—"

"What about me? What about my *issues*," Rebecca Lewis says bawling. "When was anybody ever there for *me*? All the time I was by myself, clutching my little doll, nobody there to hear my cries—"

"Times were very hard then, you know that Rebecca. I needed someone to lean on *OK*. We were struggling!" Dawn cries, trying to through to her daughter.

"Well, whose fault was that? You couldn't keep a job for your life. You were too busy looking for someone who would screw you. What would you always say? Oh yeah, 'Oh don't worry kids, mommy's going to be a big actress. Mommy's name is going to be all over Hollywood. We're going to be living in Beverly Hills,'" Rebecca says, mocking her mother with her face matted with tears. "One guy tells you you're kinda cute and you think you're Marilyn Monroe. Well guess what mom, we never got to Beverly Hills. We had to settle for an old VW van for a month in Vegas."

"OK, I've made mistakes all right. Forgive me!" Dawn begs.

"But, why did I have to suffer for that? Nobody told you to get knocked up when you were in high school."

"Nobody told you either," her mother hisses.

For a few moments, Rebecca stares coldly at her mother. She storms out of the funeral home.

"I really didn't think we would work it out yesterday," Denver's friend Liam rejoices. "New Salem has some of the best blockers. And, Sebastian's a kickass goalie."

"But, Vince can pull it out too. He has awesome instincts. You're right; New Salem has great blockers. The thing is, we have some of the best—if not the best—dribblers in the county. They say defense wins championships. Dribbling, at the very least, scores goals."

"How far did you take the ball down again?"

"I think it was 30 yards," Denver said with a shrug.

"You just juked 'em. And, you knew Sebastian wouldn't dive to the corner?"

"Nah, he's used to me playing it straight. I knew he had his eye on me the whole time I was coming down the field. I knew I had to fake him. By the time I got it in the corner, it would be too late."

"It was. Dude, 'Ninja' posted a new video for Call of Duty. We'll get some tips. I'm still trying to get past that kid in Albuquerque, 'Deuces.'"

"Honestly, I'm not sure 'Deuces' is a kid."

The two friends share a hearty laugh.

"Like that guy from Finland. Next time we sign on, I'll ask him some stuff about music, YouTubers, see if he can answer them," Denver slyly suggests.

"Yeah, if he answers the *right* way," Liam concurs.

"If he says 'on fleek' or only makes PewDiePie references, it's over."
Liam snickers.

"I still have to finish my final draft for ELA, and I have a test in accelerated math; so, we'll wrap at 4:30 OK."

"Yeah, me too. And, I'm hanging out with my dad today. I hope I get to stay with him."

Denver raised his eyebrows.

"Wait, I thought your parents were working things out? It's official now?"

"Yeah bro. They were; but, they both had kind of moved on already. My mom is seeing people, and my dad has been with a chick for a while.

After my mom got the promotion a couple of months ago, she said she was officially done."

"Seriously? How much does it suck? How's your sister taking it?" Denver asks with concern as both boys are still rapt by the 'Ninja' gameplay.

"It does man. I love both my parents. My sister couldn't stop crying when mom told her. She's just eight; so, she doesn't really know how to take it. I'm still figuring out how to take it too bro."

"Did you know when it was getting bad between your parents?"

"Not really. I mean they were fighting more. My dad started going away more. He said he had another business trip or conference; but, it was like every other week."

"Did your mom or dad ever tell you anything?"

"My mom would say stuff like, 'Sometimes, people shouldn't be together anymore.' My dad just seemed more and more irritated. And, they wouldn't spend as much time together. I would do things with my mom only, and my dad only. We weren't really doing family stuff anymore.

Got it, you got to aim straight at his chest. I didn't even know you could pick up that grenade. Thanks for telling me about this video," Liam never takes his eye off the gameplay as he and Denver talk.

"That's major key. 'Deuces' is fucked."

The two boys gamely flash each other the "peace" sign.

"He shouldn't even bother logging on," Denver continues on confidently.

"Nah, he won't. He's too busy watching PewDiePie videos."

The friends laugh as they nod their heads in agreement.

"When will you know who gets custody? It'll probably be joint custody right?" Denver asks.

"My mom said three months; but, she mentioned it might be longer. I hope it's joint. Actually, I really hope I go with my dad. My dad said they almost always give the kids to moms, only if they're completely blown."

"Does your mom pop pills?"

"Not more than anyone else bro."

"You're staying with her then."

"You're probably right. But, it's chill man."

"You sure? I think about my parents splitting up. I don't think I could handle it."

"The Lewises splitting up? Yeah right. Everybody thinks your parents have the perfect relationship. That'll never happen.

But, every dad think your mom's a smokeshow."

"Really? What do they say?"

"You're like my brother man. It'd be weird. Maybe one day. Just know they think she's hot."

Denver just shakes his head.

"My dad just texted me. Gotta go bro."

"Sure man. See you on Thursday."

Liam turns back around.

"Things'll be chill right?"

Denver puts on a stoic face for his friend.

"Yeah man. Things change, but they're always chill. You and your sister will be all right."

"Thanks man. See you Thursday."

"See ya."

Denver walks his friend to the door. He gives Liam's dad a wave. He heads to the den to get his math book; but, he turns into the kitchen instead.

"I don't know how Liam is getting through it. This family is the only thing I've got. I think Liam is the only friend I have," Denver utters nervously to himself.

He grabs a carving knife.

"The Lewises have the perfect marriage? They're showing the signs too. Mom and dad hardly spend time with each other. I only hang out with dad—sometimes. Angelina hardly spends time with any of them.

And, they all think mom's a smokeshow? Jacob's dad is pretty slick. He'll probably pick her up. I think mom and dad are heading in that direction."

He raises the carving knife.

"And, what about if Liam moves? I'll be totally by myself in school. They already target me."

Denver brings the knife to his forearm.

"Mom covers her pill-popping. She seems too functional to be 'blown,' 'blitzed,' 'methed,'...I'd have to stay with her.

It's getting harder to do this."

Denver drags the carving knife across the top of his forearm.

"That actually made it a little better."

Denver moves further down his forearm, and makes a second slit. He takes a deep breath.

He continues down his forearm stepwise. He makes a third slit.

Denver takes another breath.

He makes a fourth slot, a fifth slit. Drops of blood trickle from the knife blade.

Denver turns his arm over, exposing his wrist.

He aims the blade at his wrist, but catches himself.

"That's for when it gets really bad."

Denver rinses the carving knife clean. He tucks his math book under his arm, and heads up to his room.

V

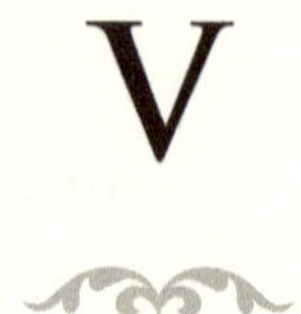

The sun's rays dance radiantly off the kitchen's green-and-white tiled floor. Scores of pristine pots and pans float above the sweeping counter in the center. Denver is sitting at the large, elliptic table in the back corner. His mother stands next to him, washing some plates in the sink.

"Well, tomorrow is the big day Denver."

"Yeah I know. I can't wait," He pauses for a moment. "Do I have to finish eating the lamb chops?"

"Well, if you could gobble up those peas, you can certainly finish my *delicious* lamb chops. You know I don't cook much anymore, take advantage. There's only a little bit left. OK honey?"

Denver reluctantly resumes eating.

"You know, you haven't been eating very much. Don't you want to be a big, strong man like your dad?"

"I do," Denver replies somberly. He tries to sound a little more upbeat. "The sales for Windows to the Soul are going to be even higher, especially after the Super Bowl."

"I hope so. We're already doing pretty well. Remember I showed you last year's earnings yesterday? Pretty big numbers huh? The Super Bowl and 'Good Morning America' should only build our momentum."

"So, you think after all that, you won't be so stressed out?"

"Oh, I'm not stressed out honey. I'm doing all right." Rebecca walks over to the table, sits on the edge, and pulls Denver toward her side. "We're all doing OK, right?" Rebecca says to her son as she runs her hands soothingly up and down his arm.

"Yeah," Denver says with a small smile.

"You know Peter, it's amazing how Denver rises to the occasion. Look how alive he is right now. He can really turn it on." Rebecca and Peter are watching Denver being interviewed by the 'Good Morning America' reporter.

"I guess he got that from you. He's slowly been coming out of his shell with soccer. I've been noticing some real changes. I know being the star of the game last week couldn't have hurt either," Peter says.

"That was good thinking signing him up."

Denver wraps up his interview and walks over to his parents.

"You did an amazing job Denver! We're so proud. They should do the whole profile on you buddy," Rebecca says excitedly.

Peter signals an enthusiastic "OK" with his right hand.

"But, I don't know why you insisted on wearing this sweater. Weren't you so warm? You know this house is always so hot. Let me take it off."

"It's OK mom, I'll do it."

Rebecca looks up at the clock near the front door.

"Damn! You've only got 10 minutes until Sam's mom gets here. Let me just help with that."

"No mom!" Denver yells uncharacteristically.

Rebecca retreats in surprise.

"I'm not a little kid. I can do it myself," Denver says calmly.

"Well, hurry on upstairs then."

Denver whips off his sweater as he walks up the stairs. He begins unbuttoning the left sleeve of his white dress shirt. He is unaware his mother is looking. She sees what seems to be a string of red wounds strewn on his arm. Rebecca is horrified.

"Denver get down here!"

"Mom, I have to get ready for school!"

"Denver, I said get. Down. Here."

Denver drags himself back to the living room. As soon as he gets to the foot of the stairs, Rebecca violently grabs his arm, and yanks him toward her. She forces the rest of his sleeve up, revealing the wounds to his father.

"Who did this to you?" Rebecca asks with alarmed impatience.

"What happened Denver?" his father asks calmly.

Denver doesn't utter a word.

"Denver, how did you get these slits?" Rebecca asks, becoming increasingly distressed.

Denver remains silent.

"Did you do this yourself?"

Denver's lifeless glower continues. Peter intervenes.

"Denver, we're going to talk about this later all right?"

Denver nods. Rebecca desperately pushes Peter away.

"Look Denver, I've been going through a lot of shit—," Rebecca stops herself. "Sorry. I mean I have been going through a lot lately, and I don't need this right now. Baby, please tell me what's going on."

Denver continues staring. Rebecca becomes angrier.

"WHAT IS THIS DENVER? I'M YOUR MOTHER! You can't tell me what's wrong with you?" Rebecca's voice starts to crack. "You're not even saying a word to me. Am I really that bad?"

"Denver, go up to your room all right," Dr. Lewis says to his son.

Denver looks at his father and then turns back to his mother.

"It's OK sport. Go upstairs," Peter assures Denver.

Denver rushes upstairs.

"What the fuck was that, Peter? He has wounds all over his arm and you tell him to go upstairs? Please, tell me you didn't learn that at Columbia," Rebecca says angrily to Peter as tears stream down her cheeks.

"Calm down Rebecca."

"Calm down, Peter? *Calm down?* My kid is fucking mutilating himself; and, you're telling me to *calm down*," Rebecca starts crying. "You're a riot Peter."

"Listen to me. He's in a lot of pain right now and he's not going to talk…"

"We're outside Ms. Lewis," one of the crewmembers says at the front door.

"OK," Rebecca says without turning around. "Give me at most 5 minutes. Is that OK?"

"Sure," the woman says and she closes the door. Peter reaches for some tissues and dabs his wife's eyes.

"He's not going to talk now. I'll take him to work with me. He'll probably open up there; and, we'll talk to him together later tonight. It's going to be all right. Just listen to me."

"Fuck listening to you! My little boy is in a fucking depression."

"Shhhh, shhh," Peter whispers while hugging his wife. "We'll get through this," he tells her and starts kissing her on the cheek. "Haven't I always come through for you? Have I ever let you down?"

"No, you haven't," Rebecca says.

"Who was the man who brought you back to life?"

"You."

"Who was the one that told you, 'Windows to the Soul is not a silly idea; it's brilliant. You should go for it and I'll support you all the way.'"

"You did. It's all you," Rebecca says tearing and laughing.

"We have a problem; but, we can handle it."

"I know Peter, but I can't do this. I think I'll tell them that we have to cancel the whole profile. Things are getting way too crazy." Rebecca turns around.

Peter grabs his wife.

"No, don't."

"Peter, our son is messed up! This is not the right time to be doing an interview. He's a little bit more important."

"Of course he is; but, this is a once in a lifetime chance. You always wanted to have this huge, successful business. And, with this, you're on the road to making that dream come true. You know what we always say: there's a reason why things happen. There's a reason why this is happening right here and right now. Take advantage of it."

"But our kid's a wreck! He doesn't want me doing this."

"Yes he does! Look at how he was during the interview. I've never seen him happier."

"He was on camera. He knows you have to look like that on TV."

"When I picked him up after the game last week, that's all he was talking about on the ride home. He kept saying, 'Mom is going to be on 'Good Morning America' and she's going to have a Super Bowl commercial! This is great!' Few times has he ever been that excited. He said that maybe when the company becomes more successful, you'd be more relaxed and spend more time with them. He wants this for you.

Again, we learned there's a problem. Now, we can do something to solve it."

"This is my fault. I should have been more attentive."

"No, I knocked you up twice and made you bring those two kids into the world," Peter says with lighthearted solemnity.

Rebecca starts to laugh.

"They're as much mine as they are yours. The very eloquent and wise Rebecca Lewis once said this—"

"What?"

"Your shit is my shit and my shit is your shit."

"Yeah, I remember that."

"We're going to get through this together."

"But I don't know what's going to happen after this Peter. You know, maybe we won't totally explode. And if we do, maybe we won't be able to handle it. I don't know if I can take all this: Denver, the IPO… And what are they going to ask me in the interview? All this crap like, 'How do you find *your* spirituality?' 'How do you keep it all together?' With Denver up there like that, I can't believe anything I'm saying. I'll be like one of those has-been celebrities on the infomercials…They know the products don't work, but it's cool as long as they're getting paid."

Peter laughs.

"I don't want to be like that Peter."

"You don't have to be. This will open up a lot of doors and a lot more responsibility. Maybe this is the push we need to both practice what we preach," Peter says while holding Rebecca at her shoulders. He gazes right in her eyes. "Get out there. They're starting to get pretty testy."

The crewmembers are yelling outside. Peter and Rebecca kiss each other.

"Bye Peter." Rebecca runs outside and begins to apologize.

VI

"Why do you think that spirituality is not the number one priority on most of our lists? Why have we, in a way, forgotten it?"

"Our society, the world, at large—especially in considering the globalization phenomenon—is more prosperous than ever before. People are so much more successful, in a professional and material sense. However, they forget that it's the Spirit that made all of that possible. I think people have also forgotten what spirituality really is. It has assumed this touchy-feely, almost caricatured image, in recent years. Yes, *The Secret* and similar works have made it more of a topic of conversation; but, many still fail to see it as an integral part of daily life. It's still seen as something remote or at the very worst, the province of fanatics or extremists. But it's not that; spirituality is about having a true sense of self. And, few people do. Our company strives to remind everyone of the true force and strength in their lives, that which has given them all their success—the Spirit. In doing that, I think, spirituality will be prioritized, as it must."

"So, you think even with how hectic our lives are, people will some day rediscover it?"

"I don't think it's a question of if they will; they *have* to. Many people strive to come to terms with and resolve a variety of issues, whether they come from their childhood, personal relationships, etc. A sense of freedom, contentment, and balance cannot be attained without a spiritual connection. Only after sorting through those issues will happiness—whatever that really is—be possible. With openness, we'll all have that opportunity."

"I know there's a lot of women at home watching now—getting ready for work and trying to get the kids off to school—wondering to themselves, how do you do it all?"

Rebecca lets out a subtly anxious laugh before approaching the question.

"I think one of the worst things that this society has done for women is create that myth: the superwoman, the woman who has everything. The truth of the matter is, Susan, nobody can do everything. One part of becoming a spiritual person is accepting, if not embracing, the condition of human frailty, the imperfection that makes up all of us. The strength, the reward, of spirituality comes from building from that incomplete foundation and striving towards completion, resolving to become a better person with every moment of the day. I always tell myself and other women, 'Don't try to do the impossible; do the best you can.' *That's* how I'm able to have the successful business, the strong marriage, the wonderful kids..."

Rebecca loses track for a moment as the image of Denver's wounded arm flashes across her mind.

"I keep things in perspective, always concentrating on what is important and what really matters. I'm thrilled that Windows to the Soul is doing so well; and, most importantly, that I'm doing my part to enable the rest of the world to get in touch with their spirituality on a daily basis. But, I also realize that this can all be gone tomorrow. This is all finite, limited. What does live on, my true essence, is within my spirit and how I use that to uplift my world—impacting others through my products, or the love and nurturance I give my family."

"Those are truly beautiful words Rebecca. I hope we all can one day fulfill those truths."

Rebecca pauses the video on her phone, and goes to the top of the stairs to check on the party. The Lewis house is boisterous and lively. Peter and Rebecca had invited some friends, including her co-workers, over to watch the Super Bowl. Peter, their friends, and the kids are all in the living room crowded around the expansive HDTV. Annie Hall is sitting on Angelina's lap.

Rebecca Lewis goes back to the bed. She will head downstairs when the Windows to the Soul ad, or any other eagerly anticipated commercial, comes up. She has never really been interested in the Super Bowl, or football, for that matter. For her, the only reason to watch is the commercials.

Rebecca resumes the video.

"She's the best mom. She's always there for you when you need her. Mom's so understanding, caring, and intelligent. I know she's the only one who could have pulled her business off. Mom would do anything for Angelina and me. She's worked so hard for her success; and, we're happy she's getting the rewards. We all love her so much," Denver says to the reporter.

"REBECCA!" She hears about 50 people scream from the living room.

"ALL RIGHT, I'M COMING!" Rebecca screams back.

She leaps out of her bed and runs downstairs. Everyone sits silently, wanting to take the whole ad in.

The team opted for an "Apocalypse" theme. The world lies decimated; once lush fields and expanses now rendered a desiccated ocean of death. Only Windows to the Soul products are left intact. The commercial rapidly cuts across the world, showing people reaching desperately for the Windows to the Soul lenses. On initial contact with the lenses, their bodies begin to morph into breathtaking, almost ethereal semblances of themselves. Their surroundings are transforming in a similar way. Then, there is an extreme close-up on one of the lenses which floats above one of the empyreal figures. "We'll help you see the light," appears like a hologram on the frames.

"That was extraordinary Rebecca," Peter says amid a resounding round of applause.

"Awesome mom," Skye says.

"Thanks, but these guys had a whole lot to do with it."

Rebecca points at Xavier, Alexander, and Mimi. The group immediately gets wrapped up in animated conversation while Rebecca sneaks dourly upstairs. Peter sees her and rises from his chair.

"Hey Pete, where ya going?" his friend Phil asks.

"I just want to check on Rebecca. You know how women can be with gadgets. I don't want her to mess up the Chromecast," Peter says jokingly. Phil laughs and nods his head. Peter walks up the stairs.

Rebecca is crouched over on the bed, sobbing inconsolably. Her brunette doll lies nestled between her left arm and side. Peter quietly closes the bedroom door and gently moves toward her. He immediately embraces her and laces her body with soft kisses.

"I think we need to call the therapist."

"Yeah, tomorrow."

VII

Long, slender fingers wipe away the lingering wetness of morning tears. Her reddened eyes are tinged with pain and swelled by worry. Nonetheless, Rebecca's eyes twinkle as they race across the page:

EXECUTIVE SUMMARY

A new day is upon us. The tragic events of this still young century have forced people not only to take stock of their lives, but to strive to change them. There's a drive to reflect upon where we are, and an undying need to understand where we are heading. Humanity is searching for meaning, truth, and ultimately the inextinguishable light of spirituality. And, Windows to the Soul has heard that call.

Window to the Soul's eye-catching designs feature uplifting, insightful, and inspirational words, enabling consumers to make spirituality not just a stylish look but, more importantly, a state of mind. Through sleek style, inspired creativity, lofty words of wisdom and quality products, Windows to the Soul is fulfilling its mission of helping everyone see the light.

That light of the future shines ever brighter for Windows to the Soul. We are projecting growth of over 28% over the next three years, on the heels of an average growth rate of 86% during the last five. The new California Dreamin' line is the premier designer sunglass line in North America and Europe. And, our Priceless line has exceeded expectations, posting $1.06 million in sales during its first week alone, with margins of nearly 45% on average. With this performance, Windows to the Soul is projected to generate sales of $194 million, $260 million, $337 million, and $411 million—with EBIT of $72 million, $128 million, $142 million, and $185 million —from 2019 to 2022 respectively, and will achieve 9% market share in two years.

The eyewear industry also presents some promising trends. It now generates over $16 billion annually, and our primary market, sunglasses, constitutes $1.7 billion of total revenue. The eyewear industry is expected to experience 7 to 10% annual real growth within the next five years. But, with the aging baby boomer population, totaling approximately 78 million, and their increasing vision-care needs, some analysts expect the market to expand by up to 15% within the next decade. The above trends, and rising spending on luxury goods in emerging markets, will provide even more growth opportunities for premium-priced prescription-lens, watch, and headband, lines. Evidently, the future's so bright, we have to wear…we'll stop right there. You can read more details about Windows to the Soul's growth prospects in the appendix.

New <u>I See the Light</u> Store Locations:

Atlanta

Chicago

Miami

Milan

Paris

As you can see, nothing but more success is on the horizon. But, your support will ensure that our dreams become brilliant realities. We're looking forward to a mutually rewarding and prosperous relationship.

Sincerely,
Rebecca Lewis
CEO
Windows to the Soul

"This needs to be tweaked; but, we should have no problem getting more investors on board. I still can't believe how much we've grown in the last few months. These numbers are unbelievable," Rebecca says with an incredulous smile.

"And, we'll just skyrocket with the retail expansions. I can't wait till the new board members see the summary," Xavier replies excitedly.

As they step out from the taxi, Rebecca straightens her billowy turtleneck sweater, and flowing ivory coat. Before entering the building, she wipes some of the late February snow off her milky stiletto boots. Xavier straightens out the golden tie atop his mocha vest, which sumptuously accents his rich mahogany skin.

He opens the doors to the Wily & Snarkson building, the advertising firm that is handling the Windows to the Soul ad campaign. As Rebecca walks through the entrance, lascivious glances follow her behind.

"Those guys are checking you out," Xavier utters intimately to Rebecca.

"Well, at least somebody is nowadays. You don't look so bad yourself," Rebecca says as she admires Xavier's person. "The success of the Super Bowl ad will give us even more leverage. I think now we can finally direct this brand on our own terms."

"You're definitely right. I have to admit, I was somewhat nervous about the ad; a lot of them have been flops over recent years. But, ours proved to be among the exceptions. Without that, we wouldn't even be here."

"I know. What a difference 30 seconds, and a couple of million, make."

Rebecca and Xavier emerge from the elevator. The bold, copperplate letters of "Wiley and Snarkson" shine like specious lights at the end of the 53rd floor tunnel. The advertising firm is vibrant and upbeat. Thirtyish man-children mill around the office in organized chaos, armed with Skechers and Levis. Some bloated, stodgy types in wool sweaters and dark suits patrol the corners.

Wiley and Snarkson is a veritable Chuck E. Cheese cradled in the stern arms of Corporate America. One guy wearing a "Maybe Still a

Boy, But Definitely Not a Man" T-shirt and an outrageous pompadour almost bounces in front of his computer. His co-worker speeds by in Heelys to give him a piece of paper. One of the corporate types is not-so-silently singing ELO's "Mr. Blue Sky" while Grey, Maren Morris, and Zedd's "The Middle" plays in the background. Wiley and Snarkson personified the odd, if not somewhat fascinating, nexus of the Millennial, Generation X, and Baby Boomer generations. Now parents can rest easy; your slacker kid, wearing out Grand Theft Auto V, does have a future.

"Ahhh, so this is where all the kids from 'Freaks and Geeks' ended up," Rebecca says to Xavier.

Xavier and Rebecca approach the reception desk. Placed prominently beside it is a sign that read "Work = Play." The receptionist is a more fashion-challenged version of Mimi. Her platinum-blonde hair (nicely complemented by dark-brown roots) is tied in shellacked bunches, forming an enameled crown. Her V-Neck ACDC shirt is holding on for dear life around her chest and stomach. A tiny diamond signals from her left nostril, slightly eclipsing the hollow piercings on her nose's bulb. But, she is conceding to the corporate structure. She also has on a short, black jacket, buttoned at the center, with matching pants. The receptionist is on her cell.

"Mmmmm… smokin' that was almost as good as suckin' on your long, thick…"

She instinctively looks up before uttering another word.

"Yo, I'll tawk to ya lata," she blurts out quickly in a mousy, Brooklyn accent.

She clears her throat and starts to speak in an almost mechanical tone.

"How may I help you?"

"We're here for the Windows to the Soul meeting."

"Of course. The board room is directly to the left."

"Thank you," Rebecca unconsciously responds with the same mechanical tone.

Xavier nods his head, while giving her a soft slap.

Rebecca is heading toward the formidable leather chair directly ahead of her; but, she sees the coffeemaker and starts toward it. Xavier comes by her side as she starts on a cup. Rebecca fiercely sips on the cup as her right eye begins to twitch.

"This is a pretty impressive room. You know, that eye-twitching thing has been going on for months. You should check it out. Maybe it's all the coffee you've been downing."

"Very funny. I'll turn away from you next time. I'm sure it's nothing."

Rebecca quickly sits in the chair at the end of the table. She absentmindedly begins tapping a little rhythm on the tabletop. Her eyes sweep across the walls of the boardroom.

"You're right. It's impressive."

Delightfully quirky pictures of eggheads in tee shirts standing with uptight executives lit up the walls as assorted Clio, ADDY, Mobius, and Webby awards punctuated the room. Rebecca's eyes fixated on a poster at the corner. It featured a dweeby-looking kid with a mushroom cut and his shoulders slouched, getting the bunny ears from a student behind him. "Don't worry, in 10 years I'll be your boss," is written on the bottom. Her hand begins to gingerly glide across the glass tabletop. Her eyes lock on the collage of top advertising campaigns from Wiley & Snarkson's history. Images from Coca-Cola, Nike, Apple and other commercials jog Rebecca's memory while a nostalgic smile waxes on her face.

"It's pretty cool isn't it?" This comes from the toothy simper of a bespectacled Wiley & Snarkson employee. His aquiline noise is precariously close to Rebecca's eyes.

"Yes, it definitely is."

"You must be the *beautiful* Rebecca Lewis," he hisses ingratiatingly. Rebecca is very amused.

"Well, I wouldn't mind being that," Rebecca replies with a chuckle.

"Whoa! When did Will Smith walk into the room?"

"Hmm, not bad; but, I would have preferred Denzel Washington," Xavier deadpans as he looks at the employee.

"Of course, my sincerest apologies," he says as he takes a seat by Rebecca.

The rest of the dweeb team begins filing into the boardroom, followed by a personable, confident man who is one of the directors. He saunters toward the Windows to the Soul team.

"Hi, Rick Shaughnessy. I know we've talked so much on the phone; but, it's *so* much better to see you face-to-face," Rick says with a charming smile and wink to Rebecca.

"Well, with that wonderful voice, I felt like I've known you all along," Rebecca replies flirtatiously as his Burberry cologne teases her nose.

Rick smiles back flattered.

"And, you must be Xavier Marx."

"You would be right."

"He's our COO and doubles as the token Black guy," Rebecca snickers.

"Hey, at least there is one," Rick rejoins.

Rick and Rebecca share a laugh. Xavier smiles.

"Hey Rick, stop hitting on the hot chick," screams one guy with slightly unkempt hair from the table.

"He's right; we better start the meeting," Rick says as he hastens to his chair.

As he lumbers toward the boys' bathroom, Denver releases a weary sigh. He takes a quick glance at his watch and realizes he only has one more period to go. His eyes suddenly shine as a relieved smile begins to light his face. Carefree, riotous laughs begin to fill the space behind the door. Denver sees three familiar boys by the stalls.

"I'd like to introduce you all to Rebecca Lewis, the CEO of Windows to the Soul and Xavier Marx, the Chief Operating Officer. It's currently the fastest growing company in the eyewear industry. We're honored and grateful to have Windows to the Soul as part of our family."

"We are as well," Rebecca responds politely.

"In my 15 years here, we've seen some success stories; but, Windows to the Soul has to be among the top in the list. We caution clients that one commercial, not even one ad campaign, can make a company; however, your organization has undoubtedly proved us wrong. It's nothing short of an advertising marvel. I understand that your projected revenues for 2019 are $192 million correct?"

Xavier answers quickly.

"That's right Rick, which will mark year-over-year growth of 23% in revenue. The eyewear industry currently grosses over $17 billion each year and with its steady growth of 7 to 10% annually, we're poised to have a strong foothold of at least 12% of the market in four years. At that rate Rick, you won't just be grateful that we're part of the family; we'll be your favorite relative."

Denver tries to dart into a stall, but the boys catch him.

"Hey Denver. Little baby gonna shit in his pants? Don't ya wanna say 'hi'?"

"Um, I appreciate that Rob; but, I don't want to be late for class. I just need to go to the bathroom and get going. I'll see you later." Denver tries to make a quick exit, but Rob grabs his right shoulder and pins him against the stall door. Denver goes into a controlled shudder.

"Don't worry Einstein. You'll get to class. We just wanted to see how your suicidal kids' program was going. Right guys?"

Rob turns around at his minions. They utter "yeah" in unison.

"So, how's that going?"

"It's not exactly a suicidal kids program Rob. It's a place for kids to do homework and hang out after school. This may be a little hard for your mind to understand; but, suicide is a point of no return, of complete emotional and psychological breakdown. I'm not there. I need to get to class," is Denver's acerbic riposte.

"Did you just call me stupid? Your ass *definitely* isn't going to class." Rob leans in closer to Denver.

"Well Xavier, you should be head of the Windows to the Soul finance department, not to mention Rebecca's personal promoter."

"He might be, once you don't try to take him away," Rebecca jests.

"Rest assured. Well with numbers like that, we want to do all we can to keep the momentum going. A new, 'viral' campaign is crucial for the expansion ventures you're undertaking this year. We want people to be crowding the website, and knocking down the doors of the 'I See the Light' stores. After they see the ads, they'll be counting down to the new designs."

"That's exactly what we want too Rick. We're opening stores in Chicago, Miami, Milan, and Paris, and adding locations in New York and LA. Since these are all cities with their own unique characters, we want the ad campaigns to reflect that. The 'I See the Light' stores will all have that signature sophisticated, 'casual cool' and serene ambience; but, we want the public to feel that this is a company that will be a part of their lives and even beyond that, a part of their spirit. Thus, we need ads that are relatable, but also innovative and creative, staying true to Windows to the Soul's place at the vanguard of the eyewear industry. I guess you're all here to help with the innovative and creative part?"

The T-shirted titans nod their heads with self-satisfaction.

"Yeah, that's what they tell me; but, I wonder sometimes," Rick says.

Rebecca and Xavier laugh.

"Of course, and that's the vision we had for the ad campaign as well. We just need to work on how to best merge Windows to the Soul's and the cities' images."

"NOBODY..." He takes Denver by the shoulders and slams him against the lockers.

"CALLS..." He bangs him harder this time.

"ME..." still harder.

"STUPID!" The impact of Denver against the lockers rings through the halls as he falls to the ground.

"Are you going to let 'im call me stupid? Are ya?"

"No," they say again in unison.

"Alright then, do what you gotta do."

The lackeys throw Denver back in the bathroom. They begin pummeling him. A swift blow to Denver's right rib sounds through his ear. His once vivid reflection on the bathroom floor begins to sink into a fog. Another thug starts pummeling his stomach, with each impact quivering through his body. The stark lines of the blue tiles begin to morph into blurred edges. A gnawing sensation starts in his groan area as another boy trounces his legs.

Denver lets out a plaintive whimper. The assault stops.

"Watcha do that for? Keep going."

"No Rob, I think he's had enough. If he gets too hurt, we'll get in trouble."

"Yeah, Mike's right."

Rob glares at his two goons for a moment. "Alright, that's enough. Next time, keep your smart ass quiet." The three boys drag Denver out the bathroom, and run toward the cafeteria. Denver lays on the floor of the hallway nearly lifeless.

⸻ ∞o❈o∞ ⸻

"I think this would be great for LA," an ad guy says with eager hurriedness under his Linux cap. "You know how LA is all about Hollywood, entertainment, etc. Well, you should give it a kind of movie theme… you have guys and girls who are like superheroes, named after your featured models. They're lined up, you do a close up on each of them and they say, 'I'm Elegance, I'm Catalina Island…' all in their voices. Oh yeah, and they each tell their power like, 'I give you sophistication, I give you casual cool…'"

"Didn't Alexander have an idea like that?" Rebecca and Xavier say to each other in quiet unison.

"Yeah, that idea is not ideal; but, I do like the movie aspect. We can use a kind of trailer concept though. We need to make the opening of the new 'I See the Light' store a big event. We can make the commercial like a coming attractions kind of thing, like it's advertising a summer blockbuster," Rebecca responds.

"Yeah, that's cool," starts the man-child with a receding hairline, wearing thick black glasses and a Superman shirt. "The first frame could be a black screen with 'I See the Light' in caps appearing gradually and, in the bottom, in smaller letters, sophistication, serenity, spirituality."

His energy mounts with every word.

"It could have rapid cuts showing clips of people feeling uplifted, fulfilled…There could be a shot of a *humongous* sun rising right behind a woman sitting on the grass in a meditative position."

He is approaching breakneck speed.

"Another one could show a man *scaling* a mountain with a breathtaking landscape in the background. We can have a shot of some cute little kids, cradled by their mom and dad, or a couple dancing with amazing energy… The last shot could be a medium close-up of someone just jumping up in the air with incredible, um what do you call it, yeah *joie de vivre*."

He comes to an energetic conclusion.

"Then it ends with the first frame, the black screen with I See the Light appearing…"

"You done running the marathon buddy?" Rick says jokingly. "We can start working with that. We got a pretty good budget with this campaign; so, we could probably get most of those shots. What could we do with Chicago?"

The only other woman in the room begins speaking. She's wearing a tan fisherman's cap; long, stringy, dirty-blonde hair; a pink T-shirt; and a white-washed denim miniskirt. Her voice has a commanding but restrained intensity.

"Along with the sophistication and casual cool of the Windows to the Soul brand, we also want people to think that the eyewear is a kind of panacea; the quiet we need in a disquieting world. Chicago's a fast-paced city; so, the commercial could take place on a crowded city block. We'll show people on the block engaged in those everyday kind of annoyances. Maybe they spilled some coffee on themselves; maybe they're arguing on their cell phone with a partner; maybe they missed the L…whatever. The last frame will show someone who is cool and collected—of course, with Windows to the Soul gear on.

"We'll zoom in on them, amidst the boisterous crowd, and then around them, starting on the top, or maybe starting from the side… We can have words from one of the hot new models appear. They'll be in warm colors, like yellows, oranges or golds, maybe with slight illumination, swirling around them, displaying the 'light' and the power of the Windows to the Soul expressions. Of course, we'll have quiet music, perhaps a classical score…maybe it can get louder as we get tight on the 'Windows to the Soul' people."

"Mmmm, nothing like a woman to give you some great perspective huh guys?" Rick asks the rest of his team.

The Comic Con denizens just look at each other and shake their heads dismissively.

"Oh sorry, you wouldn't know."

Rebecca lets out a little chuckle and gives her feedback.

"I love that idea. That's a perfect springboard for our new lines. The expression swirling around should be from one of the 'Priceless' or 'California Dreamin' lines… That's excellent."

"Do we have any ideas for the Atlanta ad?"

"Yes, actually something just came to me," Rebecca begins.

"Great, I'm sure you have some good ideas," Rick says with anticipatory pleasure and an unconscious wink.

"I was thinking of something that conveyed personal, soulful. We can take an everyday conflict or challenge as the theme. Um let's see… Not having enough time with one's family. We can show a mom who has 'everything'—a great job, a beautiful family, a great house… But, she still feels empty. In the background, we can have selected lyrics from U2's 'I Still Haven't Found What I'm Looking For' or something. We can show her at an important business meeting, then cut to her bedroom, where the camera pans revealing pictures of family and vacations. Then, we can cut to another scene where she's returning home in her BMW… you know, things that establish her success.

Then, the next shots could show the distance she has with her family. One could be very literal. She's on one side of the room and her son is on the other side, and they're just sighing, not saying anything. Another could show her turning over in bed, reaching for her husband; but, there's nobody there. In the next shot, she could be in her office, or some such place, and she's looking through a magazine. She sees an ad for a pair of Windows to the Soul glasses. They will feature words referring to her situation like, 'The world's success glitters as the gifts of the heart remain priceless.' One of her co-workers comes in and tells her she needs to schedule a flight for a business trip. She replies, 'You know what, I'll stay here at home.'"

The team reflects on her idea for some moments. Rick finally responds.

"That's a neat idea; but, the commercial is really aimed at one particular audience—the conflicted working mom. This campaign is supposed to introduce Windows to the Soul to a world stage; so, you need it to have broad appeal. Plus, it's really like all message and no product. As much as we're promoting the Windows to the Soul image, you're not really promoting the brand. It's really all about the emotional drama this woman is experiencing. The products may get lost."

"Rick that is the product. That's a valid point but what Xavier, I, and the rest of the Windows to the Soul team value is the subtle power of spirituality—not ramming it down your throat—because spirituality is essentially part of everything—whether we're dealing with work, family, or anything else that's a part of life. We don't want this to be too abstract. When we show this kind of situation, people realize that spirituality is something they need to deal with every day," Rebecca replies firmly. Her right eye begins twitching.

"And, that's the integral part of our brand. The product side of Windows to the Soul and the philosophy of Windows to the Soul are married in that concept. During the shots showing the distance with her family, words can appear at the bottom of the screen that refer to the situation like, 'The bonds of love should know no distance.' For showing more of our product, she can be going past 'I See the Light' stores or around shops where Windows to the Soul products are prominently displayed. We can definitely carry off that subtle tool of corporate advertising, product placement, all with signature Windows to the Soul style." Xavier rattles out, attempting a save.

"Got it. We can work with that."

Rebecca lets out a sigh of relief, tinged with disappointment.

"We're making some serious headway here folks. Let's check the concepts for the Milan and Paris ads."

The period ends. Angelina is walking towards Denver's school to pick him up. The back door is open this afternoon, and she hears anguished cries by the boy's bathroom. She peeks in and sees Denver writhing on the ground. She dashes in.

"Denver!"

Denver continues to agonize on the floor, his body contorted with pain. He is unable to muster the strength to utter a coherent word.

"Did the idiots from gym get you again?"

"Yep," Denver whispers.

"Sorry. We gotta get you out of that program. Come on, I'll help you up. We'll take care of those bruises at home."

"What about when mom gets back? I don't want her to see them."

"Like I'd tell her that you got beat up Denver. You got banged up during gym. You were playing football…You got sacked a couple of times… Don't worry about it."

The big sister scoops Denver up from the ground, serving as his crutch, as they slowly make their way out of school.

Rebecca's phone begins to ring to Rod Stewart's "If You Think I'm Sexy." She scurries into the adjacent lounge to take the call.

Rick enjoys a good laugh.

"Well on that note, we'll take a little break."

The group disperses as Rebecca starts talking on the phone. It's Peter.

"Hey hon. What's going on?"

"Actually, a lot. We have a spectacular new intern who's just begun working with us. I met her at the NSF conference in Chicago last month. She's very intelligent, enthusiastic and eager to learn; so, we're trying to get her acclimated as quickly as possible. We've also come across some new research on stem cells that's making Alzheimer's seem a little less daunting. Some impressive young people have worked here; but, I can already see that she's the most gifted one. With everything going on, I might stay a little later tonight. I'll fill you in on everything when I get home. I also called to let you know that Angel will be meeting with the goodwill ambassador she met through one of the AIDS projects tonight."

"How many times this week? She obviously really likes this kid."

"Yeah I know; but, she's really engaged. We might have an ambassador in the house."

Rebecca pauses before responding.

"Peter, do you remember what she was wearing today?"

"Hmmm, let me think. I think she was wearing that really snug black turtleneck, the skirt that comes right above her knees, and those long, black stiletto boots that you bought her last Christmas."

"Uh huh, I figured it would be something like that. I have to talk to her when I get home."

"When are you getting back tonight?"

"Let me see, with my appointment and traffic, probably around 9:30. Yeah I know. Hey babe, I'm still at the meeting. I'll talk to you later all right."

"OK hon. I love you."

"Love you too. Bye."

Just as she hangs up, Rebecca's cell phone rings again. She sees it is a private number and does not answer. Rick ambles toward her.

"Well, I definitely think you're sexy, and I will let you know."

"Oh really?" Rebecca says as she swivels her hips to face him. "What would you do?"

He is surprised; but, he takes advantage of the opening.

"You'd really like to know?"

"Of course," Rebecca says with coquettishness.

"Well, I can't take my eyes off that amazing blonde hair." Rick comes in close to Rebecca and begins to run his fingers through her ringlets. His fingertips leave little drops of sweat on each strand.

"Or those green eyes…" His long, strong fingers glide from her hair and softly caress her cheeks. "Along with those luscious lips."

As he uttered the last syllable of "lips," Rick's mouth covertly begins creeping upon Rebecca's face. His taut arms quickly capture Rebecca in a tight and close embrace, nestling her against his nascent hardness. Rebecca feels uncomfortable yet wanting. Rick's lips are now massaging Rebecca's with youthful passion.

It has hardly been seconds; but, for Rebecca it feels like an eternity. As Rebecca begins savoring the touch of his lips, his long tongue stealthily darts into her mouth. He penetrates her mouth like a serpent, thrusting in her throat, probing deeper and deeper, engaging more snugly with each passing second. Rebecca is moving in closer, her head moving back and forth with each thrust.

Her tongue's titillating stroke and the burgeoning hardness of her nipples spurred him on. He releases his tool from the passionate grasp of her mouth just before the tongues engage in a sensually playful swirl. A long, fluid bond continues to connect the couple for a few more moments. Rebecca quickly throws her head back, revealing her long neck for his attack. Rick starts assaulting it, grinding it, as his hands begin to grope her chest. His fingers begin to undo her shirt as Rick hears the door opening. He stops within a millisecond.

The wannabe Superman comes into the room. He could only see Rick from the back, who is completely blocking Rebecca from his perspective.

"Why don't we get back to work before clothes start coming off," he says with oblivious glibness.

"Right," Rick says with almost affected professionalism.

Rick quickly starts back into the boardroom. Rebecca stays behind for a few more moments, with eyes closed and head tilted back, as her hands run across the lingering wetness of her neck.

Angelina approaches some of her classmates.

"Hey Ange."

"Hey girls. Suh?"

"We're doing a quick Starbucks run, and heading to Jenny's house after," Lila says with her eyebrows raised.

"That was suggestive," Angelina chimes in, and drops his voice about three octaves. "What are you doing at Jenny's?"

"She's taking topless photos for her boyfriend," Adeson says giggling.

"We'll help her with the full body shot," Pamela says proudly.

"You can't come right?" Lila asks with thinly veiled disdain. "We'll love to take your picture, crop your head, and put Jenny's face on."

"Or, he can just put a filter on your body and send it to Jay."

"I could make room in my schedule for the right price…," Angelina tempts. "Sorry guys, I have to miss the sexting party. We have the UN Ambassadors meeting."

"Right. I went to the seminar; but, it wasn't cool to me. I'd rather just give," Adeson says.

"Yeah, Ange. You're putting a lot of time into this. I mean these kids are halfway across the world—"

"Pam, people have been giving money for over 30 years. There needs to be more involvement. They're halfway across the world; but, a lot of those affected are our age and even younger. Imagine losing your whole family to a disease. If that happened to someone in White Plains, wouldn't you care?"

"Yeah, you told me all that before. Didn't AIDS start in Africa anyway? I mean, from all the monkeys they have there? They kind of brought it on themselves," Pam retorts.

"And, at the end of the day, it's a shitload, and I do mean shitload, of Black people. Even if it was a lot of Europeans, I'd think twice.

Losing some of them make it a little easier for all of us. The world is overcrowded enough anyway…"

"You should totally major in sociology Lila. Actually, you don't have to even take classes…you got everything figured out. If we want to solve the world's problems, we should just kill off black and brown people.

Or, you can think about running for office.

Why do you guys do sexting parties? Why don't you just get with a guy for real."

"You mean, actually have sex?"

Angelina realizes she may have revealed a little more than she intended.

"You have sex?" Adeson inquires with almost lurid curiosity.

"I didn't say that," Angelina whispers.

"Who is it?"

"I didn't say I do."

Angelina conveniently checks her phone.

"The meeting is going to start in five minutes. I need to start on saving the worthless Black people."

None of the other girls catch the irony.

"All right. See you later," Lila says with a sneer as she, and her friends, skip away.

"See ya."

Angelina heads to the computer lab. Chris Shays is still setting up. When he sees Angelina, he decides to start.

"OK guys. We want to make sure we end on time tonight; so, let's start. As we prepare for our trip, let's get a brief overview of the extent of the age crisis in Africa." Chris begins his PowerPoint.

"Nearly 70% of the over 30 million people in the world suffering from AIDS live in sub-Saharan Africa; just under 25 million of Africa's residents have AIDS; more than one million African children and adults die from AIDS or HIV annually; and, the AIDS crisis has caused the life expectancy in a number of African countries to fall below 54-years-old, with life expectancy dipping below 49-years-old in some nations. Without adequate drugs, there is an up to 45% chance that an expectant mom's baby will contract the virus in utero.

We hear stats like these; and, it's easy to become despondent. But, what can we do to curb AIDS spread, especially in hard-hit areas like the African continent?"

Paul raises his hand.

"You can't help anyone without having enough funds to get people medicine, food, take them to services, etc. It starts with money."

"The importance of fundraising cannot be overstated Paul. Thanks for reminding us, and getting our conversation started. What else is needed? Yes Morna."

"Along with money, education also should be a focus. Even with the spread of the disease, not everyone is sure about all the ways the virus is spread, and how it can be contained. I think more education would be good for women, children, and teenagers."

"I agree with Morna and Paul," Angelina starts without raising her hand. "Funds are vital for any program or effort we undertake. That can't be argued. Many women on the continent, especially, are often at the mercy of their husbands or partners. For cultural and legal reasons, they often don't have the opportunity, the agency, to guard their sexual health. If they are more informed about the ways the disease could be spread, through a variety of sexual acts and contact, they can better protect themselves. Also, as Morna pointed out, we also need to better educate young people—children, teenagers, and I think young adults as well—so, the cycle could be broken. They don't have to be gripped by the epidemic as their parents or older relatives were.

And, I want to piggyback on that emphasis on the young people. Along with distributing much-needed relief supplies, food, and medical materials, I think we should also concentrate more resources on involving the young people through education, technology, training programs, and cultural activities. I think in expanding their perspectives, and giving them something beyond themselves they can aspire to, kids and young adults will be more likely to act responsibly; participate in less risky behaviors; guard their health; and, be more pro-active in helping family members and friends get the support, especially the health aid, that's needed. And, in coordinating with sponsors, we can have more resources for assisting those impacted.

I didn't mean to take so much time everybody. I just felt that these issues aren't brought up a lot of times."

"It's true Angelina," Chris agrees assertively. "How do you all feel about the efforts she suggested? Might there be challenges?"

Paul shoots up his hand.

"Yes Paul."

"I can think of a couple. First of all, especially for technology resources, there probably isn't the infrastructure. Second, many of the people probably don't have the skills for getting through a training program. They are probably illiterate, and an educational program would likely be impractical. Oh, and, should we really care about reading books to kids when people are dying?"

"I'd like to answer what Paul said, if I can Chris."

"Go ahead Angelina."

"In terms of infrastructure, a number of tech companies have been working on ways to provide wireless service and internet access in less-resourced, and less-developed, areas. For instance, Google's Project Loon has been working on delivering wireless access through specially designed balloons. About the skill set of the African people, Africans are among the most industrious and capable people around the world. They are the second most-educated immigrant population in the America. These individuals are just waiting for opportunities to advance themselves. And, with the right medications, that are becoming more and more available, people with HIV and AIDS can live very productive lives. Once their health is managed, growth should be the next priority. And, as I said, in providing the educational and training resources and coordinating with sponsors, we can link them up to much-needed health resources."

Paul rolls his eyes. Some of the other ambassadors do the same or suck their teeth.

"It's evident that you're passionate about these ideas Angelina, and you've been thinking about them. The sponsors will be the key. Please reach out to Google and other organizations that can assisting us in securing supplies by next week's session. You can include my name, and use the UN Ambassadors contact information. Would anybody else like to work with Angelina on this? We know things work faster if we work as a team."

"I'll help," Morna says as she smiled at Angelina.

"I'll help out too," David says.

"I can reach out," Oliver says.

"Nice, we're already getting a group together. And, as you reach out and plan, never forget our values of service, accountability, and the respect for human dignity, both for ourselves—we have to make sure the efforts fulfill the goals intended—and for the individuals and families on the ground. You guys update the group on progress next week; and, keep me updated on any developments, and any challenges, during the week.

I want us to watch a short video about Mofasa, a 22-year-old mother of two in Mozambique who lost her husband to AIDS. I want you to think about the obstacles she's facing and the support she needs. We'll discuss it in about 15.

Angelina, I actually have some literature about Project Loon and coordination efforts with local universities on the ground. Let me give you a quick peak."

Chris motions for Angelina to follow him to the corner office. She enthusiastically follows.

Chris softly closes the door.

"Here is some literature you can share with the group. The University of Cape Town has been running a training and therapy program for young people afflicted by HIV or AIDS—including those infected, and those who have lost family members to the virus—for about three years. We can look at ways to help them expand and to begin similar programs around the continent. I have some contacts at Google NYC and in Mountainview. I can help with seeing how sites can be integrated into Project Loon.

I asked the question about challenges, so you could bolster your argument. I'm proud of how you defended yourself."

"Paul likes to put down what I say. He's not the only one. Some of us are here because we really want to get involved. Others are here just to list the program on a college application."

"I know. You'll have a lot to include in apps. But, I know your heart is in it. Thanks for always being involved."

"Thanks for being a great leader Chris."

"This team is the most productive in the Northeast. It's a big part of why I got the promotion. A lot of that is because of your work, especially."

Angelina smiles bashfully.

"I also wanted to let you know that I haven't forgotten about the surprise you gave me at the end of the Skype call on Monday. I could never forget *those*."

Chris pulls Angelina towards him and starts necking her as he fondled her chest and rubs her hips.

"I think I've put on some weight. I hope you don't mind."

"What? You look amazing. You're damn sexy. I love curves anyway."

Chris and Angelina kiss each other.

"As great as this is, this is wrong on so many levels. I'll lose everything if someone finds out."

"Nobody will. My parents are hardly around, and I don't post personal crap on Snapchat and Instagram like those kids." Angelina cocks her head to the students outside. "And, I'll only do 'exhibitions' in real time—no sexting. The more time we spend together, the more you can get the real thing."

Angelina lifts up her shirt, exposing her breasts. Chris sucks on her nipples.

"We better get back outside."

Angelina curls her shirt back down, and fixes her hair. Chris begins to rub himself to release the tension. Angelina walks out first, with the literature firmly in hand. Chris emerges about six minutes later, just as the video ends.

"We'll fill Mimi and Alexander in about everything tomorrow."

"Yeah. The tour's going to start in a couple of weeks, right?" Xavier asks.

"Yes, April 16. It all came so quickly didn't it? Just like everything else with this company. It's really hard sometimes to get a handle on things," Rebecca says with grudging acceptance.

"I know exactly what you mean. So, are you heading home now?"

"Sadly, I'm not. I have another appointment."

"Oh right, with the psychologist."

Rebecca sighs in both dread and embarrassment. Her face sinks below a chagrined expression.

"Honestly, there's nothing to be ashamed about," Xavier says as he rests a comforting hand on her shoulder. "You've been going through a lot. Even the strongest and smartest among us need some help every now and then. At least you didn't wait till you were having stimulating conversations with your invisible friends on the train."

A surprised look appears on Rebecca's face.

"You mean, you don't see them too?"

They both share a laugh.

"Be proud of yourself that you knew when you needed the help; and, you didn't wait till you fell off the deep end. I've always had the utmost respect for you Rebecca. I only have more now."

"That really means a whole lot coming from you. I just wished I felt the same way about myself," Rebecca responds with unease.

"You should. Have a good night. Celebrate with Peter." He winks at Rebecca as he is getting into his car.

She shakes her head with amusement.

"See you tomorrow."

The black Ford Explorer is rendered a hulking mammoth next to the sublime tranquility of the Long Island sound. Seagulls alight on the shore as low clouds create a winsome, ethereal mist. Rebecca steals momentary glances at the lapping waves, finely caressing the rocks with fluid glimmers, highlighting the golden hue of the sundown sky. A forsaken sigh is released as her eyes return straight ahead.

Coldplay's "The Scientist" quickly rouses her from her reverie.

"Hello?"

"Hey mom, how are you doing?"

"Hey Denver. I'm doing fine. How was school?"

"It was all right, I just had a rough day in PE class. I came back with some bruises, but—"

"Bruises! What were you guys doing?"

"We had football today, and it got a little intense. We're starting to get deeper into the tournament now."

"What happened to two-hand touch?"

"This is junior high mom; it's tackle now. Don't worry though; Angelina helped me take care of them."

"I didn't even like the idea of some of those brats getting near a football. All right, but I'll still look at them when I get home."

"Are you on your way home now?"

"No honey, I need to meet with the … director of our expansion campaign for a little bit. You remember how I'll be out in LA in a couple of weeks right?"

"Of course. The rapid expansion is keeping true to the Lewis vision, right mom?"

Rebecca smiles for a moment.

"I'm trying Denver, I'm trying. I'll see you when I get home. And, I'll check out those bruises. See you soon."

"I told you I'm fine mom. See you later."

"One more thing Denver, I love you."

"I love you too mom."

Rebecca spots the nondescript, two-story brick house to the right. On the well-manicured lawns are the signs "Richard Beckman—Attorney at Law" and "Dr. Melanie Chow, PhD—Psychotherapist."

"Now, that's synergy."

She turns into the inclined road, leading down to the back parking lot. There is a space right near Dr. Chow's back entrance. Rebecca swings out of the door; locks the car; lets out a heavy breath; and readies herself for action.

Dr. Chow's door is left slightly ajar. Rebecca furtively enters. The office is almost eerily cozy. Rebecca nestles into one of the matching, overstuffed pillows as she fondles its brocade and lace. Her eyes peruse the assorted health and news magazine covers that are fanned on the glen coffee table. The sounds of the crackling fire behind her and the warm earth tones of its embers begin to lull Rebecca Lewis into a slumber.

"I'm not going to get caught in this trap," Rebecca murmurs in slurred words as her eyelids shut.

"Excuse me. Can I help you?" a spry, young voice of about 21 chirps from behind the window.

Rebecca bounces up from the sofa and walks over.

"Hi, I have an appointment with Dr. Chow. I'm Rebecca Lewis."

"Sure, just sign in. She should be with you in a few minutes."

"Thanks."

Rebecca makes her way back to the sofa and begins skimming through *U.S. News and World Report*. A nasal, monotone drawl emerges from the whir of the flushing toilet.

"Is that Rebecca Lewis?"

Rebecca, who instantly finds the timbre of the voice off-putting, tries to devise an escape plan.

"Rebecca who?"

"Ha, ha, ha," he laughs with a screechy grind. "You're very funny. I remember seeing you on *GMA*."

Rebecca nods her head while she continues to peruse the magazine.

The man moves toward the sofa and slides near Rebecca. He smooths out his gray and black flannel shirt; pulls down his excruciatingly tight jeans; and licks his fingers to straighten out his dubious comb-over. The man leans in, getting within inches of Rebecca's face, and begins to speak.

"So, what is someone like you doing in a place like this?"

If you can imagine, he leans in even closer.

"Have you been hearing them too?"

Rebecca is momentarily disconcerted by his close proximity, the large gaps between his teeth, and the putrid odor of his breath; but, she quickly regains her poise.

"Um, no I haven't. Sometimes you just need someone to talk to, you know, clear your head."

She goes back to reading the article, immediately regretting that she engaged him in conversation.

"Yeah I understand that totally. I always tell Dr. Chow that I can't understand how a handsome and virile man like me can't get a date."

Rebecca slowly turns toward the man and looks him over from head to toe with furrowed brow.

"Nor can I."

He shrugs his shoulders.

"When's your appointment?" She asks.

"It was at 3."

Rebecca quickly checks her watch.

"It's a little past 4:30."

"Oh, I was on my way out."

"Of course."

"You know, a lot of the stuff you said on that segment made sense. It *resonated* with me."

"I'm happy to hear that."

"I'm starting to wear some of your designs."

He rips a pair of pea green and navy blue shades out from one of his pockets.

"Here, take a look."

Initially, Rebecca springs back from the atrocious color; but, she then takes the shades and begins scrutinizing them for their expression. She spots a shoddy imitation of the Windows to the Soul logo.

"Crazy is in the mind of the beholder?! This isn't our design! Where did you get this? And, from whom?"

"From some guy on Canal Street, right outside of the J station."

"Hi Ms. Lewis. You're extremely early. All right Jon, I'll see you in two weeks."

A slender, middle-aged woman stands at the door. She is about 5'3 with a dignified carriage that burnished her person. Cropped, shoulder-length hair and bangs; thin, circular glasses; and a navy blue pantsuit completed her appearance. Rebecca does not waste a second walking toward the office.

"Hi Dr. Chow." Rebecca quickly turns around. "Nice meeting you."

Rebecca gives Jon a perfunctory back wave. He ogles at her rear as he nods his head and wears a satisfied smirk. Rebecca enters the office and quickly shuts the door behind her.

"You're one of the few people who are happy that guys like that are around."

Dr. Chow laughs pleasantly in agreement.

"Well, it's good to finally see you. It's been about a month since we've been trying to set a schedule, hasn't it? We would have scheduled earlier if I had known that would be convenient (wanted to keep it private). Please have a seat."

"No, it's fine. I apologize for the delay. It's been unbelievably hectic."

Rebecca sits on the plush, black, leather loveseat across from Dr. Chow. She begins surveying the office.

The therapist's office is neatly decorated with the latest psychology journals and magazines, health and wellness tapes, DVDs, and assorted inspirational quotes from luminaries. Rebecca is momentarily pulled to the striking view of the Long Island Sound as the late-evening light weaves a misty haven. Dr. Chow's desk is right near the window. Its ordered disarray of patient reports, folders, and printed e-mails is offset by a floral centerpiece surrounded by Mediterranean and East-Asian knickknacks. A picture featuring Dr. Chow embracing a tall, brown-haired woman, cradling a shih tzu, rounded out the table.

"I would imagine it has been. Well, I did see the 'Good Morning America' segment; so, I know a few things about you. But, I'd rather get it from the horse's mouth."

"Sure, well I'm 45-years-old and basically grew up in upstate New York. When I speak to people from out of state, I just say New York because it sounds a lot more impressive."

Dr. Chow laughs.

"I did my undergraduate at Brown and got an MBA in finance at NYU. The beginning of my career was basically dedicated to trying to find my way in the financial market, working anywhere from the Wall Street Journal to Morgan Stanley. I finally couldn't stand another day of drab business suits and closed-toe shoes; so, I decided to put my degrees to good use, and start making funky sunglasses."

"Well, those are very popular, funky sunglasses; and, you should be happy that you did. I was already familiar with that part; now, tell me a little more about you. What do you like to do?"

"That's getting harder to answer. I like to write, read, catch up on the latest news, watch great films, or go to the theater when I get a chance. But, you know what I really like? Just exploring and learning.

Sometimes traveling abroad is just as interesting as reading a book on quantum theory. Discovery really turns me on the most."

"I love that too. How about we do a little exploring with your family? Tell me a little bit more about them."

Dr. Chow quietly takes out her notebook and a pen, preparing to take notes.

"That was a nice segue way. Well, you probably know about my husband and my two kids…"

"Yes, I do. How about the other members of your family? Do you keep in touch with your parents, brothers, and sisters?"

"I have three older brothers, but no sisters. I touch base with them once in a while. My biological father died when I was five, and my stepfather about two months ago. My mother…" Rebecca makes a dismissive gesture with her hand.

"Why is there such little contact?"

"It's really nothing. There's no bitterness, no rancor. It's just that we all lead such busy lives. It's always a challenge to get in contact with one another. I know there's Facebook, Instagram…Windows to the Soul is active on social media; but, I'm not. #closetloner."

"I get it," Dr. Chow says with a laugh. "Were you distant as children?"

"Actually, when we see each other, everything is fine. There was never any falling out or big blowup. At my stepfather's funeral, we were quite cordial and polite. It was very pleasant conversation, trying to catch up. But, I just never felt close to them. I always felt like the odd man, or woman, out. I always did the best in school; I was always the go-getter; I was always the high-achiever; and, there was definitely some jealousy…I'm not upset though. I think we just were never able to find common ground; so, there was never any sentimental attachment.

I had no problem going off to Brown. I wasn't homesick for a minute. Honestly, that was really the first time I ever felt something close to happiness. I really discovered my abilities, my strength, and started to really discover myself while I was there. I dove into my studies and community activities, welcoming the chance to get away from, I guess you would say, the ugliness of my childhood."

"Why was it so ugly?"

"Well, as I mentioned, I was five when I lost my dad," Rebecca sits up and straightens out in the chair. "As you can imagine, I don't remember him so vividly; but, when I do think of him, I see a handsome, strong, vibrant, and spirited man. He would hold me a lot, always kissing my cheek, and playing with me. My mom would always tell me that he was *joie de vivre* personified. The only time I would see him upset was around my mother. She's always been one of those social butterflies. So, she had a lot of male friends that would come over the house, and would flirt with them. My father didn't take kindly to that; and, they would frequently be at each other's throats, screaming and yelling. Actually, my dad died in large part because of my mom's behavior."

"Why do you say that?"

"She was never content with being a housewife; she always thought that her name should be in lights. I learned from my aunt some years later that she met a guy who told her he can get her into the business. They began a relationship. The guy didn't turn out to be anything but a wannabe; but, my mom was sleeping with him and was heavily in debt before she found that out. My dad was going through my mom's stuff and find out about the guy. My dad tracked them down during one of their 'business meetings.' The man shot my dad."

Rebecca bends her head back. She looked straight up to the ceiling, hoping the tears would retreat. She sits up in her chair, collects herself, and continues on. Her voice breaks into a tearful quiver.

"He shot my dad twice in the head. He later died at the hospital. I think that's the third time I've talked about that."

Dr. Chow bends forward and puts a comforting hand on Rebecca's shoulder.

"I appreciate your sharing it. Is that when you grew cold to your mother, or did you always have a tense relationship?"

"You *really* want me to talk about her."

"I think it would help."

"Honestly, I've been pretty indifferent. For the first five years I was daddy's little girl, and I saw him as the one who would make things right. Everything was fine as long as he was around. I remember the house being in total disarray most of the day. When she got the call from dad saying he was coming home, there was a mad dash to clean up. She would delegate. I would help her with the kitchen and bathroom; Michael and Tom handled the bedrooms; and Greg, most of the time, would do the front and back yards. She always seemed to live like that… always on the edge, waiting till the last possible minute. It was never destructive until dad died.

Looking back on it, I think that's when she really lost herself. I have scenes in my mind of her sleeping with different guys every night, starting to experiment with drugs. I knew she loved my father very much, though she wasn't faithful to him. I don't think she could conceive of life without him; he's the one that kept everything together."

"And, she tried to find men to fill that void."

"She sure did. There were times she would run down to the city for days at a time. She would just leave us with friends and neighbors. She was rendezvousing with her, I guess 'sugar daddies,' you know? She would fall for it again and again, men telling her that they were big-time agents or businessmen that had connections. She finally fell for a struggling actor, this screwed-up guy named Jake."

"Was he your stepfather?"

"Yeah, I guess you can call him that."

"I presume your relationship with him wasn't very good."

"Not at all. He couldn't hold a candle to my father. He was violent, crude, and out-of-control. He was a lush, an inveterate liar… Jake was verbally and physically abusive to all of us, and abusive in all ways to my mother. He enabled her drug habit as well. I think one of the main reasons she stayed with him was because of the sex. I mean, I could hear her coming from our basement (sorry for being explicit). There were times they would leave the bedroom door open too.

Thinking about it, that's her Achilles heel; she needs someone to find her attractive. After he would beat her up, he would always bring back nice clothes, jewelry… I think most of which he stole. I'll give him credit though; he was a talented actor. But, he couldn't keep a job because of his problems. He was really a self-destructive personality; and, my mom fed off of him."

"How did your mom react when he was abusive to you kids?"

"She really didn't. She tried to pretend to be naïve, like nothing was going on. I even tried telling her about how he was fu…"

"How he was what?"

"He sexually abused me, till I was 16."

Rebecca lets out a heavy breath and stares at the ground

"I really don't want to talk about it Dr. Chow."

"I know it's painful; but, it's important to come to terms with these issues. You're a very strong woman Rebecca. We got through talking about your father's death; so, we can get through this."

Dr. Chow takes Rebecca's hand reassuringly. Rebecca continues to look at the ground and begins speaking, flatly.

"He sexually abused me, continuously, for six years. It started when I was 10-years-old. I started developing early and he noticed it. He would tell me that I have a nice body…I'm very pretty…I look older than my age. I knew he was a loser; but, he was attractive. When he wasn't high, drunk, etc. which was very seldom, he wasn't that bad of a guy. I was fond of him at the beginning. He picked up on that and took advantage of it, I think. I'm not saying I came on to him or I was trying to seduce him because I didn't; but, I just had complex feelings toward him."

Rebecca swallows before continuing.

"I was 10-years-old the first time he had sex with me. My mom and brothers were sound asleep. He got on my bed and told me he wanted to see how I was doing, spend some time with me...."

Rebecca's eyes began to twitch. She closed them for a moment and held her eyes, trying to stop it. She then swallows, attempting to regain her composure.

"I remember thinking that this is so wrong, feeling so cold and unprotected, but I didn't really fight him so hard. There was a part of me—I guess being that age, and wanting his affection—that didn't mind it. He would tell me how he loved me, he thought I was so beautiful...There were times that it was really rough and other times when it was...each time he would say he loved me, I was good to him.

Before then, I never felt such intensity and passion and I hate to admit, I got a kind of high off of it. But even during those times, I realized that this was wrong; I mean, he was violating me and violating my mother...Wow, I've never talked about this. I guess I've never really reconciled those feelings. I would wait for the nights with this haunting dread, and I don't know, morbid anticipation. After a while, as he became more disturbed and really taken by the addiction, I just began to resent him. But, after a couple of years I became inured to the abuse. It just became a routine part of my life."

Rebecca finally looks up at Dr. Chow. The pained tremor gives way to an emboldened voice, strengthened by assertion.

"I think that's what makes sexual abuse especially vicious, diabolical even. Not only are you defiling something that is inherently beautiful and loving, you're taking advantage of someone at such a delicate period in their lives…I was so relieved when it all ended."

"How did it end?"

Rebecca's eyes turn toward the ground once again. She takes a few deep breaths, attempting to muster resolve.

"I would tell him as I got older that we need to use protection, but; he never wanted to. He would even beat me when I brought it up. I've never told anyone this Dr. Chow."

"It's OK Rebecca," Dr. Chow says soothingly. "You're doing great."

"OK… Right before I turned 16, I found out I was…My mom never found out; but, I told him after about a month and half…"

"That you were pregnant?"

Rebecca opens her mouth to respond, but then turns away from Dr. Chow. She opens her eyes widely trying to rein in tears.

"He also beat me throughout. My mom worked the graveyard shift for about a year and wouldn't be back until around 8 or 9 in the morning. One of those nights he comes up to my room, bashes in the door, and just *throws* me on the bedroom floor. He starts pounding my stomach," Rebecca begins striking her left palm with a closed first, recreating the moments. "POUNDING it and POUNDING it. After about 20 minutes, I think I passed out. When I woke up, I was lying in a pool of blood—"

Rebecca brings up her left hand to cover her face, stifling tears.

"He became apprehensive after that and told me we wouldn't fuck anymore…" Rebecca says trailing off.

"During the period of abuse, did you have any other relationships? Were there any romantic involvements or even close girlfriends you could talk to?"

"I guess you could say that I had some good acquaintances, but hardly any good friends. It's not that I was particularly antisocial; it's just that I didn't meet people to whom I could fully relate. I wanted relationships that were meaningful. I know it sounds clichéd, but I wanted someone I could discuss the meaning of life with and how to make the world better…those kinds of issues. It's hard to find that among your peers at that age. Sometimes you never do.

I've never been uncomfortable with being the loner though. After a while I just resigned to the role, thinking, 'You know that this is my lot in life…this is the way it was supposed to be.'"

"I did have *one* good friend, Stacey, whom I met during a student-ambassadors trip to Washington, D.C. Well, I guess we were more like pen pals, since she lived in Arizona and I hardly got to see her. We had to settle for long phone conversations (which my mom didn't like) and letters. I wanted to arrange more trips; but, lack of money—and, I guess, my mom's fear that I might see 'greener pastures' and leave— made visiting her difficult. My mom didn't want her to visit me either. I know she went to school overseas and then I went to Brown; so, we just lost touch after a while. She was one of the few people I connected with.

Boyfriends? I didn't have any during the period of abuse. You know I would go out with some friends to the movies, amusement park, etc., but there wasn't anything serious. Right after the abuse ended, I started getting close to a kid in school, Anthony. Yeah, he was my high-school sweetheart. It was pretty intense. It was very passionate, very sexual. We both loved to experiment. That was one of the best parts of the relationship.

I think on some levels, I wanted to fill the physical void left by the end… I wanted that deep connection, to feel that intensity with someone else. I regarded him as my first time. I tell Peter the same thing. It was the first time sex wasn't manipulated; there was neither a feeling of dread nor domination, you know? We were just having a good time and expressing our love and affection for one another. I remember feeling so liberated during that first time. I'll always remember him for giving me that feeling.

It wasn't purely a sexual relationship though. Tony was very intelligent and curious. We could talk for hours and we shared a lot of the same dreams and goals. He was so thoughtful too, very sweet."

"Why did it end?"

"We just went our separate ways, figuratively and literally. He decided to go to Berkeley. I went to Brown; so, there was a considerable distance there. That, and I felt a lot of pain from the relationship. I felt I had to distance myself from it in order to move on."

"What kind of pain?"

"We were going to have a baby. I lost Lily after four months," Rebecca says in a monotone.

"You had named the baby?"

"Yeah, I really connected with her. We were even preparing for her, getting clothes and toys, even thinking about where she would go to school. I guess we were trying to convince ourselves we could deal with this, that we could be parents." Rebecca and Dr. Chow laugh.

"Do you still have any of those clothes?"

"I actually have a d—. Yes, I still have the clothes.

She starts again with renewed energy and looks straight at Dr. Chow.

"The miscarriage really marred our relationship. Tony tried to reach out to me, but I just rejected his gestures. We finally just decided to move on."

"I presume it was also difficult to forge relationships during college?"

"Yeah it was. For a year I was pretty depressed. I still don't know how I was able to do it. I was on the Dean's List, in student government, 4.0

GPA… You know everything was fine when I was in the classroom or in community and campus activities; but, when I got home, I imploded. I would sob for like two hours, wouldn't eat. But then, I would bury myself in work. It was just tunnel-vision, and I was able to forget about all of my pain. I really did miss Tony. I think that was another part of it too. I was ashamed of myself, how I couldn't move on. I was supposed to be this really strong person, completely self-reliant and independent. and I was devastated, pining for a man you know?"

"Well, there's nothing to be ashamed of. This was your first healthy relationship; and, there was really no closure. You never effectively dealt with your feelings."

"I just felt that I had endured so much; so, I should have been able to overcome this as well. I felt that I was being tested so much; my strength was always being challenged.

I did meet someone else sophomore year, Will. That relationship was also difficult."

"How so?"

"Well, Will was Black. Not that Rhode Island is racist. But, there's this insidious prejudice that penetrated the country post-Civil Rights, and that area wasn't an exception. You know how it's become overt again, since the election. You know, men don't go around with sheets on their heads and torching houses (at least not most of the time); but, now racism is more treacherous and furtive, rendering it more destructive. We would get glowers, overhear snide remarks, and of course, things that were more blatant. There were times we had to wait to be served in restaurants. For me, racism was an abstract thing till that point. After seeing what Will had to go through, and what we experienced together, I had a greater awareness of it. It's almost like a cancer; you don't see it, you don't smell it, but you know it's there destroying, ravaging each moment.

He served as an escape for me in many ways. I'm not going to say he being Black wasn't any part of the attraction—it was. I had never been with anyone outside of my race; and, I found the dark chocolate skin, and the full lips, alluring. OK, yeah and I wanted to see if the myths and stories were true (in his case they were)."

Dr. Chow chuckles.

"It wasn't just the physical fascination, but he showed me a whole new world. He grew up in San Francisco, and his parents were learned and forward-looking. They were part of the Black Power movement. He taught me a lot about his culture, art. We would travel around, exploring the club and music scenes. Most importantly, I think he introduced me to different schools of thought. He ignited my yearning for developing my spirituality, and discovering that which is beyond myself really. In a lot of ways, he sowed the seeds for Windows to the Soul. We really had a great time. I hate to use the cliché; but, he did expand my horizons."

"Did it end amicably, or did you reach some kind of impasse?"

"Honestly, I think it just ran its course. Maybe I wasn't completely comfortable with the race issue; but, at the end of the day I think we just belonged with other people."

Rebecca turns to her right, searching her mind.

"I would tell friends that Will and I we were just friends, nothing serious…Actually, I really didn't want it to get too serious; but, I think he wanted more than that. One day, I just told him things aren't really working out; and, I think it would be better for us to end it. He pleaded with me, telling me were having a great time, we love each other, and we shouldn't end this…But, I didn't want to hear it. He tried calling me a few times after that too; but, I never returned his calls. He finally got the point. I've come to terms with it; it was a long time ago."

"Hmmm. You've obviously gone through some tough times. Did meeting Peter help to alleviate the pain?"

"Yes, it did. We just connected that first night we met. I told him a lot of things I had never told anybody. He just has that kind of power. It's like a Svengali aspect; but, in the most benign sense. I automatically felt safer and more secure around him, like everything was going to be OK. I hadn't felt that feeling since my father died."

"He's about 12 years older than you correct?"

"Yes."

"How would you describe him?"

"He's just a beautiful person, inside and out. He's immensely intelligent, and has this kind of droll sense of humor. Peter's the eternal optimist too. He never lets things get him down; but, he's not manic, always on an even keel. He's loving and affectionate too. You always know that he cares. He's my biggest fan. I approached the Windows to the Soul idea with a lot of trepidation. I was thinking to myself, 'How practical is this?' 'How will people respond?' 'Even if it does work out, will this be one of those flash in the pan kinds of things?' He allayed my reservations, and told me no matter what happens just go for it—don't hold back. If you put your heart and soul into it, you can't have any regrets. Every day, I'm grateful I took that leap of faith."

"Let's talk a little bit more about Windows to the Soul. I think that's a wonderful idea."

"Thanks."

"I think many people have been hesitant to embrace their spirituality because either it seems too abstract or even formidable. Winding that in seamlessly with everyday items like eyewear, watches, and bands is a novel and approachable idea. That's a perfect way to break down those barriers."

"That's really the central facet of the *Windows to the Soul* vision. You have to see spirituality as something that's intrinsic to your daily life. It's not something you just think about on Sundays or religious holidays; it has to be a constant, internal force that motivates every moment."

"So, why were you so passionate about that idea?"

"After a number of years of being in finance, I felt that I had lost myself; I didn't feel that fire that had fueled me through school. I had done things that I wasn't passionate about, and plain regretted. I didn't want to compromise myself any longer. I was searching for a way to reconnect."

"It seems that connection has been a motif in your life, a driving force. Connection, I believe is also an integral part of spirituality. How do you see spirituality?"

"I think it's different things to different people. You can't define that kind of concept really, that would be belittling it. However, there needs to be an awareness of something greater than yourself and that your strength, the blessings, come from the Source. Also, we're all on a journey; and, you have to keep in mind that with every moment, and every experience, there's a lesson. Life is more than the car you drive, how much money you make, the kind of clothes you wear—and how many likes you get. Life lies in that which is immaterial—that which can't be perceived through the eyes of the mind, but only through the depths of the soul."

"That's beautiful. I want to add something if I may."

"Please."

"Spirituality also constitutes connecting with your higher self to ultimately reconnect with the Source. That fire that you were always craving, that feeling of 'life' is being connected with the *Energy*, the *Light*, of the higher Power. I believe that is the Entity, beyond yourself, with which you were seeking to connect."

"I definitely agree with that."

"Part of connecting with that Force is living your life fully, and meeting things head on."

"Here it comes. I think I know where you're going with this," Rebecca moans.

"Just hear me out Rebecca."

"OK."

"We're both spiritual people; so, I know you can appreciate this idea. Only the Source is perfect, complete. Therefore, as spiritual beings, we are always on a journey of evolution, hopefully growing more aware, and deepening our understanding, every day. All of us have different phases and different lessons on that journey."

"That's true."

"I think part of your lesson, on this phase of your journey, is to come to terms with your feelings and pain. Do you think that the hurt from the past has served as somewhat of a barrier to your being your best self at times?"

"I appreciate those words Dr. Chow; but, I've dealt with that pain. I know I wasn't so forthcoming about everything; but, that's because I don't want to dwell on it. What's in the past should stay in the past; and, I don't need to talk about it," Rebecca says with convincing assuredness. "Look, despite all of that, I was a distinguished student; I have a business that's exploding as we speak; and, I have a great husband and wonderful children. I've done more than all right," she continues rather peremptorily.

"There is no doubt that you have done excellently; and, you should be very proud of your accomplishments. We have to keep in mind that we can always be doing better. There are parts of ourselves that we need to develop in order to better appreciate the immaterial and, as you said, connect with that which is beyond ourselves."

Rebecca manages a nod.

"Let's talk about your husband and your children. Do you get to spend enough time with them?"

"Not as much as I'd like. We do have special days together; but, those have been rare lately. But, isn't it really about the quality of the time, not the quantity? Sure, we don't have all that much together. But, they know I love them. Love is the most important."

"Of course it is. And, you feel that going to soccer games, the school plays, having some nights with just you and Peter, and finding times for intimacy is fine. But, the most important thing is just having it there."

"That's true."

"There might be more to it Rebecca. During our conversation, there seems to be a pattern emerging here. You've tried to convince yourself that you are above emotions, and transmuting feelings into a kind of aloofness is a form of transcendence (while raw emotions lie just below the surface). Quite frankly, 'connecting to your higher self' has almost become an excuse for not living your life."

A stoic stare, camouflaging burgeoning aggravation, creeps onto Rebecca's face.

"Let's take Windows to the Soul for instance. You have insightful words of wisdom scrawled on assorted products. This is a good first step toward becoming in touch with your spirituality; but, it should not be the end all and be all. I'm sure it was supposed to be a springboard—"

"What my company does is hardly superficial. This is not supposed to be an indictment of Windows to the Soul. This is supposed to be a supportive forum for me to deal with my feelings Dr. Chow," Rebecca says with her eye beginning to twitch.

"However, those emotional complexes have hindered the growth of your relationship with your husband and children. You may have developed a fear of emotional attachments because you have witnessed how tragedy is, from what you have gone through, their natural result. Is it that you keep Peter, Angelina, and Denver at a distance because you're too afraid of losing them?"

Rebecca immediately erupts, bolting out of her chair.

"All right, I've been holding back long enough. You can say a lot of things about me Dr. Chow; but, I won't let you say that I don't love my husband and my kids."

"Rebecca, I didn't say that at all. But, you're not as close to them as you would like to be. I know some of these issues are hard to confront but we need—"

"I don't have *issues* Dr. Chow. I am doing pretty damn well OK. I don't need this, excuse me, shit. You have nutcases like Jon that need to *be one with their feelings* and *come to terms with their pain;* but, no matter what you say, I am not, excuse me again, fucked-up. I love my husband and my children very much, and they know that."

Rebecca continues with incensed fervor.

"You think I don't get this scheme? You're trying to make me think that I have some sort of complex so you can bilk me. Yeah, fatten your pocket week after week. I'm too smart for that."

"Rebecca, that's hardly what I'm doing; and, I'm deeply sorry that you're misunderstanding my words. I don't doubt your love for your husband and children; I can see it. But, you can still love people very much and keep them at a distance."

"That's not me."

"I suppose you don't love your mother."

"That's enough."

Rebecca whips out her checkbook, makes the check out furiously, and stuffs it into Dr. Chow's hand.

"People like Jon need you. I don't."

Rebecca storms out of the room. The slam of the door roars through the office. Dr. Chow sighs in disappointment.

⸺ ∘∘∘❧◈❧∘∘∘ ⸺

Denver is working on his homework at the kitchen table. He looks up as soon as the door opens and greets his mom with a bright smile.

"Hi mom! How was the meeting with the director?"

"Oh, actually it went pretty well. We're really gearing up for the new openings in LA. Then, we have Atlanta and Chicago soon after that."

"It's pretty exciting. I wish we could go with you."

"Oh I know honey; but, you have school and it'll be just a lot of tedious, business stuff. It wouldn't be that fun. So, what happened in PE? Let me see those bruises."

"Mom, I'm really OK. Angelina took care of them."

"Well, mom is back now. I'm going to see them."

Rebecca lifts up his shirt to see numerous, broad bandages concealing his wounds. Rebecca looks at them with pained shock.

"What kind of football game was this? This was more than just a hard sack."

"I'm fine mom; I'm not even hurting anymore."

"Why did they beat you up Denver?"

"They didn't mom."

"Don't lie to me."

Denver goes back to doing his homework.

"Forget about your homework for a second."

Rebecca slams his books shut.

"Did they find out about the program?"

Denver looks up at his mother with a determined stare.

"I told you that nothing happened mom. I'm fine."

Rebecca is not ready to back down.

"Who are they?"

Denver stuffs his iPad under his arm and starts upstairs impetuously. Rebecca chases him down and held his shoulders in a tight grasp. She looks starkly at Denver with eyes that begin to tear.

"Denver, please believe me; you can tell me what happened. It's OK if they beat you up. You don't have to be ashamed. I'm your mom baby," Rebecca says in a very soothing voice. She releases Denver from her grasp and strokes his blond hair.

"Mom, I'm trying to tell you I'm fine. There's nothing to worry about," Denver responds turning away from his mother. "I need to do my homework."

Rebecca throws her head back and lets out a despondent sigh. She starts again with a plaintive cry.

"Help me Denver. I'm going to ask you one more time, 'What happened?'"

Denver looks back at her and shoots an intransigent stare. Rebecca explodes with desperation.

"Why do you feel that you can't share your life with me?" Rebecca cries with a tear streaming down her face.

"You never understood it."

Denver goes into the den and slams the door. Rebecca blankly stares at the floor dejected.

Rebecca hears Angelina skipping down the stairs. She is wearing an overly snug baby-blue and white striped sweater; a denim–pleated miniskirt; and white, thigh-high, platform boots. A matching fur, baby-blue cap—that is cocked to the side—caps off the outfit. She's holding her Surface in one hand and some documents from the United Nations and the CDC in the other.

"I think I'm going to have an aneurysm," Rebecca mutters to herself.

"Hey mom, I didn't know you got back."

She notices her mom's dispirited expression.

"Are you OK?"

"Yeah I'm doing better now. You know, seeing you dressed like that just lights up my spirits."

"Whatever."

"Thanks for taking care of Denver. What happened?"

"Oh, he didn't tell you? They were playing football today in PE and he played quarterback. You know, I think soccer is really building up his confidence. He's really begun to take the initiative in everything.

Anyway, you know how guys become animals with football. They sacked him a couple of times; it got kinda rough. But don't worry, him and his team did really well. You should've been there mom."

Rebecca claps sarcastically. "That was an excellent collaboration with your brother, everything in sync, impeccable. It's late-May. Aren't they done playing football? Now, who beat him up?"

"What are you talking about mom?"

"Angelina-Skye."

"Mom, you know I'm always open with you. I was passing by the field while they were playing. I saw it myself."

"Angelina, I know Denver never talks to me, but you can. Have they been teasing him about being in the program?"

Angelina hesitates for a moment and responds.

"Yeah, a little bit; and, it might be good to transfer him. But, Denver's a strong kid mom. You don't need to worry about him."

"Would you all quit saying, 'Don't worry'! I have a right to worry. We're going to talk about this when your dad gets back. By the way, where are you going?"

"I'm meeting with Chris."

"Wait a minute, I thought it was just Thursday and Friday. How much research are you doing? Maybe you two can stop the trade war while you're at it."

"Ha ha. We just wanted to go over a presentation we were working on. You know, just a quick run-through."

"Really? What kind of run-through?"

"MOM!" Angelina says with an exasperated groan.

"In that case, why are you dressed like that? You're about to pop out of that sweater and I can spot your ass cheeks from here. What happened to a T-shirt and jeans?"

"My clothes fit fine mom."

"No they don't! You've filled out a lot these last few months and you need to get some new clothes."

"I've just rounded out mom."

"That's what I mean Angelina; you're curvy. You're naturally a very beautiful, attractive girl; and, you don't need to wear those clothes. You can't hide them; but, don't call any more attention to them."

"You're always talking about my body. Just leave me alone."

"I'm sorry Angelina; but, it's like you've grown overnight. It's hard for me to get used to."

"Well, you have to. I'll be back at 10."

"9:30."

Angelina glowers at her mother.

"You have to wear a jacket over that if you're going to leave this house."

"I don't want to wear a jacket."

"Maybe you didn't hear me. I said *you have* to wear a jacket over it if you're going to leave this house."

Rebecca throws her a light blue, spring, button-down jacket with a fringe collar and sleeves.

"Fine, but I'll take it off right when I get out of the house."

"You know that Surface sure would make a pretty good paddle."

Angelina grudgingly puts on the sweater and stomps out of the living room.

"You'll be back what time?"

"10," Angelina mutters under her breath.

"Sorry, I didn't hear that."

"9:30!"

Angelina could feel her mom's eyes burning through her as she walks out of the door and down the sidewalk. Chris's Audi is parked a few blocks from the Lewises' driveway. Rebecca turns away when Angelina leaps into his car.

As soon as Angelina gets into the car, she undoes her sweater and tosses it in the backseat. Chris's eyes fire with anticipation.

"I knew you'd love this outfit," Angelina says seductively. Chris immediately starts undoing his jeans. Angelina does the rest. Her head dives into his crotch.

Totally oblivious to what is transpiring less than a block away, Peter enters the door.

"Honey, I'm home."

Rebecca walks hurriedly out of the kitchen.

"Hey Peter," she says followed by a quick kiss on the lips.

"How was your day?" he asks.

"That's a loaded question. Denver got beat up by some kids at school. He's upstairs."

"By whom? Was he hurt badly?"

"I don't know; but, I suspect there's a group of kids bullying him. I think they know he's attending the depression program. Actually, Angelina did a good job of treating him. He's not too bad now."

"Did Angelina tell you anything?"

"They've created a little cabal. They both gave me this lame story about how his football game in PE got rough. Denver was playing quarterback and he got sacked a few times. I think we should transfer him to another center."

"But the one near the school is the top-rated in the area. They have about an 80% success rate."

"I know, but New Horizons in North Salem is excellent as well. Maybe we can schedule some weekend sessions for him there. I had a feeling enrolling him at Brighter Days wasn't the best idea. It was inevitable that the kids at school would find out. They say crap on Snapchat…Convenience is one thing; but, his well-being is paramount. He's more open with you. Please talk to him."

"I definitely will. You know what, I'll take him to the office with me tonight. We should have some good talking time on the road."

"Why are you going to the office?"

"Remember I told you earlier that I might have to stay late? I tried calling you again a couple of hours ago; but, your cell phone was off. Amber, our new intern, has been working with me on the A-Beta research and we're *thisclose* to some new developments," Peter says with almost childlike excitement.

"Oh right. It seems like you're on the cusp of a breakthrough. You have to fill me in on what you're working on. By the way, I'd like to meet Amber. Why don't you invite her over for dinner some time?"

"Yeah that's a good idea. I think you'd like her a lot. I just came back to pick up some of my reports and get something to eat at work. By the way, how did the ad meeting go?"

"Yeah, that seems like ages ago now. It wasn't too exciting, just bandying some ideas about with eggheads."

Peter laughs.

"It was pretty productive though. We settled on some good ideas for the grand openings."

"That's excellent. I'm sure Mimi and Alexander will be excited. Oh, I almost forgot. How was the session with Dr. Chow?"

"It was fine," Rebecca answers with subtle consternation.

Peter notices, but chooses not to probe.

"See, I told you it would be. I know you're thinking now, 'Why did I put it off for a month?'"

"Yeah, that's exactly what I thought," Rebecca answers.

"So, you'll be seeing her every Wednesday, right?"

"Hmmm, I don't know about that. It's going to be pretty busy from now on; so, I'll have to squeeze it in when I get the chance."

"Rebecca, we're talking about your health here. You need to make time to see her."

"Peter, I'm healthy. Besides, I made a lot of progress with just this first session. I was really able to get a lot of things out of my system tonight. I was amazed at how helpful it was. All I really needed was an opportunity to vent and clear my head. I know now I just need to do that more often."

"Good, I'm happy you had that epiphany. That's why you need to see her regularly."

"I'll try Peter."

Peter comes over, grabs Rebecca's behind and kisses her neck. He whispers in her ear.

"You've been going through my cologne?"

"What are you talking about?"

"You smell like Burberry."

"Hmmm, I don't know." Rick's face flashes through her mind. "Some crazy guy at the Dr. Chow's office insisted on hugging me. Maybe that's it."

"I told you you were like a magnet. I'll see you around 10. Let me get Denver."

Denver is already coming down the stairs.

"Hi dad, I just heard you now."

"That's OK sport. Hey, you want to come to the office with me? I want to show you some of the cool stuff we're uncovering about Alzheimer's. You can finish your work there."

"I'm already done; but, I'll come along anyway. Maybe I can help you look up some things on the Internet."

"That's a great idea. Hurry up and get your coat."

Denver runs to the coat hanger.

Peter mouths to Rebecca, "We'll talk."

"I'll see you later hon," Peter says.

"Bye babe. Bye Denver."

"Bye mom."

"When we get back today, I'm going to show you some moves to protect yourself. All right?"

"OK."

"Those kids shouldn't be messing with you; but, that doesn't mean you don't stand up to them. With those moves, they won't be able to take you down. Stand up for yourself; we'll deal with the suspensions later."

Denver starts laughing.

"Thanks dad."

"No son of mine is getting his butt kicked. They'll be cowering from you in no time.

"We're going to move you out of Brighter Days anyway. I think you'll be going to New Horizons in North Salem. I have to check it out later this week.

"Another thing, you need to talk more to your mom. I know she's not always the most affectionate; but, she loves you very much and she wants to get close to you. It really pained her to see you hurt today. She feels that both of you kids are moving away from her; and, that gives a mother a lot of grief. You need to try reaching out to her."

"I'll try."

The red BMW pulls into the Westchester Neurological Sciences Center. The white, seventeen-story building is almost completely dark, save for the illuminated room on the fifth floor. Amber is waiting for Dr. Lewis there.

"Hey Amber. How early did you get in?"

"Oh, about an hour ago, not too long. Who's that handsome, little man giving you a run for your money?" Amber says affectionately to Denver. She brushes her sideways bangs to the right repeatedly, making sure they are not covering her face. She subtly primps her ponytail as well.

"I'm Dr. Lewis's son, Denver," he responds with a satisfied smile.

"He's always wanted to see the office; and, he volunteered to help us do some research on the Internet."

"Awesome! We're finding out some really cool things about Alzheimer's every day. Hopefully, you won't even have to think about it by the time you get older."

"Thanks for the good work Amber," Denver says as he gets lost in her large, brown eyes.

"Anytime Denver."

"OK sport, now it's time for you to work. Remember the links I texted? Please go through as many of these websites as you can, and put in 'Alzheimer's - astrocytes' OK? Print out some of the best articles and we'll talk about them later. You can use the computer in the back room over there."

"Sure dad."

"It seems like you made a new friend there," Peter says to Amber.

"I think so. You have quite a kid. I think you're molding a future neuroscientist."

"He's brilliant. His IQ is over 160. He doesn't want to do that though. I think he wants to be a writer. His mind is insatiable. He loves to learn; so, I share a lot of the new developments from the office with him. Maybe I should bring him here more often."

"I'd like that a lot."

"So, Ms. Overeager Beaver, you've been here since an hour? You really don't have to work so hard anymore, you've impressed me enough."

"It was really nothing Dr. Lewis—"

"You can call me Peter."

Amber gives him a little smile.

"It was really nothing Peter; I just wanted to get an early start on finishing up my reports. I just got through the last one about 10 minutes ago."

"I admire your diligence; but, I thought we were supposed to work on that together tonight."

"Oh, I know, but you've been working really hard today. I thought it would be easier if we just reviewed them together. I reworked the SEM. Maybe you can help me revise the discussion."

"Sounds good. Let's start on that now," Peter responds.

"Oh, I wanted to tell you, you were *outstanding* at the conference today," Amber starts. "You're really good on your feet. Some of that information just appeared in the Journal today. It was impressive how you were able to integrate it into your presentation so quickly."

"I appreciate that coming from you Amber. Well, we conducted a few of the previous studies that were referenced in the article. We also know the researchers; so, I've been keeping abreast of the developments."

"You're the consummate professional. I just hope I could be as good as you one day."

"No, you won't. With the way you're going, you'll probably be better."

"Wow," Amber responds with flattered, yet nervous, laughter.

"I also found some new information about temporal lobe distribution in schizophrenics. There was a new study about subtle gender differences. I'll give you a synopsis tomorrow."

"You're always working hard. Well, let's get to your reports now. I'm sure they don't need that much revision; but, the sooner we get on them the better."

Amber grimaces.

"What's wrong?"

"I don't know... I've been having this awful headache."

"It's probably due to how you've been pushing yourself so much since you've gotten here. Just take a few minutes all right? I think you need a little time to clear your head. I'll go check how Denver's doing." Peter begins to rise from the chair.

"I wish it were that easy."

"What's that?"

"Sorry Peter, I was just talking to myself. I was saying that I wish it were that easy for me to just clear my head."

Peter signals to Denver to wait for a moment.

"Is there something going on?"

"No, just some personal things that have been weighing on me a little bit. I know you have to focus on Denver. I'll get the reports."

"Well, we won't get much done with the reports if your focus isn't here. In 56 years, I know about personal problems. What's the matter?"

"I've just been feeling kind of empty these last few months. Don't get me wrong, I'm really grateful for this internship—especially having the opportunity to work with you— but I think I've just been pouring all of my energies into this to distract myself from everything else that's going on. Or isn't."

"I'm sure an intelligent, vivacious young woman such as yourself has a great group of friends she can hang out with, right? I'd be very surprised if there isn't a man in your life."

"Yeah I do have great girl friends; but, I need intimacy Peter. I miss the flowers, the kisses, the romance. You know, that, that intensity. The sense of merging with someone, almost getting lost in them..." Amber says to Peter as she turns toward his face.

"I understand. It sounds like your last boyfriend was definitely the romantic type."

"He undoubtedly was. I'm the same way too; so, we indulged each other. I know this is going to sound kind of corny—"

"No, go ahead."

"I felt like our love was something magical; it was spiritual. We just had this incredible connection. It's almost ineffable how close we felt to each other. There were times we even finished each other's sentences. It sounds really stupid; but, at times we would even dream of each other and hold conversations. We would see each other the next day and realize that they didn't happen in reality."

"That's amazing," Peter says longingly.

"And the sex..." Amber begins as she tosses her neck back, her eyes almost reaching the back of her head. "I can't even begin to tell you

Peter. It was like there was neither 'him' nor 'I,' we were just 'one.' What we had was greater than us. Have you ever had that?"

Peter is contently lost in his own mind before he returns.

"Honestly it's been a while. I know how it is to feel like you've lost someone you really love. But, you have to cherish those memories without getting lost in them. The future is always better, if you let it be."

"I'll try to remember that."

"You know a lot of men, actually a lot of women for that matter, are scared of that kind of love. It's hard when someone can look inside your soul when you're not comfortable with what's inside there yourself. That's probably the reason why he left."

"I think you're right. I mean it wasn't always perfect. There were times we got into pretty heated arguments, most of the time because he was trying to lie to me. I would think, 'I know you, why aren't you being open with me?'

I know he loved me; but, he had so many issues he needed to deal with. I don't think he was fully able to appreciate what we had. I'm still wishing that—I'm too embarrassed to say."

"That he would come back."

"I'm pathetic right?" Amber says with chagrined laughter.

"It's not. When you had something like that, there's no way you won't be experiencing any longing."

"But you know, over these last few months I've been thinking to myself, 'Maybe it wasn't all that great.' Maybe it was just this splendid fantasy that I crafted in my head."

"Well, that's a lot of what goes on in a relationship anyway. An integral piece of keeping one together is striking that balance, getting lost in the fantasy while you're grounded in reality.

You always need to remember that people are just that, people. You can't apotheosize them. The higher you exalt them, the harder they tumble down. But you have a sublime imagination. You're definitely going to need that."

"You've got 20 years with Rebecca. I guess you've crafted the fantasy."

"Ha, I would hardly say that. I think I could use a little bit more of your imagination lately."

Amber lets out a little laugh.

"Honestly, no relationship is perfect. It's kind of like going to the museum. You don't look at everything; you just focus on the good parts. Sometimes, that's really all that keeps it together."

"Wow, I guess I need to get out of my bubble."

"I know this won't do much to pacify you; but, if you're meant to be together, you'll meet each other again. But, do keep your heart open. The love you had with him could just be preparing you for an even greater one in the future. The Universe won't let a woman as wonderful and beautiful as you stay alone that much longer."

"You're too sweet Peter. Thanks so much." Amber says adoringly to Peter. She then gives him a quick but very affectionate hug. Peter then cradles Amber's face in his hands. Denver stands up a little from the computer and begins looking at his dad and the intern.

Peter leans into Amber's face and sweetly kisses her.

"That's so the wait won't seem as long."

Peter and Amber just look into each other's eyes for what seems to be forever. Denver runs out with some papers in hand.

"Hey dad, hey Amber."

Peter and Amber hurriedly start going thumbing through the reports.

"It's starting to get late. We should leave soon if you want to get home by 10:00."

"You're right sport. Time goes by so quickly when you're working hard. You'll see that in a few years. Hey Amber, let's just go through the first three paragraphs, and finish up the rest tomorrow morning. You can also e-mail me the slides you were working on; and, I'll look at them tonight."

"Thanks a lot Dr. Lewis. I really appreciate all of your help."

"That's what I'm here for."

"Will you have time to show me the moves you were telling me about?" Denver asks.

"Of course. I'll finish reviewing the slides after."

VIII

The once modest interiors of Windows to the Soul have been usurped by the hallmarks of capitalistic sprawl. The cluttered head office once buzzing with childlike excitement and web 2.0-era (or web 3.0-era) derring-do is now an electric, muted version of corporate structure.

The fab four have even remodeled to their offices. Xavier's still has its modern elegance and refined urbanity; Alexander's still has its sophomoric charm; and Mimi's still has the twinkle of her Bohemian bonhomie. But, the décor—instead of revealing many of the team's idiosyncrasies and peccadilloes—now reinforced the company brand. A stylish hodgepodge of model expressions, from past and present, begin to create a unique mosaic, and conveniently serve as ad hoc wallpaper. Rebecca's office, sparked by a pastel ottoman and a post-modern chaise longue, and replete with "paper gold"—the mishmash of company earnings reports, articles, and pictures featuring Windows to the Soul products and designs. Right above Rebecca's chair is the Wall Street Journal article with the headline "Windows to the Soul Closes at $92" from May 19th.

The Windows to the Soul suite is quickly becoming the busiest office in the 46th street building. Their new receptionist, Indira

—cosmopolitanly dressed, honey-voiced stunner—was busy manning the phones, as she was also helping with configuring the new servers. The company associates dubbed it the second Grand Central station as everyone from studio heads setting up product-placement deals to New York and LA socialites (just wanting to say "hi") dropped by. This morning, Rebecca is meeting with Ed. They are reviewing the company's stock options and projected revenues.

"Ed, I just have unbounded optimism for this company. I know, we always need to be conservative with our projections; but, I think we're starting a revolution here. Before it was just a vision in my head. But, after looking at these numbers, it's this much closer to reality. We've obviously tapped into a deep facet of the public's consciousness; and, the sky's the limit. I don't think there's anything we can't do with this company."

"We're about 18.25% above the IPO price; so, we're in an excellent place. I have to say though, as valuable of an asset as optimism is, we have to look at these reports with restraint if not sobering temperance. No matter how much research we do for these reports and how many times we refine the data, they can't—and don't—prognosticate. A lot can happen in the market, with this company for that matter, over the next two quarters. Once you keep that in mind, this may very well be the year of Windows to the Soul," the CFO admonishes, cautiously rejoicing with Rebecca.

"I know Ed, but these figures certainly bode well. The year of Windows to the Soul… you don't know how long I've wanted to say that."

"Let's just take it day by day. So, I'll see you Friday, 9:30 right?"

"Yeah, that's right. I think that's a good plan with the call options. Let's talk about the hedge funds too."

"Sure. I'll give you a call before I come by to make sure you're available. I know you always have people stopping by."

Rebecca laughs.

"Good idea."

"Take care."

"Have a great day Ed."

Rebecca walks back into her office with a jaunty bounce. Mimi skips into the office eager to share in the excitement.

"How was the briefing Bec?" she asks brimming with excitement.

"It was fabulous Mimi. Ed will be stopping by again on Friday."

"That's Angelina right?" Mimi asks as she turns Rebecca's monitor in her direction.

"Yeah it is. She just got an article published on amnestyonline. com about how the biggest victims of the AIDS epidemic in Africa are children. She was selected as a student ambassador for the United Nations. Actually, Angelina will be in Africa—Congo, Mozambique, South Africa and other countries—tending to children who have been orphaned by AIDS," Rebecca tells Mimi proudly.

"You're lucky you have such great kids."

"Yeah I am. It's just that she's been growing up so quickly... she looks like she's 21 now. Now she's getting some 'extra lessons' from a junior officer at the UN's Social Policy and Development Division."

"Have you talked to her about it?"

"I've been trying to broach the subject with her; but, I don't want to interfere too much and drive her away. I'll tell Peter to have a discussion with her. Maybe if she hears from a man how she needs to constrain herself, it will make more of an impact than if I were talking to her. I think we need to have that sex talk again."

Rebecca quickly glances at her watch.

"It's time for the meeting."

"Great, I'll get the team."

Rebecca makes her way toward the front, thumbing through the Windows to the Soul financial documents.

The threesome assembles around the oval table in the meeting room, and about fifteen other members of the finance and sales departments also join.

"Guys, we have a lot to talk about today."

"Alright, I'll grab the cognac from my desk," Alexander says dryly, and immediately starts walking from the table.

"This one will be good," Rebecca says.

Alexander returns back to his seat.

Rebecca begins sauntering about the room with authoritative self-assurance, eyeing her team, as an excited smile illuminates her face. She seems as if she is warming up for a sermon.

"Anyway, as you all know, I was having my weekly meeting with Ed; and, we were reviewing some prospects." Rebecca picks up the executive summary and begins to quickly flip through it. "We thought we had impressive numbers before." She stops flipping through the report and looks up. She cavalierly tosses the report to the back of the room. "That's *nothing* compared to what we have now."

The Windows to the Soul team sit up straighter in their seats, unconsciously edging forth with anticipation. Rebecca leans in toward the flock. She starts speaking in an enticingly deliberate voice.

"With the advanced sales from our website; the new deals with the retail stores; the buzz percolating in the satellite cities…" Rebecca's voice begins to rise and muster strength with each passing word. "And, of course, with our scintillating new ad campaign, our projected 2020 revenues are now estimated at $435 MILLION!"

Mimi almost shrieks with euphoric delight. Xavier and Alexander look around at the team with approving head nods. The faces of the finance managers present polite smiles.

"This is a hypothetical number. But, that shouldn't temper any of your enthusiasm," Rebecca says to her team with almost affected forbearance. "We don't have that number yet. It's just waiting for us to take it," she follows with cocksure casualness.

A vociferous outcry of agreement rumbles from the crowd.

"But team, we can't rest on our laurels. I mean $435 million minus costs of operating, financing, etc. hardly leaves a large profit."

The team nods in agreement.

"So, we need to set our sights on reaching a higher pinnacle. We're blowing that $435 million straight out of the water! We're hitting 520 baby!"

The sales team erupts into euphoric squeals. Xavier, Alexander, Mimi, and the finance team wear encouraging grins.

"We're going through the pearly gates this year. But, it won't be easy."

"No, it won't," Xavier says in a half-whisper. Rebecca hardly hears it. She starts darting around the front of the room with fervor, alternately looking around the room and intensely gazing at her team.

"We not only have to KEEP this tremendous momentum, we need to BUILD it. Our company is built on tapping into a deep *yearning* of the collective spirit, of *igniting* a deep longing in the public consciousness."

The team is in agreement.

"But, a lot of other companies have done that. This is what *we* did differently: We touched the longing heart while lighting the benighted soul," Rebecca says with pretentious conviction.

About four of the members break out in rousing applause. The rest of the team claps politely.

"*We* blazed a new trail. *We* entered uncharted territory. *We* were the benign renegades who shepherded corporate America from the slums of avarice, stuffy suits, and cutthroat tactics to the pastures of higher chakras, meditation, and a clear chi."

The team responds in good-natured laughter.

"I mean, I started this company because I had a vision; actually, I had a mission."

Rebecca then walks back to the head of the table. She leans forward with her palms, pressed firmly downward, looking at her congregation.

"I wanted to make the whole world feel that spirituality was within reach. It should be an integral part of their daily lives. I know that you're all on that mission with me; and, I thank you for that.

"Spirituality should also be the salve for all of your pain, the panacea that will absolve you from your heaviest burdens, the most cavernous emptiness, and even the most anguishing tragedy. Windows to the Soul needs to assert those tenets in all that we do."

"Are you thinking of changing the product direction?" Xavier asks.

"No, I think we've definitely hit our stride with that. But, I'm thinking of changing the direction of our upcoming ad campaign."

"It's cool how you want to be bold with the Windows ad campaign Rebecca; but, I think what we're working on now is really good for the post-Super Bowl period," Alexander starts. "We should continue to establish our image with the public, and allow the consumers to become familiar with our brand. We don't want to ram it down their throats," he continues with understated forcefulness.

"You're right Alexander; and, I don't want to make any changes to the current ad campaign. This is for the upcoming campaign, set for the fourth quarter."

"Do you have some ideas already?" Kurt, a sales manager, asks.

"Yes, I do. Though the economic reports are promising; they are still many who are treading water. They're not just asking about how they're going to pay their mortgages; if they'll have health insurance; or how they're going to be able to retire. They're also questioning their worth, and, in a larger sense, their faith. Few things in life make you question your ability more than being in a dead-end job, living from paycheck to paycheck, or not being able to find a job. The questions of 'Why me? and 'Am I good enough?' inevitably crop up. Not only that, others will start asking, 'How did God let this happen?' and feel such a sense of loss and desperation that they reach that proverbial point of no return and take actions that, under normal circumstances, they would never have even considered. There's still lingering pain from 9-11, the Financial Crisis, the spate of natural disasters across the country...People need to be shown the way forward; and, our products—our vision—puts us in an extraordinary position to do just that."

The team begins to look at Rebecca with blank stares. Their once bright faces are now dimmed.

"This pain—for better or for worse—gave Windows to the Soul even more relevance. In this time when the world is coming to grips with an atmosphere of uncertainty, high alerts, and overall unrest, Windows to the Soul could be the handle that they can hold on to. It can be the crutch that helps them to move forward. Honestly, I feel it's this 'Age of Uncertainty' that has allowed Windows to the Soul to be such a phenomenon now."

"I think it's awesome how you see Windows to the Soul being at the forefront of this kind of spiritual rebirth and everything; but, these issues are still so raw. Even 9-11 is still a touchy subject, even though we're approaching 20 years since the Attacks. If these issues are not handled *extremely* delicately, I feel, they should be left alone," Mimi politely opines.

"That's an excellent point. It's true; brands tweak their images and 'bring it up a notch' all the time. But, we have to remember that we've just come to the forefront of the eyewear industry in about the last year.

Yes, we are marching to the beat of a different drummer; but, we're still a business and we have to adhere to some conventions. This is just my opinion; but, I think we need to take a little bit more time to mold our image with the public before we make especially bold moves," Xavier adds.

"Well I'm happy we have this kind of open atmosphere at the office where we can just tear down the boss's ideas before we even hear her out," she says with wounded sarcasm, glaring at the whole team. A subtly icy stare was shot at Xavier.

"I'll tell you guys the very *rough* idea that I have in my mind. You have shots of about five very diverse people. They're having these torturous nightmares about the Dow falling 900 points, losing their jobs, and scenes from a battered economy. They each get up to a brilliant sunny day. Windows to the Soul lenses are each on their windowsills. They get up; walk toward their windows; put them on; and look at the sun. It fades out. In the last frame of the commercial we could have posted at the bottom of the screen, 'There is a bright day. We'll help you get there.'"

"But that —," Alexander starts but Rebecca abruptly cuts him off.

"I also have another scenario I've been playing around with. You can just have two people's stories. We can follow one from the beginning of the day—watching 'GMA,' hearing about a new round of lay-offs, etc.—to the end of the day when he or she gets 'the pink slip.' Images of the person losing the house, being rejected again and again for jobs, seeing the bills mount, etc. could flash through his or her mind. We can flash back to September 11th and follow another person's story. They're busily getting ready for their day as the news of the disaster emerges on the screen. He or she is at first in disbelief, as we all were; but, as the coverage proceeds, the news sinks in. The person is trying to get in touch with loved ones who were either working in the World

Trade Center or were in the lower Manhattan area during the time of the Attacks. In the next scene, we have a funeral in which a victim is being laid to rest. The person gets home, sits on the couch, and picks up a Windows to the Soul watch (we should also be promoting the new products) scrawled with an expression that befits the occasion, something like 'Spirituality will temper your wounded heart.'"

"Rebecca, those definitely pull at the heart strings; but, Windows to the Soul might be diving into the deep end with that," Alley, a senior sales manager, offers.

"What?" Rebecca responds with a subdued scowl.

"I mean, you're just setting yourself up for some serious backlash. You're using very painful chapters in America's consciousness, that are touchy—and, for many, sacred—for financial gain —"

"Alley, I know you've only been here for a few months; but, please don't forget that at Windows to the Soul, we care about a lot more than the bottom line."

"We understand and respect that Rebecca. What Alley is saying is that it comes off a little like Windows to the Soul is the answer for tragedies. Accessories are one thing; but, being foreclosed on, or national catastrophes like September 11th, are critically important," Madison, a senior finance analyst, says in support of her friend.

Rebecca bristles.

"I think you may want to reconsider that Madison. Let me ask you, what could be more important than what we're working on here?"

"Now, we'll hear from Angelina Lewis. She'll read an excerpt from her published essay on the effects of the AIDS epidemic on Africa's children, and discuss this summer's UN Student Ambassador program. Come on Angelina," Principal Doherty says enthusiastically.

The audience applauds as Angelina ascends to the podium. She is wearing a long, caramel, suit; white blouse; and golden high heels.

"Thanks Mr. Doherty. Hi everybody. How you all doing today?"

The crowd breaks out in adulatory hoots and hollers.

"Ready for my speech?" she asks cutely.

"Yeahs" erupt from the crowd.

"All right, I'll try to make it good," she says. Then, Angelina begins.

"You have probably heard the astounding numbers on the evening news. You have heard the plaintive cries from humanitarian organizations and civic leaders that resound loudly from the channels of mass media. And, of course, you have heard the debate within our country about the rise in HIV cases, and about how much more we can do—with our tremendous power and resources—to alleviate the effects of this catastrophe, even within our borders.

These are all stories that are familiar to your ears and eyes; but, I will tell you some stories that maybe you are not so familiar with. Every 13 seconds another African child is orphaned by AIDS. Every day there are children born—damned to a short and agonizing life—afflicted by the debilitating condition. Each passing day, families are disintegrated because its center, the parents, is stripped away. Each day, due either to the formidable nature of the task, the high demand of resources, racism, or just plain apathy, we are allowing a continent's vitality to come ever closer to being extinguished.

Not only is the AIDS crisis killing bodies; it is destroying our humanity. Children are left without role models to teach them about their heritage, to instill values in them, and to mold a sense of self which will allow them to be viable members of both the African and world society. If we do not combat AIDS and nurture these children, we will lose the vital links to the cradle of civilization. If we let Africa go extinct by the way of AIDS, we can lose a continent and a part of ourselves.

I, and the other United Nations student ambassadors, will not cure AIDS when we journey to Africa; but, we will help the fight by tending to the orphans that now overrun this beautiful land. We will volunteer in the schools, hospitals, and all around the communities trying to fill the tremendous shoes that mom, dad, and their caretakers left behind. We intend to show these children that family transcends race, blood, and continental borders.

I am, *we are*, fortunate enough to live in a blessed land where an epidemic of AIDS' magnitude is relegated to science fiction dramas and Hollywood movies. I am also fortunate enough to live in a home where I can experience every day the importance of the family unit. Unfortunately my parents could not be here today—"

Angelina stops and takes a sigh.

"My mother is working on expanding her spiritual wellness company, and my dad is diligently making breakthroughs in Alzheimer's, and other neurological disorders. However, I don't feel alone here. I have the support of all of you —"

The students roar and applaud. Chris waves to her and gives her a "thumbs up" from the back.

"And, I also have the love and support of my parents. You see, even if they're not here physically, they're always here in spirit; and, their love transcends miles. I want the kids we will help to feel that too.

I know all of you cannot be student ambassadors; but, we can all do our part to help. As of tomorrow, we will begin collecting donations to help us with our effort. It doesn't necessarily have to be money, though that would be the best."

The crowd responds with laughter.

"But, it can be anything that you can give—clothes, canned food, even toys. Think about what makes your home feel like home and give those items to us, so the kids could have 'home' too. We will have special jars and bins in each classroom starting next week, April 21ˢᵗ. Tell your friends and relatives around the country too. We want this to be a nationwide project. We will give all the information to the teachers tomorrow; and, they will distribute it during class. Thanks so much for your support and cooperation. You've been an awesome audience!"

The students rise to their feet, giving Angelina thunderous applause. She nearly leaps off the stage with excitement.

"Thank you very much Angelina. Though Dr. and Mrs. Lewis couldn't be here, I know they're just brimming with pride at their daughter.

Enjoy the rest of your day and remember tomorrow's early dismissal."

Dr. Lewis scurries into Scalini Fedeli. He spots his booth tucked away in the back-left corner.

"I thought you stood me up," Amber growls.

"I apologize Amber. You know I had to brief Dr. Lynn about the progress of the experiment and that interview with the Journal today ran a little long. I missed one of the trains getting up here..."

"Shhhh," Amber says to him resting her pointer finger tenderly on his lips. "I'm just playing with you."

"No, I should feel badly. I should have called you, and let you know I was running late. I can see the maître d' glowering at us. The waiter's coming over."

He hands them two menus.

"Thank you sir."

Peter takes a look at Amber. She is wearing a form-fitting, lavender satin dress with a scoop neck and a prominent, purple quartz necklace on her chest. Small white flowers loll out of her flowing, brunette curls. White and blue eye shadow is blended on her eyelids, and complement her wine lipstick.

"You look great all the time; but, you look especially ravishing today."

"I try," Amber says as she twirls a lock of her hair around her finger.

"You did a great job girl."

"Thanks," she says with a satisfied smile. "I know I told you already; but, thanks a lot for talking to me last night. You have no idea how much those words meant."

"I'm just doing my job. Remember I'm your mentor; that means more than helping you revise reports. It also means helping you through the personal issues and well, life. So, what would you like?"

"Let's see…"

Amber opens the menu and starts perusing the offerings.

"Wow, I know you're a hotshot doctor; but, this is extravagant. I don't deserve all of this."

"Please Amber. You've made the office so much brighter. I wish I could give you more than this," Dr. Lewis begins caressing Amber's hand.

"You're too much Dr. Lewis. Well, the braised snapper sounds pretty good. You have any recommendations?"

"The langoustines are delectable; but, the foie gras is positively indulgent."

"OK, we can share that then."

"I think I'll have the pappardelle. It comes with some wine, and a tangy chocolate."

Amber nods in approval.

"It's *fantastic*," Peter says in an excited whisper.

"I'm sure it is. Do you come here often with Mrs. Lewis?"

"We used to; but, things have gotten so hectic. I don't have nearly as much time as I'd like with her, much less my kids."

"I bet things have been really busy for her too. Windows to the Soul stuff is the hottest thing right now."

"Busy is not even the word… I'm almost getting whiplash with how fast checks are coming in."

Amber giggles.

"Now, I'm living with a top CEO, an accessories magnate. It's great," Peter murmurs.

"With the demand of both of your careers, it must be difficult to balance things."

"It has been the last few years. Things used to be a lot simpler. I remember when Rebecca was doing her graduate work at NYU; and, I had started at New York-Presbyterian. We would come down here every Friday and have dinner—eating the cheapest things on the menu."

"She must have loved that. This is such a romantic place."

"It sure is. The times we felt like splurging, we would cut back on the food and order the best wine. Oh, I almost forgot to ask you, what would you like to drink?"

"Oh, water would be fine."

"Water? I didn't bring you here to get water! Try the merlot. They serve some of the finest wines in the city. I think the chardonnay would be delightful with the pappardelle."

The maître d' saunters back toward their booth.

"Would you and the beautiful lady like to order?"

"Yes, we would. She'd like the langoustines and foie gras. I'd like the pappardelle."

"What would you like to drink?"

"She'll have the merlot. I'll have the chardonnay."

"Perfect choice. I'll be with you shortly."

"Rebecca is the luckiest woman on earth."

"Why do you say that?"

"She has a man like you who's so generous and classy, not to mention intelligent and accomplished."

"You know, I never tire of hearing compliments like that from you."

Amber blushes a little bit while giving Peter a satisfied smile.

"I'm a very lucky man too. She's vibrant, extremely intelligent, witty, and beautiful. There's a great heart inside of there too."

"She sounds wonderful."

"That she is. I love her very much."

"It's a shame that you don't spend more time with her. I bet even with as busy as you are with work, you still miss her."

"That's for sure. It seems as of late, we're just falling out of sync. When I want to do something, she's too tired. When she wants to go out, I need to be at a conference. Sometimes, I wonder if it'll always be like that."

"As great as she is, she should make more time for you. I could never think of being away from a man like you. I don't know how she stands it."

Peter laughs bashfully.

"No, I mean that Pete. Excuse me for saying this but if I were her, you'd never be missing me."

"I really appreciate that Amber," Peter says modestly.

"I know she's very grateful to have you in her life; but, she needs to show you that every day. You can't take a perfect man for granted."

Peter begins looking around the restaurant. He sees the waiter, a poised young man in his early 20s, making his way back toward their booth. He is placing down the appetizers and the wine.

"Merlot for the beautiful lady."

"Thank you very much."

"Chardonnay for the gentleman."

"Thank you."

He also left the couple a plate of cheese bread. Peter took a slice.

"I'm sorry if I'm making you uncomfortable."

"No, that's OK Amber. It's just that I haven't heard those kinds of words for a while."

Amber's arm extends from her lap and rubs Peter's hand under the table. She starts to stroke it with her thumb. Peter looks at her. She begins to whisper to Peter:

"I don't know how she doesn't crave to be held in your strong arms. Or, how she doesn't get lost in those piercing blue eyes—"

Peter looks down.

Amber's right hand is now gliding over lips.

"Or, how she goes without feeling those full, sexy lips sucking her body."

Amber sits up in her chair and leans toward Peter. Their lips embrace. For a brief moment, he savors the softness of Amber's lips before their tongues engage in a playful tango. His fingers press firmly down her neck as his body warms with each passing moment. Peter's fingertips bathe in the beads of sweat forming in the center of Amber's chest.

Peter abruptly pulls back. Amber looks at him with a glance of desire and uneasy anticipation.

"Not right now."

Rebecca is holding some magazines from her custom aqua Porsche. She does not know that Peter is following her behind. Finally, she hears some footsteps and turns around.

"Hey hon," Rebecca says cheerfully.

"Hey babe," Peter says without looking at his wife.

Rebecca walks toward her husband.

"I don't get a kiss."

"Sorry hon."

He gives her a quick peck on her lips.

"What have you got there?" Rebecca looks at the bags.

"Oh, they're just some leftovers from Scalini Fedeli."

"You were there today?"

"Yeah some of the doctors and I were in the city, briefing the groups on our Alzheimer's experiment. We figured we'd celebrate there with lunch before heading back to the office."

"Thanks for bringing some back." Rebecca opens the cardboard package and sees the leftover from the meal.

"I love their foie gras. And some pappardelle too? Thanks for being so thoughtful babe." She gives him a kiss on the cheek.

"That's the least I can do. How did your day go?"

"It was pretty busy at work," Rebecca answers through foie gras.

"As always right?"

"Yeah, but today was really good. I met with Ed, and our projected revenues for the year are up by nearly 46%! Because of advanced sales from our websites, all the buzz the new stores have been generating, and the launch of the ad campaign, we should hit $435 million this year!"

Peter scoops his wife up.

"That's great!" Peter says while twirling his wife around. "Didn't I tell you it would be like this?"

Rebecca jumps from Peter's arms.

"I know! You always had the vision. I'm finally seeing it too. Oh, more good news. You know Angelina gave her speech in front of the school today."

"That's right. I have to ask her how that went."

"Well, Chris was there and he posted a clip on Instagram. He posted the full video, and some awesome pictures, on Google. He told me that she was *outstanding*. I think our little girl is the next Margaret Thatcher," Rebecca says proudly.

"I sure hope not," Peter quips.

"Oh, you know what I mean," Rebecca says as she playfully slaps Peter on the back. "I'll make some time tonight to do a collage for her. I'll put in more of the borders later. I want Angelina to get a sneak peek."

"She's going to love that."

Rebecca starts up the stairs. Naughty laughs and satisfied moans begin to punctuate the creek of the stairs. Instinctively, Rebecca begins to walk more quickly, pouncing up the staircase. As she gets nearer, she strategically slows down. The sounds from her daughter's room emanate like a sordid cacophony, piercing her ears.

She inches up the flight of stairs leading to the third floor. She walks on her tip-toes down the hall. Her daughter's voice becomes louder as Rebecca grows more disturbed. She goes by the master bedroom. She then passes the study, and sneaks into the bathroom.

Rebecca immediately grabs the knob leading into Angelina's bedroom.

It is locked.

Angelina stops for a moment.

"Oh nothing baby, I thought I heard something. Sorry to stop the flow."

"There isn't going to be any flow," Rebecca utters under her breath. She backs out of the bathroom going toward Angelina's other door.

"My tongue is sliding down your stomach. I can feel you getting so hard against me baby. My huge, round breasts are squeezing your thick, long, hard cock, my hard nipples rubbing against..."

The other door is locked too. Rebecca takes a few steps back and rams into her daughter's bedroom. She breaks the lock. Angelina screams, and drops the phone to the ground. She turns around.

"MOM! WHAT ARE YOU DOING?"

"You better hang up that phone."

Angelina anxiously picks up her left hand while straining to cover her body with her right.

"Yeah… I'll talk to you later," Angelina says in a furious tempo.

"That's what you think."

Angelina shoots a livid scowl at her mother.

"What the fuck mom? You didn't even knock."

In two steps, Rebecca came over to her daughter's bed. Rebecca smacks her daughter across her face.

"You *never* talk to me like that. Hurry up and put on your clothes."

Angelina snatches her bra and panties from the door and nervously begins to put them on.

"Mom, please calm down."

"CALM DOWN? A *man* is fucking my daughter. You're lucky I haven't gone over there and cut his dick off."

"It's not as bad as you think."

"I come up here thinking my daughter's the next UN secretary; and, instead, I find a whore," Rebecca says angrily to Angelina as her eye begins to twitch.

"I'm NOT a whore. I've only been with Chris."

"That pedophile is not getting near you again. His ass is going to jail."

Rebecca whips out her cell phone. Angelina runs to her and wrestles it out of her hand.

"Mom please don't do that. You can beat me up as much as you want; but, don't report him. Please, don't report him," Angelina is kneeling on the ground, crying at her mother's feet. Rebecca places Angelina's phone on the bed.

"I won't call them now. Get up."

Her daughter's chest heaves with anxious breath as Rebecca glowers at her.

"When did this happen?" Rebecca says as she eyes her daughter with a bemused glance.

"We didn't start having sex till about 4 months ago."

The twitch becomes more rapid as her eyes redden with anger.

"Angelina, you don't see anything wrong with this? You're a fuckin' minor! This is statutory rape."

"I'm telling you mom it's not like that. He didn't force me into anything. Chris's a great guy."

"He's a smart guy too. Fucking you is more fun than helping refugees."

"Go ahead mom, make jokes. I knew you wouldn't understand."

"Angelina, *you're* the one who doesn't understand. He's taking advantage of you. You were easy prey for him."

"He didn't come on to me mom. I came on to him."

Rebecca turns around slowly and looks at her daughter.

"What?"

"I wanted him. He tried to dissuade me, telling me that it really wasn't ethical…I'm too young…if anyone finds out he'll lose his job. I told him don't worry about it, I won't let anyone find out."

"Why Angelina?"

"I started feeling really close to him. I fell in love with him."

"Love? Like you know what that is."

"Didn't you know what that was when you met Anthony?"

Rebecca is stunned.

"How do you know about him?"

"You've mentioned him to dad once. He's the one who made you laugh, who made you feel safe. Chris did the same for me."

"Why did you need that?"

"I've just been feeling so alone, you know. I mean, I know I'm always getting straight As and I'm really involved in school. But, it's just like a distraction from everything else. It's weird with a lot of the girls at school. I mean I talk to everybody and everybody knows me; but, I feel like I don't fit in. And, don't think this body isn't hard for me to get used to either. All the guys at school stare at me…I hear them talking about me; and, then I have to hear it from you. It's a lot of stuff."

"It's always seems like that at this age Angie. I know everything seems to be in flux. Honestly hon, that's how life is. But you're never alone. Your dad and I are always here."

Angelina looks at her mom with a cold stare.

"You weren't there today."

Rebecca turns her head down to the floor and closes her eyes.

"Sorry mom, I didn't mean to make you feel bad."

"No, it's true. You feel like you have absentee parents. He's filling a void."

"Chris sees me as a real person. I know he loves my body; but, he also loves my poetry, how I laugh, how I want to change the world… He loves *me*."

"I don't doubt that. But, he's also someone who makes you feel safe and gives you some kind of stability, like a father would."

"Is there something so wrong with that?"

"It doesn't seem like it; but, you're putting someone on a pedestal that they can't stand on. He can't be your savior. A relationship shouldn't be based on that. I know what I'm talking about; I've been there. You remember how I told you that my dad died when I was a little girl?"

"Yeah. That must have been so hard to deal with it."

"It was; and, there wasn't a day that passed that I didn't wish he were there. I just plunged into school, getting involved in so many different activities to get away from it. On most nights, I didn't know what man my mom was going to bring to the house. Sometimes, I didn't even know where we'd live…"

"Wow, I didn't know it was that bad."

"It was. Then when I was about 10, Jake came into my mom's life. He was terrible—heavy drinking, did drugs, abusive…but, underneath that was a decent man. He knew I knew that—"

"And he took advantage of it."

"Yes."

"He molested you?"

Rebecca looks at Angelina with an expression of vulnerable honesty.

"He was a monster! I had no idea. Honestly, if it's too hard for you to tell me, you don't have to."

"No, I do. I do."

Angelina moves closer to her mother, and places her hands on her mother's lap.

"It was so complicated. I felt violated, dirty…but at the same time, this almost addictive feeling of intensity. There were times I couldn't bear to look at myself in the mirror. I couldn't reconcile those feelings; and, honestly, I still have problems doing that."

Angelina raises comforting eyes up to her mother. Rebecca is encouraged.

"Anthony helped me to get over it."

"You loved him so much."

"I did. I remember telling him that I was a virgin. I guess I didn't want to admit to myself what Jake and I had done and also, I think, I really felt that way. It was the first time I had experienced pure love.

I began to find myself again. Something else helped me get through it too."

Rebecca gets up from the bed and Angelina follows behind. The mother and daughter walk through the bathroom and open the corner door, entering the master bedroom. They both walk to Rebecca's bureau, and open the third drawer from the top. She pushes away the linens to reveal a tattered, yellowed doll. Her fingers gingerly slide across the doll's glazed eyes. Angelina gazes at her mother, arrested by her rare show of vulnerability.

Rebecca slowly lifts the baby out from the drawer, and places it in Angelina's arm. Her daughter instinctively cradles the doll. She turns to look at her mother.

"Does she have a name?"

"Yeah, Lily. That was going to be the name of our baby."

"You were pregnant?"

Rebecca nods.

"Did you have her?"

"No, I had a miscarriage."

"Wow," Angelina says looking at the doll. "Is this the way you remember her?"

"I think so."

"How did you get through that?"

"Losing her was devastating to me. But, pain can at times be odd comfort. When I look at her, I see sadness and hope at the same time."

"Do you see us that way?"

Rebecca stares with poignant surprise at her daughter. She gets closer to her and begins running her fingers affectionately through her daughter's hair.

"Angelina, I don't want you to have a Lily. I don't want you to be the way I was, hell, the way I still am.

"I know that you love Chris, and, I'm sure, in his way, he loves you too. But, I don't want you to put him in a place where he doesn't deserve to be in. Where *you* don't deserve to be in."

"I know mom."

"I know that euphoria that you feel when someone tells you that you're beautiful; that you're brilliant; and, they see you as special. It's so empowering when you realize that your body can totally consume him, turn him on. That point when they're completely under your command because the energy between you, your love for each other, is that strong. You feel like you're one with them. I know; it's amazing."

"It's not just about the sex mom. It's everything."

"I know it's more than that Angelina, but that's an integral part of it. He's the first one who made you feel like that; and, he'll always be important to you because of it—no matter what happens. Do you guys use protection?"

"Mom, he doesn't run around; and, I don't either. I know when I'm ovulating—"

"You still need protection. OK."

"OK."

"You can get some at school right?"

"Yeah, I'll get some tomorrow."

"No, a whole lot."

"Fine, a whole lot."

"I'll give you some money to get some at the store too. I know I can't stop you from seeing him Angelina. You're an intelligent young woman; and, you're very mature for your age. But, you need to be safe."

"Thanks."

"Remember, he's just a person. There are times when you'll feel alone; but, you just have to find the strength to keep fighting."

"How do you do that?"

"It's different for everybody Angel; there's no handbook. Though self-help books will try to tell you differently. You have to find your own best way."

Angelina sits up slightly on the bed.

"Isn't spirituality a key to that? It's like you're always championing with Windows to the Soul: a strong spiritual connection is the key. I mean, with that, you're never *really* alone right? No matter what, God's always there. He's always your best friend."

Rebecca is pleasantly surprised by her daughter's insight. She feels a sense of pride, tinged with envy, wishing she had said it.

"Of course."

"And a great love, like you have with dad, or what I feel with Chris, could be an avenue to realizing His Power. Love can open the doors to your spirituality, bringing you toward connecting with the Source, right?" Angelina says as she turned to her mother.

Rebecca proudly looks at her daughter with a sense of longing.

"I'm still trying to realize that myself."

VIII

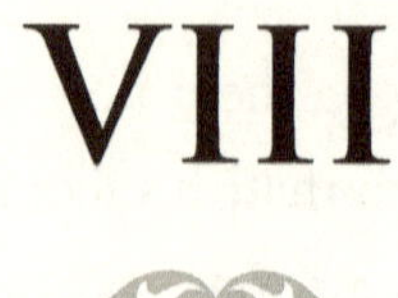

The Westchester Center of Neurological Sciences lays silent, save for the rustling on the fifth floor where Amber Ferrer is snapping on her bra and buttoning up her blouse. She sashays over to Peter, and begins to massage his shoulders delicately, as she whispers in his ear.

"You sure it's going to be safe in your house sexy?"

"I'm sure. Rebecca is going to be running late at the office. Well, she always is; but, since she told me that she will, she'll definitely be back pretty late."

"How about your kids?"

"Oh, don't worry. Angelina has a meeting with the UN group tonight at school. I have to remember to pick her up at 8. Denver might be in the house; but, he has a long day. He has to go to New Horizons, then he has soccer practice immediately afterward. I'm sure when he gets back, he'll just plunge right into his Latin project. He was really eager to get that started."

"Good," Amber says. She licks his neck and rubs his stomach.

"I love a man who likes to finish what he started."

Peter turns around, grabs Amber and bends her over the computer table. He starts unzipping the back of her skirt.

Fifteen children scamper into the meeting room at New Horizons. They quickly begin arranging the chairs and desks into a circle. Denver takes his customary seat next to the door. Ms. Stone, their counselor takes her seat.

"Hey guys. How's everyone doing today?"

"Fine."

"That's good to hear. Yesterday, we had a great discussion about our hopes and dreams. You guys had a good time, right?"

"Yes," they say in unison.

"Good. Well, communicating your ideas is always a good way to bring them into reality, especially writing. Every day when you come in for the session, I want you to sit at your seats and write a little. This could be anything from your hopes and dreams, like we were talking about yesterday, to a memorable experience in your life—whatever you want. It could be in any form of writing too—a journal, a short story… I'll give you guys a chance to start on it now. If you need me, I'll be in the book room."

Denver sits for a while, his elbow to his knee, his chin resting in his palm. Then, he begins to write:

What would you think about this family? The mother is a hotshot, entrepreneur, trying to foster her own spiritual revolution. The father is a leading neuroscientist, moving with leaps and bounds toward a cure for Alzheimer's disease. The daughter is a beautiful teenager who wants to change the world, waging war against the needs of a 14-year-old girl in the body and mind of a woman. And, then you have a pretty bright, sensitive 12-year-old boy who feels that he'll be hopelessly lost in the storm. This seems like it will be an interesting story right? Well, it gets better.

We have the white picket fence, the nice cars, almost the 2.5 kids, and the dog. We're ostensibly(?) living the American dream. It's hardly that simple though. Trust me, I wish it were that simple. Let me begin taking you through the Denver stops writing for a moment. He then brings his pen to the top of the page and fills in the title:

The Perfect American Family

—∘∘◦❯◉❮◦∘∘—

"I'm really sorry about what happened during the meeting several weeks ago. It was completely unprofessional. I honestly don't know what came over me."

"Well, I'm sorry for putting you in that kind of position. I think the receptionist with the shellacked hair and all those eggheads put me off balance."

Rick has a relieved laugh.

"Now that we got that out of the way, let's get to business."

"Yeah, I'm developing a premise for the new Windows to the Soul ad campaign. I think it will really put us over the top."

"I can't wait to hear it."

"Well, part of Windows to the Soul's success is centered on connecting with a deep part of the human psyche, whether that's longing for something beyond oneself, emptiness, or even pain. Ads that show how the Windows to the Soul products can get you through tragedy will reinforce that idea."

"That's a good starting point. Do you have any scenarios in mind?"

"I want it to center around financial uncertainty, and perhaps link it to September 11th."

A look of reservation grips Rick's face.

"Really?" he says with evident trepidation. He gets up from the top of his desk and begins walking around the room. "That's a pretty dicey area to say the least. If you *are* going to approach it—especially with something that hinges on public appeal like advertising—you're going to have to do it—"

"Delicately. I know that Rick. But, these ads are not exploiting the tragedy in any way; they're acknowledging it. The people in the ads didn't seek the Windows to the Soul products themselves; they sought them for the connection to spirituality that they represent. These ads go beyond Windows to the Soul; they speak to a great need that we all have. It's, at heart, a testament to spirituality."

"I hate to say this Bec, but that 'no-exploitation' defense isn't gonna fly. The Windows to the Soul logo will be prominent, the products will be in full view. Plus, this is a really big-budget, flashy ad; and, with the effects of the recession and the bailout stuff—but, no bailout for families—still in the country's memory, this might be seen as ostentatious or out-of-touch ... Your noble intents notwithstanding, this is a for-profit campaign using painful national events as vehicles."

"It doesn't have to seem that way Rick; it all depends on how we deliver it. Here's the treatment."

Rebecca hands him the outline for the ads. His eyes race as he skims the page.

"These are good ideas Rebecca; but, no ad campaign is a success—no matter how well-conceived—if the people don't respond. This has the potential, at the very least, to rub consumers the wrong way."

Rebecca shakes her head wearing a contemptuous smirk.

"Why does it always come down to that? What people think, how they feel? What happened to truth? That's what's paramount."

"Rebecca, you're not in the clergy; you're in business. Perceptions are paramount."

Rebecca turns away sullenly.

"Look, I didn't get to this point pissing people off. We weren't middle of the road either. We became famous for making ads that were innovative and creative. There were times they were funny. There were times that they were even poignant. But, we never did anything that was outright offensive."

"These ideas may be heart-wrenching; but, they're anything but offensive. There's no doubt that the public will have a very strong reaction to it; but, I strongly believe that that response will be positive. I feel a great cry from people to raise their consciousness, and get to a higher level. These ads will speak to that."

"This is the same society where 20 million people watch reality shows per week. Let's face it—not everyone is looking for a higher purpose. Honestly, this is a risk that I, and frankly you, can't afford to take."

Rebecca fires back with dogged conviction.

"Rick, Windows to the Soul isn't the new kid on the block anymore. Our products are starting to be everywhere, from the faces of Hollywood stars to the heads of high-school kids. We've established ourselves *firmly* in this industry."

Rick shrugs his shoulders.

"Remember those numbers we talked about at the last meeting? We've blown them out of the water. We're projected to make $435 million this year; and, we can easily make that $520 million with buzz from an ad campaign that truly breaks us away from the crowd. You're not taking a huge risk here; you're making a sure bet."

"Rebecca, you're a capable, intelligent, creative woman. I mean you're one of the few people who could have gotten Windows to the Soul off the ground; but, I've been in this business for a long time. You were in finance; you know about projected revenues more than most people. Those are your numbers once things go smoothly; basically, once execs don't make any major missteps. One bad move can make all that go up in smoke. Sure, you may hit it out of the ballpark with this one; but, you could just as quickly sink like the Titanic. I'm not talkin' about lofty ideas here. I'm talkin' about the bottom line."

"Rick, I'm talking about more than that. I know about the bottom line; for years, the bottom line was stuffed down my throat. Minding the bottom line allowed me to start Windows to the Soul. But, I didn't start this company because I espoused the 'central tenets' of capitalism; I vowed to be true to myself. This is what Windows to the Soul is about. Yes, truth can be painful. It can be searing, and it can be cutting. But, the incontrovertible fact is that we all need to come to terms with it."

"And, *you're* the one to help them do that."

"Well, I can guide them to look at the truth head on. Yes, these are painful chapters in our country's history; but, we can't cower from them, nor can we cower from any issues with which we're still struggling. We need to overcome our fears, our sense of loss to connect with something that is greater than us, that which is vital. Besides, we've gotten some distance from the tragedies, especially September 11th; so, this campaign shouldn't be a shock. I'm just trying to remind people about the work that has yet to be done. That's all that I'm trying to do."

"I admire your conviction, and wish you the best on the Crusade; but, I have to say we can't go with you on this. I can't put my company on the line."

"You already have."

Rick looks at Rebecca with irked resignation.

"I thought we were passed that."

"And, I thought we were partners."

Rick lets out a labored sigh.

"You're gonna play by my rules," Rick says authoritatively. "And, you're covering all operating."

"Whatever it takes to get this on the air."

"When are we starting this?"

"I'll be leaving for California in a week; but, I want to start as soon as I get back. I'll be working with my team in the interim."

Amber giggles like a schoolgirl as she and Peter enter the Lewis home. She could not help but ply him with eager kisses.

"OK babe, just hold on a little bit. Denver might be around."

Amber whispers "oops" as she covers her mouth with her palm. Peter is rubbing the sides of her torso.

Denver has just finished his homework in the den, and resumes working on his story, "The Perfect American Family." He hears the door and starts walking out.

"Hi dad, hi Amber."

"Hey there little man," Amber says.

"Hi sport. The office was really hectic today, getting ready for the conference next week," Dr. Lewis says as Amber had her hands folded atop his shoulder, her chin resting on her fingers. Peter tries subtly tapping her to get off. Denver catches it.

"We didn't get a chance to finish working with the reports; so, Amber and I are going to work on it here. I might head back to the office."

"Does mom know she's coming over?"

"I told her earlier in the day; but, she might have forgotten. We'll be finished by the time she comes back anyway. You get back to work all right."

"See ya later Denver."

Denver gives her a perfunctory wave as she rushes upstairs with his father. Denver drags his feet back to the den and continues writing his passage:

I've always wondered about my parents' relationship. I wonder, what are the mechanics, the inner workings? What makes it tick (so to speak)? I know they love each other and have a tremendous amount of respect for one another; but, they're hardly ever together. Well, they've been married for 19 years; so, they have to be doing something right. But, at times it seems like they're just hanging on. I see how dad savors that rare, long kiss from mom, or mom loves to thumb dad's hair while nestling on his shoulder.

I'm only 12-years-old and I haven't had anything CLOSE to a girlfriend; but, I've thought about love too. How can people really keep it together like that? I mean, when there isn't much togetherness, hardly any intimacy (I'm guessing) and the affection is at best, subtle? There needs to be an "it" to keep it together, right?

I've seen too many kids in school go through the horror(?) of divorce. I've seen them experience the guilt and become overwhelmed by uncertainty. I guess because they realize that sometimes "till death do us part" doesn't really mean much. I wouldn't even wish that on the kids who beat me up at school. But, where's the glory in sticking it through? I know parents say they stay together for the kids; but, if you're kids know that there's not much there, aren't you just doing it for yourself? Maybe they're just too weak to move on. I shudder to think that my parents will suffer the same fate (rework this).

"Oops, need 'your' there," Denver says to himself. As he erases, he's distracted by the squeals and yells he hears from upstairs. They do not sound particularly ominous or threatening; but, they were nevertheless intense. He figured he would go up just to make sure.

As Denver moves down the third-floor hallway, Amber's squeals became louder. They are peppered with breathy cries and groans. She would also spur his father on, goading him to do more, to go faster. After slapping sounds, she would cry out in delight.

"So, it does sound like that," Denver whispers to himself.

He got to the master bedroom door. It seems to be closed but on second glance, he realizes it is ajar. Denver peers inside. For a moment, he considers taking out his smartphone.

He sees Amber and his father atop his parents' now disarrayed bed. His father is kneeling. Amber is lying down, her legs astride his father's shoulders. Her breasts were tossing in the air as she grinds on Dr. Lewis's thrusting tongue.

A grimy feeling of discomfort overcomes Denver, but his curiosity subdues it. He leans in closer to the door and continues to watch.

Peter wipes his mouth. He allows Amber to breathe for a few moments before whisking her up from the bed and swiftly turning her around. She mounts on top of him, her legs bent on the sides of Peter's body. He held her tightly, his thumbs caressing her breasts as she rides him. Peter marvels at her torso as he roars in impassioned abandon.

Denver turns away and almost gallops down the stairs. His mind is racing with stimulation, anxiety, and disquiet. He plops back on his chair in the den. He stares at the paper for a moment and then begins writing.

> I think people have different ways of dealing with it. They may resign to a union without any passion or fire. However with others, those human needs cannot go without being fulfilled, and they seek it outside. Even with their strength, they're no exception.

Rebecca Lewis opens the front door with a little spring in her step. Denver is making his way out of the den when Rebecca spots him.

"Hey Denver. How's it going?"

"I'm doing pretty well. How are you?"

"I can't complain. I got a lot done at work today. We're gearing up for our new openings in LA and San Francisco next week; got some new ideas for product lines; and we're getting this great new ad campaign underway at work. How was school today?"

"It was fine, kind of slow though."

"I know, it's always like that for you. Everything was all right?" Rebecca asks him with an inquisitive glance.

"Yeah mom, don't worry about those kids. Dad showed me how to deal with them; and, they don't bother me anymore."

Rebecca nods her head with an amused and pleased smile.

"Well I'm happy to hear that. How was New Horizons?"

"It was actually good today. Ms. Stone added a new component to the sessions. Every day, for the first 10 minutes, we're going to write. It can be in whatever form and about any subject you want, just as long as you're passionate about it."

"That's a great idea. You know, writing is one of the best ways to deal with your feelings."

"Yeah, it definitely is."

"So, what are you writing?"

"It's just a little story."

"Well, I'm sure it's outstanding already. Could I see it sometime?"

"Maybe."

"OK, I'll settle for that. I have to make some phone calls. I'll be upstairs."

Denver sits silently thinking.

"Hey mom, I kind of want to talk to you."

"You do?" Rebecca says with surprise.

"Yeah."

"OK. I'll be right down; let me just put my things away upstairs. I promise, I'll be right down."

Denver starts planning.

"Oh you know, I have to go upstairs anyway. I'll take your shoes. I want to share what I was doing for my Latin project with you."

"Wow, aren't you being helpful. But, I need to take off this suit; it's really hot."

"You've had a really long day; I'll get everything."

"Is there someone upstairs Denver?"

"No, but..." Denver stands staring at the ground with shallow, anxious breaths.

"Denver, remember one of the things we always told you and Angelina; if there's something going wrong, speak out. You can tell me Denver."

"I just don't think you should go up there."

"What do you mean?" Rebecca says laughing. "What happened?"

Denver is silent.

"What happened Denver?"

"I think you need to talk to dad."

"Talk to him about what?"

"Talk to him about you guys."

"Why do I need to do that?"

"I saw him with…I can't."

"You can't what? You saw him with whom? Just spit it out Denver."

"I saw him with…"

"Come on Denver!"

"I saw him with Am…"

"Amber?" Rebecca asks with rising indignation.

Denver gives his mother a knowing glance.

Rebecca turns away from him, her face reddening with anger and embarrassment. She begins sucking her teeth.

"You know, I know it's been hard lately; but, you don't need to make up stories to get attention—"

"Mom!"

"You've hurt me before, but this has to be the worst—"

"Me?"

"Yes, you. You actually approach me for once, wanting to talk to me, and you give me this. How could you say such a thing about your father?"

"Mom, I know this is hard to believe; but, believe me, I'm not trying to hurt you. I love dad too. I would never say this if I didn't—"

"It's not my fault that you don't feel close to me. I'm trying to do the best that I can. It's one thing for you not to want to share your life with me; but, don't lie to me. Just because you're depressed doesn't mean everyone else has to be.

Denver is taken aback. His eyes well with tears.

"I'M NOT LYING TO YOU! I saw them!"

"That's it Denver, GET OUT!"

"Mom, please believe me!" Denver says with tears streaming down his face.

"Have you no shame? Do you want me to tell your father what you said?"

"MOM —"

"Just leave," Rebecca utters quietly with simmering rage.

Denver bolts down the stairs in a fit. His cries linger in Rebecca's ears as he moves toward the first floor. He notices his mom left her purse.

He starts rummaging through her handbag. Denver feels the bottles of pills.

"Oxycodone, Vicodin, Percocet…how many things is she on? How does she even get through the day?"

Denver googles each drug. He reads, "can cause…death when taken in high doses or when combined with other substances, especially alcohol" for all of them.

"I'm small enough. I'll take four of each, and take vodka from the cellar to make sure it takes me out. Slitting my wrist would be too messy; and, they might find me before I lost too much blood."

Denver rushes down to the cellar and takes a bottle of Absolut 100. The bottle is about a quarter empty. He bound back up to the kitchen. He puts four Percocets in his mouth, takes a big swig of Absolut. He puts four Vicodins in his mouth. He takes another big swig. He puts two Oxycodones in his mouth. He takes a huge third swig. Tightly he closes the prescription containers, and places them, meticulously—despite his shaking hands—where he found them in his mother's purse. He musters enough balance to place her handbag on the bottom stair. He stumbles back to the kitchen.

"There's no turning back from this. It has to work."

He looks up.

"Nobody wants me here. Please take me."

Denver starts chugging the rest of the vodka. He gets to about the bottom eighth of the bottle, and cannot stomach anymore.

He can hardly breathe. He writhes violently, contorting in abject pain. He begins vomiting.

The kitchen is becoming foggier and foggier. The lambent pendant lights descend into darkness.

Denver Toulouse Lewis lies lifeless on the kitchen floor.

Rebecca emerges from the bathroom.

"Are people in there?"

She moves closer to her bedroom; but, something catches her step. Wearily, she heads back to the bathroom to get her phone. She scrolls through the newsfeed on her phone.

"Category 5 typhoon in Thailand? Wow, it must be horrendous."

She quickly taps on the link. Rebecca skims the Associated Press article.

"At least 250 confirmed dead…and Northern Malaysia was hit pretty hard…

"Malaysia…"

Rebecca quickly calls Angelina.

"Hey, did you hear about the typhoon in Thailand?"

"No, wow, not yet. Put down my phone for a while. How bad was it?"

"It was a category 5, at least 250 people dead."

"That's terrible. Were other places affected?"

"Yeah, Northern Malaysia was slammed."

"I can only imagine. We'll start a drive at school."

"That's definitely good, but they may need some on the ground help."

"Oh sure, Red Cross is probably already there."

"And, they may need some companies to mobilize—"

"You think Windows to the Soul can help?"

"Definitely. And, we can be there. You'll get a crash course in relief work."

"Wow mom, that's great. How about all the openings and stuff?"

"I'll show up for one of the LA ones, you come along with me, and we'll head out to Malaysia. We'll be there for a week or two."

"This is a different side mom. This is too cool."

"I'll see if I can get in touch with the offices of Thailand's and Malaysia's foreign ministers tomorrow. I'll pick you up from Chris's tonight so we'll talk more about it."

"Great. Can't wait."

"Yeah, if you want things done, you got to be on the ground. See you in a few."

"Later."

Rebecca snatches her bag ("*how did it get here?*" she thinks) and scurries out to the Porsche, avoiding the kitchen. Peter and Amber quietly tiptoe down the stairs.

"That was so close. I told you."

"She shouldn't have been back that early."

"Well, she was. This isn't safe Pete."

"It won't happen again," he says as he walks to the foot of the stairs and peers out the window.

"All right, it's clear. Let's go."

Peter turns around.

"Let me grab some water."

He gets into the kitchen and sees his son's blanched body.

"Denver!"

He bolts toward his son. He feels for his pulse. It is faint. He begins giving Denver CPR.

He stops for a few seconds.

"Amber, call 911. Denver isn't breathing. Tell them to come immediately."

Dr. Lewis resumes CPR.

"Yes, we're at Monroe and Ridgeway, 10605. He's only 12-years-old. Please come immediately."

Within about two minutes, Peter and Amber hear sirens.

Denver begins coughing.

"How the fuck did this happen?" Rebecca asks her husband desperately.

"The doctor's coming."

"You're Denver's mom?'

"Yes, I am. We sped over here. What happened doctor?"

"It was an opioid overdose and alcohol poisoning. He got the Narcan" just in time. With Denver's age and small frame, he's lucky to be alive. He also has a resourceful father. I say it seldomly; but, you can call this a miracle."

"We have alcohol in our cellar that we never thought about locking up. How did he get opioids?"

"He had high doses Oxycodone, Percocet, and Vicodin in his system. Who's taking these medications?"

Rebecca takes a few moments.

"I am doctor."

Peter looks at Angelina, and then looks at his wife in complete bewilderment. He does not utter a word.

"But doctor, they were in my purse—they're always in my purse. I don't know how he even knew they were there, or how he got to them. None of this makes sense to me."

"Those should also be under lock and key. All three of those are highly addictive, and should not be taken together. How did you get those prescriptions? Honestly, you could have ended up here."

Rebecca forewarns her husband and daughter, with a cautionarily steely glance, before starting.

"I was in a pileup on the West Side Highway about three months ago. I could barely move for weeks. I was in excruciating pain. My doctor was telling me the same thing—this can be unsafe, these are highly addictive, etc.—but the dosage has been carefully titrated."

The bewildered stares continue.

"You can see me doctor. I am no addict, nor is my son."

Peter finally breaks his silence.

"This was an apparent suicide attempt?"

"There are all the signs doc. With his size and the alcohol in his blood, he must have drunken at least ½ of a bottle of vodka. And, with the opioids in his system, he had to have swallowed about 10 pills. He knew what he was doing; and, he didn't want to make it.

Unfortunately, we're seeing this more and more; but, it's usually among those at least twice his age. There are issues here that have to be addressed."

"He's attending counseling doctor, and he seemed to be improving," Rebecca starts quietly. "He's *never* been suicidal."

The marks across his arm that Rebecca and Paul spotted a couple of months ago race across her mind.

"We're all shocked," Angelina says plaintively.

"Do you know if he's getting bullied at school? Kids can be merciless, especially online. He might have had an especially bad day; and, they might have told him to kill himself. There's no end to what these kids will say."

"We have to find out," Paul intones without looking up from the floor.

"We'll keep him here overnight. We should report this to DCS—especially when minors overdose. But I know Peter, I know you…you're a good family. You have to keep these substances—all of them—locked. You have to promise me that neither Denver, nor you," he exhorts as he points his finger squarely at Rebecca, "will be back here."

"Again, he should have been dead. Someone was looking out for you. You should be planning a funeral."

"We know Dr. D'Oro. And, we are eternally grateful. That's said with the utmost sincerity."

"Thank you for saving our son."

"I'm just as glad we could save this one. He might be up. You can start, gently, asking what happened."

"Thank you, tremendously, Randy. Have a good night," Peter says quietly.

"You were the first line of defense."

He gives his friend two hearty and congratulatory pats on his shoulder. "Be well."

Dr. D'Oro marches down the hall. Peter waits till he rounds the corner.

"I'll check on Denver," Angelina says. She pulls away.

"The pileup on the West Side Highway that you walked away from. So bad that we never knew about it; but, you still needed to be taking three of the most addictive medications simultaneously.

How are you even standing? Is that why you've gotten so thin? You probably pop like 10 a day. I know Dr. Schleindman didn't prescribe these. How did you get your hands on them?"

"You remember when I broke my wrist in 2017. Dr. Schleindman prescribed the Oxycodone for that."

"And, how about the other medications? Is the Fentanyl subscription coming next week?"

Rebecca is silent.

"You have to come clean about this. We're getting you help; but, you need to come clean about this."

Rebecca refuses to look at her husband.

"You know what, a part of me is actually happy this happened. We never would have known if Denver didn't overdose. We got two problems do deal with it."

"I'm beyond fine Peter."

"Everyone thinks that. Somehow, Denver knew better. He usually does.

How do you get through the day?"

"I told you I'm fine," Rebecca asserts indignantly.

"He inherited that from you. He can down 100% proof and 10 opioid pills, and live to tell you. Dawn gave you good genes."

Rebecca scowls at her husband.

"Only I can mock my mom."

Peter is chastened.

"I'm sorry for being glib babe. Our son just tried to commit suicide—in our own house. I'm trying to make sense of this. Did Angelina mention anything?"

"She still hasn't admitted it; but, the last thing she knows about was Denver getting roughed up. She would have told me about this."

Rebecca remembers how she rebuffed her son before she left tonight.

"He wanted to tell me; but, I didn't want to listen."

"He wanted to tell you what?"

Rebecca looks at her husband.

"I really need to use the restroom. Angelina and I just jumped in the car."

"The ladies' room is the second door on your right. I'll check on Denver."

"I'll be there in a couple of minutes."

Peter walks down the hall and makes a left. His son is in the fourth room on the right.

Denver and Angelina are laughing at a video on Tik Tok. Denver senses his father at the doorway and looks up at him. He is giving his son an expressionless stare.

"Come on dad," Angelina coaxes as she motions for her dad to enter the room.

IX

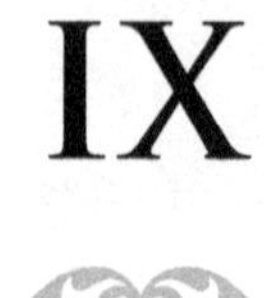

"You really wanted to end it?" Angelina inquires searchingly.

"At that moment, I did."

"Did you think about me? Dad? Mom? Did you think about Liam? We would have all been crushed man."

"Frankly, I wasn't thinking of anybody or anything. Now, I know how it was the worst decision; but, then, I wanted anything to get out. I asked Him to take me out."

"Wow."

"You know, if it wasn't for one of dad's doctor friends, they would have taken us out and placed us in foster care. A minor overdosing on opioids, in their own house, is no joke. You were popping 'em boy. You made mom look like a fuckin' stoner."

"She might be. How did she get her hands on all those medications?"

"We're still trying to figure that out. But, you know when mom wants to keep stuff on lock, she keeps them on lock. We may never know. Mom always has hook-ups. She finds contacts for everything. Or, she just got fake names for prescriptions. Whatever it was, it was slick."

"And, it's dangerous, especially when you got a fragile kid like me around. I can't be doing this. I'm sorry for hurting all over you."

"We're sadder than we are angry. We never knew it was that bad."

"What did you tell the school?"

"We said you had a severe anaphylaxis, a really bad reaction to antibiotics. You were in the hospital for precautionary measures, just for observation. Once Dr. D'Oro, and the nurses, assured us there wasn't any lasting damage, we felt comfortable telling the story.

Your welfare was the first priority. But, honestly, we were thinking about how to cover it up the whole time."

"I know how dad, and especially mom, are. I'm not surprised at all. I promise it won't happen again.

I never thought it would ever happen. I just couldn't take how mom acted."

"What do you mean?"

"Dad; Amber, the intern; and, I came back early Thursday night from the research center. Dad said he was coming back to review a report with Amber."

Angelina begins shaking her head.

"You already know. It was a lame excuse. They just came back to—"

"Fuck."

"Exactly."

"Are you serious?" Angelina asks her brother while they sit in the living room.

"Yeah. I mean I saw the signs. While we were at the office the other night, they kissed each other and were staring, lost in each other's eyes. I broke them up by telling dad it was getting late and we needed to go. Then he brought her back here and then I saw them upstairs…"

"I took out my phone for a split second. It would have been all over Snapchat…I would have been the most popular kid in school—"

"For pimping out your distinguished neurosurgeon dad. Anything works now. Man…Was it like just a make-out session, oral, or full-on fucking?"

"It was both, oral and full-on…"

Angelina leans over to her brother and gives him a pat on the shoulder.

"Denver Toulouse Lewis, today you became a man."

"Shut up Angelina, this is serious."

"I know Denver; but, I just can't believe it. How long do you think it's been going on?"

"Well, she started working with dad like six months ago. I don't think things really started until they got together to 'review' her reports last week. She's such a whore. I know she planned all that just to get some time alone with dad. And, dad, unwittingly, went along with it."

"Maybe all this wasn't done so unwittingly."

"What are you talking about? Dad would never want to cheat on mom."

"Yeah, I thought that too; but, nobody's perfect Denver. I mean dad's a really great guy; but, he's human. He has needs. I know with mom being so caught up in Windows to the Soul they hardly spend any time together, much less have sex. He's a man; he's a sexual person. If he can't get it from mom, he'll get it from somebody else," Angelina says cavalierly.

Denver shakes his head.

"When you get a little older, you'll understand," she tells her brother condescendingly.

"Dad's not like other guys; he's better. He's moral… he loves mom. He wouldn't do this to her."

"But, he did. He's all of those things; but, he's not perfect. Nobody is Denver."

Denver remains silent.

"Her name's Amber?"

"No, her name's 'slut.' She lured dad in, manipulated him—"

"It takes two man. Dad's a very intelligent, discerning 56-year-old man. He knows exactly what he's doing."

"She knows he's vulnerable; and, she's just playing with him," Denver mutters.

"Dad's not perfect. Get over it."

Denver releases a pained stare from his eyes. Angelina bends toward her brother, and gives him a tender hug. He tenderly lays his head on her shoulder as Angelina rubs his back.

"There comes a time when every kid has to realize that their parents are just struggling to figure things out like they are. Last night was that time for you. Don't lose respect for dad; respect his frailties. I realized a long time ago that we don't have the perfect American family."

Denver moves away from his sister's embrace, looking at her poignantly.

"Maybe we won't even have a family after this."

"What are you saying? Does mom know about this?"

"I tried telling her the other night."

"You did? I bet she blew up."

"Yeah she did. She just started yelling me at me, saying I was lying. She told me to get out of the room. That's when I decided I didn't want to be here anymore."

Angelina hugs her brother tightly.

"I'm not surprised. She doesn't want to believe it."

"I know. I'm just scared Ange. I can't forget how he looked at me last night."

"How?"

"It was this cold-blooded, emotionless stare. I felt like he was burning a hole through me. I couldn't tell if he was angry at me, angry about the situation, or trying to come to terms with what he did. He's never looked at me like that before; and, it terrified me."

"It could have been all of those things. I don't know what's going to happen Denver; but, it'll be all right."

"How could you be so sure of that? I know so many kids in school whose parents got divorced and it's a mess. I don't want to go through that."

"You don't have to make things so dramatic Denver."

"The picture I had of my father has been shattered and this family could fall apart. How isn't it?"

"If it happens, we'll deal with it then."

"She might have lashed out at me; but, she's suspecting something now. She'll find out."

"This might be their test."

"Test?"

"Yeah, every relationship has at least one. It's that decisive moment—a death, loss, or some kind of betrayal—that tests how strong your relationship is. If your love is strong enough you get through them, and it becomes stronger than ever."

"What about if they get through it?"

"It wasn't worth keeping."

Peter is lying under the covers with his left arm bent under his head, and his right arm lying straight on his side. Rebecca comes out of the bathroom and plops on his side. He moves toward his wife and rests her against his naked torso. He places his right hand under her nightgown and begins sliding his middle finger between her breasts.

"I thought you'd never get out of there."

Rebecca turns to his side and picks up the down comforter. She notices that there's nothing between him and the sheets.

"Where are your pajamas?"

"They're not there, but something else is."

Peter begins maneuvering his hand between her thighs. She pushes it away before he thrusts his finger.

"No Peter, I have the opening tomorrow."

"Come on, just a little bit."

"Sorry babe, I really want to be ready for this opening tomorrow. I want to have my mind clear and be in touch with my *inner self.*"

"Yeah, well I haven't been in touch with your inner self for a long time."

"I just walked straight into that one didn't I?"

Peter makes a walking motion with his fingers.

"Why are you so horny today?"

"I want you every day. I love you."

Rebecca gives him a sweet kiss on the cheek.

"And I love you too; but, I really need to get to bed."

Rebecca begins to curl up under the covers.

"When I get back, we'll make up for it," Rebecca says in a seductive tone. "Good night, sexy."

Peter turns over and lies atop his wife. He sneaks his tongue under his wife's top and begins to swirl it around her nipple.

"Peter stop, you know I love that."

He thrusts his finger inside of her as he continues to work on her chest.

"Mmmmmm."

He begins moving down her body.

"Baby…"

He is moving still further.

She feels him rub against her moistening hardness. He starts entering deeper inside of her.

"Oh Peter," she whispers.

She feels him pulsing and hardening, slowly consuming her. Rebecca lies, staring distantly as her husband rocks on top of her.

—∘∘⊱✦⊰∘∘—

The faint, pre-dawn light cascades through the kitchen windows, lacing the room with a rarefied air of calm and serenity. Rebecca sits at the table, sipping on coffee. Peter walks quietly down the stairs.

"You were going to leave without saying good-bye?"

"I was going to after I finished drinking my coffee," Rebecca says very matter-of-factly.

"Was everything all right last night?"

"What do you mean?"

"You seemed distant, like you weren't really into it."

"Didn't I tell you that I didn't want to?"

"I know; but, you needed a break though. What were you thinking about?"

Rebecca slowly turns to her husband and stares at him coldly.

"Whatever I wanted to," Rebecca answers acerbically.

Peter replies with a wounded, puzzled glance.

"Rebecca, please tell me what's wrong?"

"I think you have a pretty good idea."

Peter stares at his wife as the phone rings. Rebecca springs up from her chair. Her husband starts making his way up the stairs.

"Hello."

She hears nothing but silence.

"Hello."

"Hi Rebecca."

Rebecca is silent for a moment.

"Mom?"

"Yes, please don't hang up the phone."

"I won't. I just didn't expect to hear from you."

"I had been meaning to talk with you after the funeral; but, then I had second thoughts. The thought of calling you has been nagging me all of these months; so, I finally decided I'd do it."

"Sorry mom, but I have an early flight this morning. I have to start leaving for the airport. I'll catch up with you when I get back all right."

"I know you won't Rebecca. Just give me a little bit of your time now."

"Mom honestly I can't."

"I said, 'I need to talk to you.'"

Rebecca gives an exasperated sigh.

"Fine mom. I only have a few minutes."

"I just wanted to say that I'm sorry."

"Sorry about what?"

"Sorry about everything."

"Mom, I can't give you money right now. We can discuss that when I get back. I'll talk to you soon—"

"No, I mean it this time Rebecca. I didn't realize how much I had hurt you over the years until I saw you at the funeral. I know you don't have the time right now; but, I think there are some things that we need to talk about."

"Things we need to talk about? I think we aired all that out during the funeral. It's over mom."

"No, it isn't. Look Rebecca, I'm tired of us running away from each other."

"Or, you running away from me. There were a lot of times I tried reaching out to you mom, tried to develop a real relationship; and, all you cared to do was to tell me about the new clothes you'd gotten, how great of a lover one of your boyfriends were… I gave up on that a long time ago."

"I know, and I'm sorry for all of that Rebecca. You're the only daughter I have. I'm feeling so alone. I need you right now."

"Mom, you were always alone. You were just too high or drunk to notice most of the time."

"Please Rebecca. I know you tried reaching out to me before; but, now I'm reaching out. Please hear me out."

"Why all of this now mom?"

"Because I've been looking back on my life and I realized that I've lost the two most important things to me."

"What are those?"

"Charles and you. Lord knows that I'm not getting any younger; and, I need to make some changes. I can't get Charles back; but, I still have a chance with you."

"I've always been here; and, I will be here mom. We'll talk later."

"I know you're so busy with Windows to the Soul; and, you've got the openings today."

"Yeah, that's why I need to go now."

"OK, well I wish you, Peter and the kids a safe trip."

"Oh, Peter and the kids aren't going with me."

"How come they're not?"

"Peter has a conference next week, and the kids have school."

"But, this is a really special day for you. Everybody should come along."

"Wow mom, you're all about family values all of a sudden. Angelina is actually coming. We're heading off to Malaysia early tomorrow morning, your time, to help with hurricane relief. Peter will hold down the fort for two weeks."

"That's good. I bet Denver would have liked to come too. You were always going off, doing things by yourself."

"What are you talking about?"

"You just didn't want them to come."

"That's completely untrue mom. I wish they could all come; but, circumstances don't allow it."

"Peter can miss one conference. Denver is brilliant; he could have gotten the work from his teachers in advance."

"As usual mom, you don't understand."

"I understand perfectly Rebecca. You always knew how to push people away. Don't do that with your family."

"I'm not pushing anyone away… why am I even talking about this? I have to leave mom. Good-bye."

"Don't get angry Rebecca. I know what I'm saying. I just don't want you to end up—," Rebecca's mom says plaintively.

"Like what mom?"

"Like me."

"I really have to go mom. Take care."

Rebecca hangs up the phone.

The view of the Rocky Mountains removes Rebecca temporarily from the confines of her first-class seat. Her head is cocked against the window as reflections of the western landscape run across her eyes like a miniature film. Angelina is sleeping in the aisle seat to her left. Xavier turns back to talk to her.

"We got the free hats we're giving out right?"

"Yeah, I checked with Laura at the airport, everything is set up," Rebecca tells Xavier as she's looking outside. Xavier moves his hand back and forth in front of her glazed eyes. Alexander and Mimi are sitting to the side of them, across the aisle.

"Are you OK?"

"Yeah I'm fine; there's just a lot of things on my mind."

"I know, it's been pretty hectic; but, it's been excellent. I'm so excited about these openings. Now, when they say 'I See the Light' in Cali, they won't be talking about chronic."

Rebecca laughs.

"Yeah, I hope so."

A young Native-American man, sitting across the aisle from Xavier, turns around and looks at Rebecca.

"Hey! Are you Rebecca Lewis, the Windows to the Soul lady?"

"Yeah that's me. How are you?" Rebecca says to him with a little wave.

"Really good now. You have awesome products. I really like what you're doing."

"Thanks, I appreciate it. You have our watch on now, right?"

"Yep, this is my favorite one."

He bends his arm toward his chest and begins reading.

"It says, 'You measure a life not just by the Love one receives, but also, by the Love one leaves behind.'"

Rebecca gives him a small smile.

It is an uncharacteristically chilly, overcast day in Los Angeles, but the eyes of the crowd—lit by anticipation and the yearning for renewal (or maybe it is the free stuff?)—helps to lighten the dense air. The Windows to the Soul team ascend the podium directly in front of the "I See the Light Store" on Wilshire and Robertson. Two young women walk passed, looking curiously at the crowd.

"What's all this about?"

"See, it's the new Windows to the Soul store. The ads are all over. That's the CEO right there. She was on *Extra* yesterday."

"Oh her. That hypocrite."

"What do you mean?"

"For someone who says they're so into spirituality and everything, she seems to be way into the business. I mean, she was saying all of this new age-y stuff; but, talked a whole lot about their returns and how rapidly they're expanding. She didn't talk about charity work, contributing to humanitarian organizations, not even about her family."

Her friend shrugs her shoulders.

"She's already given like a million for the Malaysia hurricane effort. I think she's leaving to go over there right after this. Oh, she's coming up to the mic."

Rebecca catches the leer from the woman as she begins to speak.

"How's everyone doing today?"

The crowd of about 500 breaks out in a rousing cheer.

"Yeah I get it. You're all just excited about getting the free stuff."

Rebecca receives laughs in response as well as some enthusiastic "yeahs" from the crowd.

"Well, thanks so much for coming out today. I know when it's not at least 70° and sunny it's considered a bad day here; but, I applaud your resolve to participate in this momentous occasion. Today, we're not only celebrating the opening of the 'I See the Light' store—"

The crowd applauds.

"But more importantly, we're also celebrating a new day in which the world will be steered in a more fulfilling, spiritually oriented direction. And, that's what I wanted to talk a little bit about today.

Windows to the Soul is not about catchy slogans and cool designs; it's about allowing all of you, and the whole world, to get in touch with that most vital part of ourselves—the spirit. All of you have come out here because you yearned to reconnect, you strived to find meaning, and you needed to be one with the Light. You heard the reverberant cry that is sounding not only here in America, but around the world, heralding a time of higher consciousness and spiritual awakening. This period is long overdue. Gone will be the days when the dollar is the deity; now, spirituality will be the sovereign. You have been summoned; and, thank you for answering the call."

The crowd whoops and hollers.

"We've heard that cry loud and clear as well. When we open the doors to this store, we will be doing our part to further this burgeoning spiritual revolution. Let the glasses be windows to your vibrant soul, the headbands wrap around your expanded consciousness, and all of these products be the avenue for unlocking the doors to a greater life, and your greater self.

However, these products are only justified by your service, and fulfilling your promise. This enlightened awareness must permeate all aspects of your life; it must galvanize every moment of the day. One committed to the ideals of Windows to the Soul—one committed to the ideals of spirituality—is a person who is a contributing member of the community. This is a person who is dedicated to doing their best work every day. This is a person who is devoted to their families, friends and communities, leading everyday with love, respect, and wisdom."

Rebecca stops for a moment. Images of Angelina, Denver, Peter and her mother flash in her mind. She quickly regains her concentration.

"Ultimately, this is a person who passes on the gifts of spirituality to others. I have realized these treasures of spirituality for myself; and, I can't wait for you to experience them as well.

"Now, let's unlock the doors to your greater selves."

Rebecca signals to Xavier, Mimi, and Alexander to move toward the door. She takes the key out of her pocket, unlocks the doors, and swings them open. The crowd cheers.

"You have all seen the light. Thank you for being such a wonderful audience."

"See, I told you she was full o' shit," the skeptical woman says. "Let's go." She and her friend walk away from the gathering. The crowd charges the entrance doors.

"Pick up your free 'I See the Light' hat on your way out," Rebecca screams over the excitement of the crowd.

"I think that went pretty well," Xavier says patting Rebecca on the shoulder.

"Yeah, the crowd seemed really pumped," Alexander chimes.

A man walks out with a pair of shades, a watch, and some containers of acai and papalo.

"Looks like you're our first customer," Mimi says cheerily.

"If we continue like that, we can move to Rodeo Drive," Rebecca says. "Okay, you guys are heading downtown. Ange and I are going to LAX."

"You checked with Ed on the numbers for SF?" Xavier asks Rebecca.

"Yeah, we're doing outstanding business there. The Embarcadero store should kill it. Berkeley is looking like a great location. He and the finance team have been running numbers. I'll check with him when we touch down in Kuala Lumpur. Come on Ange."

Angelina skips over, wearing two Windows to the Soul hats. Rebecca shakes her head, and they begin walking to the limo. She feels her cell phone vibrating.

She checks the phone. It is Peter. She lets it ring.

"We need to bring out 150 more cartons of MREs before the next bus arrives," Angelina says as she jogs toward her mother. She and her mom are caught in a swirl of 130 relief workers setting up food, shelter, and medical-service stations for over 1,200 hurricane victims in Kuala Kerai. Rebecca has just finished setting up a tent and is unloading syringes.

"No problem. There are about 600 left in that van over there. We have time; the next group should be coming within an hour."

"That's awesome how you were able to coordinate with all these companies. These should last for another three weeks before they need reinforcements. #shiningthelight is trending on Twitter. Do you really want to go ahead with that whole deal though? Number one, it's against what Windows to the Soul stands for. On top of that, the Feds can find out."

"They won't if you don't talk about it. Can you be any louder Ange? I'm 'greasing the wheels' with the foreign ministry; so, we should be fine. Plus, with all the good press, we should be fine."

"You better hope they all keep it on the dl. When's your accomplice coming anyway?"

"Shhh," Rebecca says curtly as she glares at her daughter. "Actually, he should have been here by now."

A Range Rover featuring a Malaysian flag pulls up.

"That's probably him. OK, you set up the MREs. After, check if they need any more supplies in the clinic. There's still a lot to do. I know you know how to make yourself useful. I'll be back in about 40 minutes."

"OK, just make sure nothing's being recorded."

"I told him to leave his cell. I'll check him again before we start. All right, do what you got to do. I'll meet you back here in about an hour."

"All right," Angelina says as she heads toward the van.

Rebecca rushes over to the Range Rover.

"Hello Minister Teuku. Thanks for taking the time to come. How is Kota Bharu looking?"

"It is well-stocked just like this one, and the medical clinic is up and running. They are expecting about 200 more victims; so, we do need additional personnel."

"I'll get in touch with the team up in Pasir Puteh now," Rebecca says as she takes out her walkie-talkie.

"Mohammed, can you take a few minutes and call the team in Pasir Puteh? Please tell them to assign 18 more volunteers in Kota Bharu. They're expecting about 200 more survivors. I'm with the Foreign Minister."

"Thanks. It's being handled right now."

"Please radio when it's confirmed."

"I will."

Rebecca places her walkie-talkie back in her front, right pocket. "And, we just needed to clarify some issues. Care to walk to the trailer?"

"My pleasure," Minister Teuku said.

The CEO and the Minister walk about 50 yards to a white trailer, about 700 square feet, located in the northeastern corner of the site. Rebecca walks in first, and Minister Teuku closes the door.

"All the money came through?" Rebecca asks earnestly.

"Oh yes. The accounts have been secured. All the paper work has been secured; and, they'll begin breaking ground on the Kuala Lumpur and Kuantan stores next week. I know you'll be meeting with the Thai minister tomorrow. He assured me the Bangkok store will be among the first buildings established once they clear the debris. He faxed the certificate of occupancy and proof of insurance."

He passes the documents over to Rebecca.

"Thank you," Rebecca says as she files it in her attaché. "That saved me about three months."

"Actually, with this disaster, much more."

"You're right. Over 900 people dead…it'll take years for the nation to truly recover. But, we can get off to a solid start. Now, we can establish schools here and around the North. We can also expand the medical clinics, as we discussed. Do we have assurances about the tax situation?"

"The corporations will be registered with the State within 48 hours. With your firm's gift, you should have amnesty for at least four years; but, with changes in administrations, there may have to be some modifications. Nevertheless, I'll assure you're grandfathered in. All limits on repatriation have also been lifted. That can begin immediately upon store openings." Minister Teuku lifted a file from his suitcase.

"Thank you so much Minister. We'll begin getting in contact with NGOs down South, the Education Ministries in Indonesia and Cambodia, and even some educational programs in Australia tomorrow to ensure we meet staffing needs. Organizations in the network will be able to donate supplies within five days."

"You are saving a nation Ms. Rebecca. I hope this relationship can continue."

"Oh, it will. We'll talk more about this over dinner; but, we can start reviewing the details now."

"Surely."

Rebecca sees Angelina outside the trailer. She holds up her right index finger to her daughter who is waiting anxiously.

X

The warm July breeze blows through Rebecca's hair, whispering enticingly in her ear. As she steps out of her corvette, the warm, crimson orb looms behind her with simmering intensity. It slowly submerges into the horizon as it clears the shadows of the past, and augurs the promise of a new day.

Rebecca tip-toes to the front door. A baby blackbird alights on the door knob as she turns the key.

An austere calm gilds the air of the Lewis home. Chimerical images of adolescent feet gamboling up the stairs, the allegro tempo of Peter's fingers skipping on the computer, and booming beats of rock and hip-hop flit in Rebecca's mind as she hangs up her coat. Even after a six-hour flight from Seattle, she is feeling surprisingly energetic (must be the plush first-class seats). Rebecca saunters toward the kitchen.

As she opens the door, Rebecca spots Denver writing at the kitchen table. He slowly lifts up his head. Rebecca blinks; it is only a specter. She walks toward the kitchen table to get an apple. There is an open notebook lying on it. Rebecca begins reading it:

> Is she being too ambitious? Perhaps she's becoming
> so drunk with her own success that she feels she's

invincible, impervious(?) to the public's sensitivity and response that her business is based upon. I think that's really the sin of overconfidence; you forget where your strength comes from, how all you have comes from the Almighty. That's the way she is a lot of times—always trudging ahead no matter what is right, what is left, what is in back, and, especially what is ahead (rework). She always stands up firmly for her beliefs and for herself, and that's why she's where she is today. I wish I could develop some of that myself.

However, that fierce single-mindedness may also be her Achilles heel. She becomes so involved in her own affairs at times that everything else is invisible. At times, I wonder if she realizes if we're all here, if she considers how we're feeling, and if she notices how things are slowly beginning to crumble under pressure.

She obviously understands the virtues of life, the things that are truly important in an intellectual sense; but, isn't it more important for those ideas to be experienced inwardly too? They must live on a visceral level. They must not only be thought of, but, more importantly, they must also BELIEVED. I think deep down inside, she knows that; and, she strives for it. This is her way of trying to achieve that; but, she's not doing all that she can. Consequently, there's always a vague melancholy that lingers, an irrepressible longing. I think being actively connected to something that's greater than herself—though she already thinks she is—may alleviate it.

The sound of adolescent feet bounces down the stairs. Angelina greets her mom excitedly.

"Hey mom. I didn't hear you get back."

"It was so quiet in the house. I thought nobody was home."

"No, I was busy on my tab researching some more about HIV/AIDS for our trip."

"You're really getting ready."

"Actually it's for this little girl, Dafina, who's here from Tanzania. She's suffering from AIDS and we were able to raise enough money for her to stay at one of the city's hospitals. She'll be getting treatment here for a few months. But, we're trying to keep her here for as long as we can."

"I forgot about that. I know you and your friends were working very hard on that for so long. Have you seen her?"

"Actually no. I wanted to go tonight, but I forgot to get a Metro Card. I'll go later in the week."

"Let's go tonight. I'm sure she'd love to see you. We'll get cards at the station."

Angelina's eyes light up.

"Really mom? Great! Let me get my bag."

Rebecca and Angelina descend from the cab, right in front of New York-Presbyterian Komansky Children's Hospital. The mother and daughter walk toward the building.

"The new Windows to the Soul commercials are supposed to debut tonight right?"

"Yeah they are."

"You're going to miss them. By the time we get back to Grand Central and catch the train it will be so late."

"Don't worry about that. This is more important."

Angelina leans her head affectionately on her mother's shoulder as they walk into the hospital.

The walls are merrily decorated with pastel colors, children's drawings and pictures of cartoon characters. There are TVs mounted around the ward and in the rooms, with the majority on the Cartoon Network or Disney Channel. Nurses (though exhausted) walk around cheerily, always ready to greet little faces with a smile.

Rebecca and Angelina are still growing accustomed to the setting. They thought of the struggles that are these children's realities. Nevertheless, they cannot help but be lifted by the glimmers of joy—the ever-present hallmarks of childhood—that shine so brightly from their smiles and laughter. Their artless serenity graces them with an inner strength that surpassed that of those four times their age. And, their light hearts enliven the ward's atmosphere, as well as the spirits of the two women who come to visit.

One of the nurses walks with them to the end of the ward. They peer inside the door to see a seraphic seven-year-old sitting up on her bed. She is playing with a group of stuffed animals, affecting voices for them in her native tongue. Dafina is a black beauty, endued with the richest, dark chocolate skin; large, boundless almond eyes; a keen, regal nose; a long swanlike neck; and succulent lips bespeaking of African splendor. Her young body is rendered somewhat gaunt by the inner battle it is waging; but, she wears its delicate tautness and raw vitality as badges of honor. She greets Angelina and Rebecca with a delightfully curious stare.

"She's absolutely beautiful. Can we talk to her? Does she speak English?" Rebecca asks the nurse.

"She speaks a little bit. You can ask her how she's doing, how her day was. Daffy is a very quick learner. She loves for me to talk to her on the phone, so she can pick up new words. I can't tell you how excited she was when I told her you were coming. I'll come back in about 20 minutes."

"Sure," Rebecca answers.

"Hey cutie," Angelina says as she sat on the bed.

"Angelina?" Dafina says with a melodious voice.

"Yep, that's me. It's great to finally see you in person."

"I like seeing you too. Thank you."

"You're very welcome. Here's my mom."

"Hi Dafina. I have to tell you that you are a beautiful girl," Rebecca says as she pulls tenderly at her thick, raven coils.

"Thank you. You too, and Angelina."

"I love her already," Rebecca jokes.

"Do you like it here?" Angelina asks.

"Yes. It's very nice. America is very nice."

"Well, we think you're very nice too. How are you feeling today?"

"Good, but tired," she said, making a sleeping motion with her head and hands. "I've been feeling a little under the…"

"Weather?" Angelina offers.

"Yes," Dafina says with a smile, rejoicing in her remembrance.

"Well, you're a very strong girl," Rebecca bends her arms inward, forming muscles to simulate strength. "And, you're doing very well. You like your toys?"

"Yes, they're very fun."

"Do you want more?"

Dafina nods her head with excitement.

"Well, I'll bring you some later OK."

Rebecca gestures to Angelina to follow her to the back corner of the room.

"She's an adorable little girl," Rebecca says.

"Yeah I know; you just feel like taking her home."

"How long is she going to be here?"

"For now, we only have enough money till September. The Seavers, the Dixons, and some other families in the area pledged to make some monthly contributions. We're also getting some donors from throughout the country and overseas. But, we still have a big balance to cover."

"I'll talk to the hospital about the costs. Tomorrow, we'll figure out what we can do to cover the balance. I want her to be around as long as possible."

"I think somehow she understood what you said."

Rebecca turns to Dafina. Her angelic face is beaming with a smile that expressed a heartfelt thank you.

"We'll see you again really soon, OK Dafina."

"OK, love you."

Rebecca tenderly places her left hand on her heart. She walks over to Dafina and kisses her forehead.

"Love you too Dafi."

She and Angelina are waving good-bye.

"Hey Ange, I got to catch up on a couple of e-mails and make some calls. Could you wait for a little while in the lobby?"

"No problem mom, but we don't want to get back too late."

"We won't. I'll make it quick. Thanks honey."

"All right."

Rebecca waits till Angelina gets on the elevator. She opens her e-mail. The account information for the Thai minister of commerce is attached to the latest message.

"Perfect. This should really grease the wheels."

She calls the Minister on Skype.

"Thanks for taking the call Minister. Yes, you're account information just came through. The 1.025 million USD…actually, we can make that €1.025 million for you. It'll be sent as soon as the status of the corporations has been confirmed, and we receive the first payment. Could you forward their registration with the Ministry?"

"That'll be done this morning, along with a transfer of $3,500 into the account to demonstrate our good faith. That will be deducted from the first transfer from the stores."

"The €1.025 million will be wired as soon as the funds are received in that case. Thank you. I wanted to talk about the repatriation schedule."

"Thank you for the confirmation. We settled on bi-weekly, correct?"

"Actually, we don't want it to be too frequent and raise suspicion. Let's have it the third Wednesday of each month, starting next month, August 21st. And, we have a fixed exchange rate?"

"Yes, we have cleared that with the banks. You'll get that confirmation, along with the registration confirmations for the corporations."

"Thanks so much for that. I haven't forgotten the funds for the clinics. We needed $4.2 million didn't we?"

"3.75 million will go to the clinics, and the remaining will go to schools in the area."

"Thank you for your work on that. It's sorely needed. How quickly will the Bangkok store be open now?"

"Oh, before scheduled, on July 31st. You'll get a full three weeks before the first transfer."

"Brilliant. We'll arrange for at least another $1.5 million in relief funds next month. Isn't this better than working with the Red Cross?"

The Minister chuckles.

Rebecca sees an alert on her phone. The $3,500 had been sent.

"You are efficient. You know it's still night here; but, you'll receive your funds before 9pm ICT tonight. We discussed from which account the funds would originate?"

"We did. Thank you Mrs. Lewis."

"Thank you Minister Buapoke. You are a treasure to your people."

"And, you are a blessing to us. I'll confirm when the funds arrive."

"Yes Minister. Enjoy your day."

Minister Buapoke signs off.

Rebecca goes back to Dafina. She is still up. Dafina's eyes light up when she sees Rebecca again. Rebecca blows Dafina a kiss; and, Dafina "catches" it.

Rebecca heads to the elevator.

───∘∘∘❖∘∘∘───

A man sits on his couch, eating from a bag of potato chips. He is flipping through the channels when some disturbing images suddenly stop him.

"Is this another special about how we're in a 'Constitutional Crisis'?"

His wife comes out from the kitchen wiping her hands on a towel. "What's goin' on?"

"I think it's another one of those shows about how everything's went to shit. You know how those snowflakes are. They got September 11th stuff in there too…"

"No, I think it's an ad. You see the little logo in the corner? I think it's for that new age, sunglass company."

"Fuckin' liberals. How do you make an ad from that?…They need to shut that shit down."

───∘∘∘❖∘∘∘───

A woman sits on the windowsill of her Tribeca apartment, sipping on green tea, as she clicks on a link to a TED talk on YouTube. The new Windows to the Soul ad has to play before the ad. Tears begin to well in her eyes.

As the commercial ends, she places her cup on the windowsill and begins walking to her coffee table. She picks up a black and white photo of a young, vibrant-looking man, and begins running her hands over his image hopelessly. Tears run along the frame.

"I'm sorry," she utters with quiet regret.

⸻ ∘∘○ ▶◀ ○∘∘ ⸻

"You were talking to Lisa at lunch today?"

"Yeah, she's feelin' me. Who doesn't want all this?"

"Honestly? Everybody."

The two boys start pushing each other. Their friend is watching "Stranger "Things" on his Chromebook.

"Hey guys, check this out."

The three teenagers stare at the Windows to the Soul ad.

"That's messed up," Lisa's admirer says.

"It was hot though. Windows to the Soul always does pretty cool commercials," the teaser opines.

"It looks like they spent a lot of money. Why would you care about a watch if you're homeless though?"

The boys start laughing.

"I guess that's where all the Malaysia cash went. I hear they're killing it there."

"I know," one of the boys said with a laugh. "But, people are gonna hate this yo, especially all the 9-11 families and disaster victims. I know it's all over Twitter."

XI

*"The new Windows to the Soul ads just began two days
ago; but, they're already sparking a lifetime of controversy.
The new-age eyewear company used economic uncertainty,
natural disasters, and the 9-11 attacks as themes…"*

These words are scrawled across the towering Times Square Jumbotron as the livery cab makes it way to 46th and 9th. Rebecca nervously straightens her dark shades as she emerges.

"You should rot in hell," a man snarls under a bedraggled baseball cap and torn, wet jeans. On "hell" he hurls a rock in the CEO's direction. Instinctively, Rebecca moves her head away as the rock misses the side of her neck by a nail's breadth. The man darts down the street.

She gives herself a little shake, trying to hide her apprehension under a steely, if not awkwardly, poised posture. She scrolls through the new set of memes—a picture of the "I'm Always Angry" Hulk smashing scene from *Avengers: Age of Ultron* accompanied by "what you should do with your Windows to the Soul stuff"; the words "all Windows to the Soul ever was" with a picture of the Fortnite hype dance emote; etc.—as she soldiers on to the newsstand.

"Hey Uri, how's everything going?" Rebecca manages to say with a smile.

Uri could hardly make any eye contact with his acquaintance. He hands her a copy of the New York Times, and raises a hesitant finger to the front page of the New York Post. There is the following headline:

BLINDER THAN BATS

How did Windows to the Soul's Idiotic Ad Campaign See the Light?

Rebecca gets into the suite and goes straight to her office. She checks her messages. Xavier, Alexander, Mimi, and more than half of the staff called again to say they would not be in. Xavier continues to caution her to stay home as well. She sees a litany of hostile e-mails with subject headings like "capitalist pig," "Windows to the Soul Should be Torched," and the plain and simple "Fuck You." However, within the hostile mix, there are a select few more encouraging lines like "you have guts," and "That Really Touched Me." She deletes the rest of them and saves those, making a mental note to read them when she is more collected.

Another e-mail comes in as she is reviewing the messages. It is from Paramount:

Hey Rebecca,

It's Joel. We're thinking about going in a different direction with the product tie-ins for Long Road Home. I know a lot of people are probably bailing on you now, but…

Rebecca sighs and stops reading. Her phone rouses her from a melancholic fugue. It is Indira.

"Ed's here to see you."

"Thanks Indira. Tell him to come straight back."

"Hey," Ed says somberly.

"Hey," Rebecca almost whispers as she reaches for a large Evian bottle and takes a big swig.

"I know things have been trying lately."

"Trying? I'd hardly say that. I was almost taken out by a rock on my way to work; I've been receiving death threats; and the Times has appointed me the embodiment of capitalist greed. All is right with the world."

"Well, I'm happy you've retained your sense of humor," Ed says, managing a laugh.

"That's really all I've got now Ed."

"I hate to be the bearer of more bad news, but—"

"How bad is it?" Rebecca asks as she looks up at him with a plaintive glance.

"Let's start with the new stores. It's a little bit of a mixed bag. San Francisco is still doing strong business. Net income rose by about 44% over the last quarter, and revenues increased by about 35%. You remember how Seattle got off to a shaky start? It really came up this summer, mostly due to the 'Priceless' line and excitement about 'Greener Pastures.' The sponsorship for the eco-event up there was great PR for us. The LA store is continuing to show significant growth. Marketing found that in this particular store and actually, throughout all the stores, the customer base is skewing younger, particularly 18-34. This group now comprises 65% of our base; so, that's more good news. And, of course, the health and wellness products in the stores have proved to be a boon."

"And, what's the bad news?"

"I'm just trying to lay it down easy Rebecca."

"I know. I appreciate that."

"Well, like I said, the stores are a mixed bag. The Chicago store is doing disappointing numbers to say the least. Quite frankly, we're just operating on margin there. Our lead store here in the city is just weak. If things don't turn around fast, we're going to have to close it by the end of the year.

"It's also been vulnerable to vandals in the last few weeks."

"Yep, that's a big part of it; and, we've lost a lot of revenue through theft. You know how H&M and Nordstrom have taken the products off the shelves—"

"The product placement deal with Long Road Home fell through too. I just got the e-mail a couple of minutes ago."

"Really? Well, that's not surprising… Some more bad news about the stores. Miami hasn't been performing as robustly as we've hoped. I know you've been trying all kinds of advertising techniques, sales specials, etc.; but, the public isn't responding. Atlanta, well I can't think of a better way to phrase it other than D.O.A. It doesn't look like it can be salvaged. Plus, the internet sales, which aren't abysmal,have nonetheless slowed drastically. Additionally, the stock has plummeted about 85% and EBITDA is expected to fall by 62% by the end of the year."

"I guess the next three months are mostly going to be spent on restructuring. I'll loan some money." Rebecca laments as she closes her eyes, trying to stop them from twitching.

"It would help; this isn't the best time to be looking for more financing. With the rising interest rates, and the bad press, we're lucky if the line of credit gets extended. Well, you know, from being in the business for a while, that things could have been a lot worse.

There are salves for this though. The Chicago, Miami and Atlanta stores have basically been standing on one leg; and, we can just move forward on closing them, and cutting our losses. That'll save about $15 million in labor and administrative costs. I know you hate when I say 'layoffs'; but, we just need to make our operations lean as possible. But, I have to say that the majority of these losses have come within the last few days, when the ad campaign began running. With pulling the campaign—across all media and platforms—we can really nip everything in the bud. If we stop the bleeding now, we may be able to keep our net income intact. We can really start on damage control next quarter. We won't make projection; but, we'll have a good chance of still being in the black."

"We've put so much time and money into that ad campaign. That would be such a loss."

"Rebecca, it's going to be even more of one if you keep them on the air. Anyway, the networks are refusing to run them now. I know from watching the coverage, not everyone thinks they're despicable. Actually, some people have applauded the ads. However, if those people were buying truckloads of our products, we wouldn't be having this conversation."

Rebecca lets out an exasperated chuckle.

"They'll pro-rate and refund the money. I know you believe in those ads and I admire that; but, the issue at hand now is to save your business. You need to do two things: pull the ads and issue a mea culpa. You can release a lengthy, apologetic statement today (longer than the weekend's) and post a sincere video on YouTube. You can throw in an interview with 'GMA,' '60 Minutes,' wherever, so you can air your apology, and show some kind of contrition. I know PR has been saying essentially the same. You don't have to completely capitulate. You can say that coming to terms with dark issues like the financial crisis or

September 11th is integral to the Windows to the Soul philosophy; however this wasn't the best way to do it. You know, something like that. Like, I said, it's all about damage control."

"You're right; it is. I'll call Laura this afternoon and see what we can set up."

"Actually, there's something that might even be worse."

"What's that?"

"Something you just happened to forget to tell me."

"Ed, what are you talking?"

"Your 'Oil-for-Food Scandal'?"

"What?" Rebecca asks with a puzzled laugh. "Was I appointed a UN ambassador amid all this?"

"Hardly. It's what you did to have six stores set up in Thailand and Malaysia within three weeks after a category 5."

Rebecca looks at Ed with a shocked stare.

"You can lie to everyone else; but, you can't lie to me."

"Where's it going to be?"

"It's going to be in the Journal tomorrow. The Times will probably pick it up too. You know it'll be all over the 'net."

"How much do they know?"

"The bribery, dummy corporations for taxes…I have to admit that a part of me was impressed you did it so quickly," Ed says as he leans in. "You were that determined to open there?"

"Ed, you're the only exec willing to come up here. Don't judge me please."

"I'm not. I'm just trying to figure it out."

"I knew it would be a great area, for production and sourcing, and retail. I really wanted to help, and I knew it would be an opening."

"You definitely swung that door open."

"What can I do?"

"Disband the shell corporations and tell your contacts at the Ministry to get rid of the paperwork—before anybody can verify, and even though they're not due till the end of the quarter, make the tax payments now. We can talk more about tax havens way after this blows over.

We'll do our best to make it a three-day story. Those stores are a big part of the reason we'll be in the black, if we take prudent measures now. If we give the Feds some cash, and keep up with the relief effort—with no strings attached—we can keep those open. Call Ira to bring in some more lawyers just in case (I'll follow up with him too). I'll touch base with contacts at BDO. We just need to have the arsenal ready."

"You'll get your money Ed."

"Why do you think I'm working so hard?"

Rebecca lets out a full-throated laugh.

"We can handle this. The worst is over. Here's what I was presenting to the Board. I did my best to clean it up."

Ed takes out his tablet, displaying charts and spreadsheets detailing Windows to the Soul's decline.

"We need to cancel the meetings with the London and Paris investors," Rebecca says to Xavier matter-of-factly.

"No problem. So we're closing Chicago, Miami and Atlanta?"

"I hate to say it; but, the store here as well. I was looking at the data and we're just operating at such a severe loss. We have to do it to stay afloat. The good thing is, we can make a strong recovery for next year and put this all behind us."

"I'll be back in a couple of days. Hang in there all right; it's going to be fine."

"Thanks so much Xavier. I'll talk to you later."

"Take care."

Alexander sidesteps into the room.

"I know that meeting with Ed was hard. Things seem really bad now; but, we're going to work through it."

"You can say I told you so."

"What are you talking about?"

"With this ad campaign. I mean I know all of you had misgivings, exhorting me not to do this; but, my pigheaded ears didn't want to listen."

"Hey, you were true to yourself, you did something different."

"I should adopt that positive attitude," Rebecca says to Alexander with a smile. "Have you seen the Journal and the Times?"

"Yeah I have. Xavier and I were talking about it. That's how you got the stores in Asia set up huh?"

"Yeah."

"You didn't do anything else?" Alexander asks with a playfully searching glance.

"Nah, cash is better than head."

Alexander ponders for a moment.

"I guess. Are there former bosses and professors who would be proud?"

"Probably. Maybe, I'll get an honorary doctorate from this."

Alexander smirks.

"You and Ed worked this out right?"

"Yeah, we got rid of the shell corporations, made some more payments...the story will be in circulation for a while though."

"I think we should pass this expression on to the Creative Team. You might like it too."

Alexander passes the piece of paper to Rebecca. It reads:

The umbra gives way to a new dawn.

"Great job. I needed that. Send it to over now. Let them know I approved it."

"Sure. By the way, I'll go home with you tonight. I don't want you alone."

"Thanks so much Alex. But, I'll be fine once I'm in the cab."

"No, I'll go back to White Plains with you. I want to make sure you're safe."

"You don't need to do that Alex."

"I know. I want to."

—∘∘○ ▐◯▌ ○∘∘—

Denver walks from the kitchen to open the door. He peers through the window and sees his mom.

"Hi mom."

"Hi Denver. How was your day?"

"All right. How's everything with you?"

"It's been challenging."

"I know," Denver says to himself quietly.

"Is your dad home?"

"No, he said he was going to be back late," Denver says matter-of-factly.

"Did he?"

"Yeah," Denver says with some resignation.

"Where's Angelina?"

"She's doing UN stuff with Chris."

"Is that what she calls it? Of course. I'm going upstairs. I need to lie down for a little bit. But, we have to talk later OK."

"OK."

Rebecca lumbers up the stairs. The three flights loom like a mountain as she strains to catch her breath with every step. Rebecca finally gets to her bedroom, turns on the light and lies supine on the bed. She closes her eyes to catch a few moments of rest; but, her somnolent body soon succumbs to a deep sleep.

A tall, young man, standing about 6'2" with broad shoulders; curly, golden-brown hair; friendly cinnamon eyes; and strong arms taps her on the shoulder. He appears like a vision, shimmering with an ephemeral quality. Yet, his energy is so strong. Rebecca turns around.

"Dad!" She exclaims.

"Hey sweetheart! Let's go play," Charles says as he gestures to his daughter.

Rebecca jumps up from the bed; but, her dad is already in the hallway. A white halo is crowning the back of his head. A warm, aureate light permeates the hallway, serving as an alluring backdrop to his seraphic air. He continues to gesture for her to come with him.

"Hurry up baby. Don't you wanna come down and play?"

"Yeah, I'm coming."

Rebecca runs to the door; but, her father disappears. Childlike fright fills her as she turns to him. Her father is about 13 feet ahead of her.

"I'm still here baby. Come on."

Rebecca begins running toward her dad to get close to him. She stops. He seems to be maintaining the same distance from her. She tries running again as she rounds the railing of the stairs. Again, he remains 13 feet away, nearing the bottom floor. With a child's optimism, she tries again to run. Her father enters the living room as a fulgent, white light—tinted with a sublime blue—bathes him.

She leaps down the stairs to meet her father. Rebecca is mesmerized by the blue and white light. The light grants the living room a heavenly serenity, and enchanting wonder. Her father is in the middle of the room, sitting with his legs folded, across from a blonde-haired girl about five-years-of-age. They had a bouquet of lilies between them that is forming a heart.

Charles turns toward Rebecca as if inviting her to join them. She moves toward the living room. Something stops her, as if there's a transparent wall between her and the space. Her father keeps motioning for her to come.

"I can't get in," Rebecca says despondently.

The resplendent light begins to fade in the living room as her father and the little girl continue to form their heart. Trepidation begins to her overwhelm her. She hears the front door opening. Her mother walks into the room wearing an overcoat and bellbottom jeans. There seems to be a bulge at her side; but, Rebecca cannot tell what it is.

Her father turns around. His naturally rosy face turns into a flaming red.

"What the fuck are you doin' here?"

"This is my house. I can come whenever the fuck I want!" Dawn answers with impassioned defiance. The little girl looks up at her parents with childlike innocence.

"No, it's not," Rebecca snarls.

"You can bring that shit to me; but, I don't want it around my daughter."

"You're the only piece of shit around here."

"Aright, get out!" Charles screams.

"Fuck you!" Rebecca howls back.

"I said GET OUT!"

"Make me asshole!"

Charles charges toward his wife. With mercurial quickness, Rebecca draws a 9mm pistol from her right side. She shoots her husband in the chest instantly.

"NOOOOOOOOOO!" Rebecca says helplessly as she falls to the ground. She and the little girl begin crying in sync. She looks at her father in desperation. Her father recoils in slow motion. Then she hears another shot. He begins falling back again. She hears a third shot. Again, the recoiling resumes like a

frame caught in her mind's eye. Her father finally falls to the ground. At the moment of impact, the little girl disintegrates, evaporating into small white-blue glimmers. Rebecca feels as if the life had been stripped from her.

Dawn begins turning toward her. Instinctively, Rebecca turns away, moving up the stairs as the first floor descends into darkness. She stammers about, clambering up the flight of stairs when she senses a flash of light. She looks to the top of the stairs. The light doesn't have the sublimity of what illuminated the living room. However, there is a glitter to it; and, the light is just as bright. It beckons her.

As she lands on the third floor, she realizes that the light is coming from her bedroom. A man with dirty-blond hair to his waist, a mustache, and goatee sits on her bed smoking a joint. His wiry body bulged through his light-green, short-sleeved shirt and dark-blue, denim jeans. His piercing hazel eyes seem to penetrate her weary soul.

"Come over here beautiful. I'll make you feel better."

Rebecca reluctantly sits by him.

"Your father just died huh?"

"Yes, my mom killed him," Rebecca mutters through tears.

"Well, I can't bring him back; but, I can help take away the pain."

"You can?" she says, her eyes filling with hope.

"Oh yeah baby. I'll show you how." Jake begins kissing Rebecca's neck and unbuttoning her shirt, as she morphs into a pre-teen girl. He rips her shirt off, and lays her on the bed. He furiously unzips her skirt and tears her underwear. He quietly forces himself inside of her. She feels the violent thrusting inside of her, tearing her, as blood streams down her thighs.

"No Jake, I don't want it! Stop!"

"It's always painful the first time baby; it'll get better," Jake says soothingly.

The young Rebecca begins to relax. He is entering more easily, aided by her growing wetness as she snugly embraces his hardness, grinding her hips toward him, allowing him to plumb her, penetrate her. She bates her breaths in ecstatic delight, spurring Jake on as he forges deeper, faster. The pre-teen girl begins to morph into a 15-year-old girl as he gets deeper.

"I love you."

"I love you too," the teenage Rebecca says breathlessly. She feels him becoming more rigid as she tightens around him. Drops of his fluid flare her passion as Jake becomes louder.

"Come on baby."

He quickly releases and erupts on top of her. The flood of passion glistens her body, leaving her in the balmy aftermath of rapture. She is quickly overcome by a feeling of violation and regret.

Rebecca senses a presence and turns to her side. Dawn is there. She is standing at the foot of the bed, wearing an expression of stunned resignation. Tears are streaming down Rebecca's face.

"I'm so sorry," Rebecca says as she turns back to Jake. "You bastard!"

She bolts out of the bed moving toward the bathroom. Jake yells at her.

"Come back here ya whore! I have more for ya."

Rebecca slowly walks back to Jake. He hands her a bundle wrapped in a blue towel. She takes it. The coldness of the object unnerves her. She unwraps it. It is a dead baby girl, with two heavy rocks depressing her shoulders. Rebecca immediately collapses into tears. She slowly rests the baby down and runs out of the room.

The door of Angelina's room is ajar. A ray of fluorescent light and voices of teenagers emanate from the classroom. She is drawn toward it.

She opens the door to reveal a classroom. Calm and confidence instantly grace her. There is a golden seat in the center of the front row. Rebecca scurries toward it.

"Who performed the first open heart surgery?" The teacher asks.

Rebecca shoots up her hand as the rest of the class remains idle.

"Dr. Daniel Hale Williams."

"What did Einstein call the repulsive force that acts concordantly with gravity?"

Rebecca's hand is once again the only one to rise.

"The cosmological constant."

"What is the longest river in Europe?"

Naturally, Rebecca's hand is the only one to rise.

"Yes Rebecca, once again," the teacher says wearily.

"The Volga."

She hears derisive laughter from the back of the room. Rebecca turns her head to see her brothers pointing at her and taunting. She then feels a warm hand on her arm. It is from an olive-skinned, young man with sharp features.

"Don't worry about them; they're just jealous," he says with a comforting voice. "You're very intelligent."

"Well, you are too. You're always getting great grades."

"Yeah I do all right; but, I'm just a little quieter about it."

Rebecca laughs. He coaxes her. Anthony holds Rebecca's hand as they walk toward the wide-open window. They step outside.

When Rebecca looks up, she finds herself in a breathtaking paradise. Nobody else is in the eden save for a little girl who resembles her doll Lily, frolicking through the fields of lilacs, roses, and buttercups. Woodroses and bamboo orchids line the assorted tropical scene. As Rebecca and Anthony walk down the emerald and ruby path, a twinkling golden lake appears with regal swans, swimming in luminous bliss. Mangos, papayas, blueberries, and strawberries caress its shore. Bushes of hanging ambrosia dot the verdure. A kaleidoscopic butterfly lands between her naked bosom.

Rebecca and Anthony amble toward their little girl. Just as Rebecca extends her arms to pick her up, she becomes pallid and lifeless. She sees Jake emerging, like a serpent, behind the moribund girl. Rebecca snaps back. Her daughter's numb body tips back into the lake, turning it black as *it submerges. The resplendent arcadia is rendered desiccated, turning into shades of gray. Anthony holds his outstretched hand out to her; but, she feels herself moving further and further away.*

"Rebecca, Rebecca," he says as the sound of his voice dissipates in the zephyr.

The wind becomes stronger around Rebecca as the sky becomes ominously foreboding, suffused with a deep gray. She tries with all of her might to hold on to the trunk of the sprawling palm tree; but, the raindrops relentlessly pummel her face. The monsoon sweeps her away, putting her into a ferocious 360° turn.

As she emerges from the twirl, she finds herself on the stage of Brown University's Meehan auditorium. She welcomes thunderous applause and a standing ovation. Rebecca looks down toward the podium and sees a pile of index cards. The speech is entitled, "Walking Toward the Light." The speaker walks triumphantly off the stage. A group of girls stand at the foot of the stairs.

"I didn't think it was going to go that well."

"Well, everything you do comes out great," one of the girls says with a grudging smile.

"You guys want to go to the movies today?"

"Sorry. Midterms are next week and I really need to study."

"Yeah, I've got some presentations I need to work on."

"Me too. We'll catch up another time."

"Since when did you guys care so much about work?" Rebecca asks with derision.

The three girls walk away, leaving Rebecca by herself. She sees them meet with another girl.

"Sheila's party's gonna be dope. You guys hafta come." The three girls cheer in agreement.

The speaker walks back with heavy heart to her apartment. She opens the door to a cold, spartan room. Rebecca opens the refrigerator to reveal a collection of schoolbooks. She takes one out and sits on the black futon, completely bare except for the wilted rose on her pillow. Rebecca feels herself sinking into the futon. She tries to get up from the bed; but, she only sinks deeper.

The mysterious force plunges her into a spiraling hole. She's thrown into a brown leather chair. A graying, paunchy man with large, thick glasses stares at her. His slimy comb over slithers toward her face. His suspenders strain to cradle his protruding belly. He pushes a list of PE ratios toward Rebecca. Her client's name is scrawled on the top.

"George, I can't tell her to invest in these. They've been hemorrhaging money the last three quarters. You know these are all overvalued. It's just a matter of time—"

"Rebecca, just close your eyes and do it, just like you did with the Shenzhen deal."

"You always throw that back in my face! I'm not doing that again."

"Maybe you should take your small, uppity ass out the door."

"I will."

Rebecca bolts from the chair and walks toward the back of the room. A young, debonair man with mahogany skin stands at the open door. She sees a magnetic light toward the end of the hallway.

"Will?"

"Come with me."

Will embraces Rebecca, holding her by the shoulder as the hallway becomes a majestic temple. The couple is surrounded by philosophy books, doves, and irises. Lao-Tzu, Mohammed, and Buddha look protectively down on them. Will leads her to the pulpit. On top of it lies the key to the Manhattan Windows to the Soul office.

"Follow the light," Will says as he points to a luminous door ahead.

Rebecca takes the keys off of the pulpit, and walks toward the incandescent doorway. She feels a light force lifting her hand toward the knob. Rebecca unlocks the door. There is a sense of warmth supporting her from behind, enveloping her. She knows it's Will. He lifts his hand to her cheek and begins stroking it tenderly with the back of his hand. Will removes it. Rebecca feels a lingering wetness on her cheek. Her fingers wipe it. She sees a smear, like dark chocolate, across her fingertips. It disconcerts her.

"Let me go with you."

Rebecca looks at her hands.

"No, you can't."

The door opens and Rebecca closes it on her love.

The office's size is the same; but, there is an expanse to this, promising freedom and vitality. An exhilarated super-physical feeling overtakes Rebecca, like a fantastic reverie. Rebecca takes a seat at her desk. The sun beams with exalted intensity, encircled by a corona of light-blue rays. Five doves fly by the window, each holding a banner with a single word between their beaks. They form the following phrase:

YOU MUST EMBRACE THE LIGHT

Xavier, Mimi, and Alexander are busily working at their desks. She sees some of Windows to the Soul's best expressions swirling around them. The expressions are dropping off golden coins as they glide around the room, forming gleaming hillocks around the office.

Rebecca is prompted to turn to the window. She is surprised to see the World Trade Center looming over the skyline. A rumbling begins as two planes crash into the towers and come crashing down. Rebecca is petrified. Heavy dark clouds eclipse the brilliant sun, as the sky is enveloped in a carapace of darkness.

The rumbling roils the office, growing louder, coming closer, as Rebecca's body shakes with terror. A stampede knocks the door down charging vehemently toward Rebecca's desk. An unsettling hybrid of abject horror and primal rancor fester on the hellish faces. They carry their loved ones across their arms. Some are gruesomely disfigured while others had limbs hanging only by a single tendon. Still others are engulfed in flames. Rebecca turns back and is arrested by skeletons caked with soot, and other horrors she could barely stand to see. She catches familiar faces in the horrifying crowd crying at her with extended arms. Rebecca tries to move towards them; but, the crowd is too great. The haunting lament from the macabre lacerates her ears. She jumps out the window.

Somehow, she makes a soft landing. She is in the middle of a tent city filled with families scrambling to get food. The men and women are dressed professionally, many holding signs reading, "Will Work for Anything." One man is sitting on a bench reading a newspaper dated September 15, 2008.

The angry crowd of the walking dead and despondent workers besieges her. The closer they get, the colder the atmosphere becomes. They begin pummeling her as the floor beneath goes up in flames. Her beaten body falls to the ground, which is now a burning arroyo. Strangely she is not being burned; but, the heat is searing. The flames finally subside; but, the cracks become larger, and the ground begins to give way. Rebecca falls headfirst into the enormous rift, the echo of the lament stalking her as she somersaults down.

She drops on her living room sofa. Relief soothes her as she realizes she is back at home. She walks toward the first-floor bathroom.

Attempting to regain her composure, Rebecca places her palms under the faucet, cupping a small puddle of warm water. She splashes it on her face. As she wipes her face, she looks in the mirror. Rebecca is horrified. The mirror reflects a lifeless wraith of herself.

Rebecca stumbles toward the kitchen. A boy who resembles Denver is sitting there; but, there's no sense of familiarity. The young boy is writing in his notebook. His chest seems strangely heavy. Across his head run images of boys beating him; of the family literally collapsing; of him holding a gun to his own head; and him standing alone in darkness. The mother is immediately assailed by anguish. She runs toward her son. But, he lifts his hand and erects an invisible wall. He slowly lifts up his notebook to show a page that is blank, save for these words:

EVERYTHING MUST BECOME NEW

Puzzled and dismayed, she turns away from her son, and walks from the kitchen. She sees a little Angelina, about 3-years-old at the top of the stairs. Rebecca eyes illume with nostalgia. Her arms reach out to the baby, longing so much to hold her. As the little girl descends down the stairs, her person flickers, developing, growing, and maturing with each step. Rebecca is dejected. When Angelina arrives at the foot of the stairs, she stands as she appears today.

Her daughter smiles at her as she rounds the railing. When she backs her mother, a shocking sight appears. Angelina-Skye is an adolescent Janus; the back of her head is that of a totally different girl. The woman/girl heads out the door. Chris is there to greet her. They hug each other, the two becoming one.

Rebecca staggers up to her bedroom. The door is wide open. Her heart skips a happy beat. She sees her father lying again in the middle of the bed. As she walks toward the bed, her father's visage flies away, revealing a nude Peter. Pangs of pain immediately begin to assail her heart. He is furiously wiping his wedding ring, trying futilely to rid it of a heavy residue. Peter looks at her with tormented eyes. He cocks his head to the bathroom, communicating to go inside.

Rebecca gingerly makes her way. It seems that someone is lying in the bathtub. As she gets closer, the bathtub transforms into black, satin. Her arms pull back the curtain and her head bends over.

She snaps back, wailing in mortified horror. A weathered, lifeless semblance of her present self lies in wait. Images of her mother, Jake, her dead children, and two skeletons etched in relief surround her.

Hot tears sting her face as she sprints out of the haunted bathroom. Quickly, a small, soft, ebony hand intercepts her and wipes away her tears. It is Dafina. The Black angel takes her hand and walks her to the window. She points upward.

The night sky is giving way to bright daylight. The sun bursts forth from the clouds. A resplendent rainbow appears behind the sun. Rebecca discerns the outline of a beautiful baby on the sun's surface.

Rebecca springs up. She left a moist imprint running from her pillow to the center of her bed. A cold sweat glistens her body as beads stream down her back.

Her eyes dart around her bedroom, eager to reacquaint herself with her surroundings. Her eyes have not suffered the blurriness that is the usual attendant of awakening; they seemed to be sharpened by a new clarity.

The moonlight dances through the curtains. The sparkling twinkles shower over her, imbuing her spirit with burgeoning ethereality. Lightness surges within her. Her eyes close. She retreats into a place of earnest rumination. She prays to the Light-Father to lead her on the right path. Rebecca could not remember the last time she had.

She picks up her phone. She spots "SOUL down 74% in wake of humanitarian scandal" in the news crawl. Rebecca closes her eyes to collect herself.

The phone rings.

"Hello?"

"Hi Rebecca, it's mom. Is everything all right?"

At first, her mom's voice compounds her apprehension; but, she is then subdued by tranquil comfort.

"I think it's starting to be."

"I just got this intense feeling, like something was happening."

"Yeah, it was. My life literally flashed before my eyes."

"Oh no."

"No, I wasn't hurt or anything like that; I just had this incredibly vivid dream revealing…everything. It was so real, and surreal, at the same time."

"What was in it?"

"It's all too much for me right now. I need to absorb it."

"OK, well tell me when you're ready. I know I haven't been there before. But, I'm here now."

"I know mom."

"I just wanted to make sure everything's all right."

"Thanks so much. I love you."

"I love you too," Dawn says with a smile in her voice.

Rebecca drops the phone and grabs for the notepad on her nightstand. She furiously begins writing.

Rebecca pages through the Wall Street Journal as she awaits the reporter. The New York Post headline catches her eye.

CAN'T THEY SEE the LIGHT?

Windows to the Soul struggles to find life after blunders

"I had a feeling we should have selected another slogan."

Rebecca hears shoes unevenly clacking against the hallway floor. At first, she thinks it is an intern. When the young man gives her a strong wave and watches an assistant set up his microphone, she realizes he is the reporter. He looks as if he had just graduated from John Hughes High School.

He looks older on TV, Rebecca thinks to herself.

"Hello Ms. Lewis. Michael Regert," he says with an overly firm handshake.

"Hi. Just call me Rebecca."

"I know it's been a pretty hard couple of weeks."

"Yeah, it's been a challenge."

"Don't worry, this isn't going to be a witch hunt. It's merely a chance for you to come out, explain the company's stance, and set the record straight. It's going to be a cake walk."

"Those are some of the most encouraging words I've heard in weeks."

"Great. You've been miced already right?"

"Yeah I'm all set."

"Cool, let's roll."

"*Yeah, this should be easy*," Rebecca says to herself.

The director cues the reporter.

"Let's just start off with the question that everyone is asking, and you might even be asking yourself, 'Why did you do it?'"

Rebecca confidently laughs.

"First off, why the ad campaign? Second, why the alleged bribes and shell corporations in Thailand and Malaysia?

"I need to start off by saying that we didn't launch this ad campaign with the intent of hurting, tormenting or bringing any more anguish to the families, and individuals, those who were devastated by the recession, disasters, and September 11th. What we were trying to say with the campaign, and all we were trying to say, is that spirituality —the cornerstone of the Windows to the Soul brand— is what can help you get through such times of darkness and tragedy. With regard to the bribery and evasion allegations, there were issues that came to our attention that have been rectified. Some matters are still being investigated, so there isn't much I can say; but, any problems are being ethically, and expeditiously, resolved. The testimonies of our customers before these events, and the support that we still have now—and let me express a heartfelt thank you to all of our customers—attest to the valuable work that we do."

"But, I'm sure you're very well aware that even with some years after the tragedies, America is still grappling with them. Some families aren't back in permanent housing after the wildfires and hurricanes. For those who lost family members and friends in the Attacks, September 11th seems like yesterday. Why use that pain?"

"Now, I wouldn't say that we were using it; we were merely observing what was going on with the culture, and we made a statement. There's no doubt that these events have shaken us forever—and there's no going back. Things are difficult. People have to choose between medicine and food; a college degree may only be good for a job at a fast-food joint; armed men and women in fatigues now walk around ballparks; and people are being 'profiled' because of their name and the color of their skin. This is our new reality.

The nation has gone through some traumas over the last two decades. What we discovered, and continue to discover, from events is truth. That principle of truth is at the core of spirituality—thus, the Windows to the Soul brand—and that was the thrust of this campaign."

"Why choose to make the images so true to life, so close to the tragedies?"

"It's not always easy to look at the truth. The truth hurts many times; but, we need to both learn from it and get through it with the adequate tools. People are realizing that by using their innate strength, learning from all of life's experiences, and allowing Light in your life, any event can be a formative one. One can always move forward."

"Those are all valid points; but, with the severe backlash that you have experienced, is that really the best way to have gone about it?"

"We're all human and that means we're not perfect. There's nothing that I've done that I can say I couldn't have done better. Part of being a spiritual person is always evolving, always striving, wanting to be better than you were before. Hindsight being 20/20, this was not the best way to have done it. I don't regret the *intent* of the ad campaign. I do apologize for the suffering we added to the unimaginable anguish individuals and families, around the country, have already suffered.

Let me make it clear, I have also been affected by these tragedies. I know family members and friends who have lost jobs. I also lost people on September 11th. And, I have family and friends who were impacted by the disasters. I felt the pain that so many of those condemning us felt. Many of us are also feeling that yearning. We earnestly tried, in our small way, to fulfill that need."

"Windows to the Soul has taken a huge hit. The rapid gains this year have all but totally evaporated in less than two weeks. Your stock is down about 90%; many of your new franchise stores have closed; you've lost movie and retail deals; massive layoffs are on the horizon; and you'll suffer huge losses this year. How do you stop the bleeding?"

"First of all, massive layoffs are not necessarily on the horizon. Actually, it looks like we'll finish the year in the black. And, this is possible because of our firm's hallmarks of foresight, creativity, and innovation. Those extend to the products we create; and, how we run our business. We're already stopping the bleeding. We've pulled the ad campaign; we've rolled back on overseas expansions; we're ramping up online sales; and we've closed down select stores to give our company some time to recuperate. We're also trying some new design techniques. I know the Street has been betting on how hard the fall is going to be. Well, I'll tell you right now we're back on track; and, we're entering the fourth quarter in an excellent position. Actually, with the changes we've made, 2019 is still poised to be a strong growth year."

"You've gotten a lot of press over the last few weeks, a lot of outlets naming you as the quintessential symbol of what's wrong with Corporate America. Allegations of malfeasance have cropped up from your finance days among other things… how do you respond to all of this?"

"I've come across some of those articles myself; and, it's amusing to me how most of it comes from unnamed sources and hearsay."

"These are reports from reputable outlets."

"Look, Windows to the Soul is a company borne from my vision, and stands as an extension of my spirit. I stand by it in all of its integrity, honor, and virtue. Windows to the Soul, if I say so myself, is a paragon of corporate ethics; and, I take the utmost pride in founding it."

"You are in many ways the face of this 'paragon' as you call it; and, that brings a lot of responsibility. I've heard how your son is near suicidal; you're in therapy yourself… how do you reconcile all this with a company that stands for serenity, strength and striving toward —"

"I thought this was a reputable news magazine, not a tabloid rag."

"All this isn't true?"

"These issues, untrue or true, are not relevant to this conversation."

"Well, as a reporter upholding journalistic integrity, I have the duty to give the public the information they need to form an educated opinion."

"Those are salacious details for a gossip column, not a network news program. My personal life is not on trial here. If you want to continue this interview in that vein, I'll end it right now."

"Now, Rebecca—"

"Ms. Lewis."

"I'm sorry, Ms. Lewis. OK, let's talk about the company then. Windows to the Soul doesn't really practice what it preaches. It only ran a handful of community events last year; there weren't outstanding contributions to charities until the Thailand/Malaysia affair—"

"Windows to the Soul forges new partnerships with community leaders and organizations every day. We're also developing a scholarship fund that will be available to students by next year. We have a strong tradition of charitable contribution; you can check our financials for that. Our company works every day to embody the ideals that Windows to the Soul represents," Rebecca answers with restrained acrimony.

"From our analysis, your record of giving pales in comparison to others in your industry…"

"I'm sorry. I'll have to end this."

Rebecca takes off the microphone and stomps out of the office.

—∞◦❖◦∞—

"How was the interview?" Angelina asks as she walks into the house with her mother.

"Horrible."

"Really? I hope they don't air it."

"My walking out should be good TV."

Angelina starts laughing.

"Why did you walk out?"

"This Ryan Seacrest look-alike starts talking about Denver, me… basically interrogating me about my personal life."

"That's wrong. Well, you did the right thing then."

"Hey Denver," Rebecca says. Angelina heads into the den.

"Hi mom."

"How's it going?"

"It's going."

Rebecca lets out a dispirited sigh and heads upstairs. Denver quickly maneuvers to stop her. He remembers her interview.

"How was the interview?"

"It didn't go too well actually," Rebecca says as she proceeds up the stairs.

"What did they ask you about?"

"Not much, basically, 'Why are you the embodiment of corporate greed?'"

"Ouch."

"Yeah, and they started talking about the family. That's when I started to get angry."

Rebecca starts back up upstairs. Denver's scrambling.

"Mom, you've had a long day, you need to unwind. You know, they're showing a re-mastered version of Metropolis on TCM right now."

"Oh really?" Rebecca hears a peculiar noise from the 3rd floor. "Let me just check that out, and I'll come right down."

"I'll go with you." Denver sprints up the stairs to meet with his mother.

"What's going on Denver?"

"You don't need to go up there yet. I'm sure everything is fine."

"Look, I have to find out what's going on. If you want to come with me fine but —"

Denver's hand grabs his mother's with an iron grip. Rebecca is becoming irritated.

"Denver, what's wrong?" she asks curtly.

"You don't want to go up there."

"Just tell me what's up? Why am I always left in the cold in this house? What is it?"

Denver could only look at his mother. His sorrowful eyes stare at Rebecca with foreboding anxiety. Rebecca bounds up the stairs. Denver walks slowly behind her.

Rebecca is right at the door. She turns the knob. The door is locked. She grabs a hammer and bashes the knob. Furiously, she shoves the door.

Her husband is on top of a strange, young woman.

With solely instinct propelling her, she runs to her bed. Amber looks up and Peter turns around to see her ramming toward them. Denver stands by the side of the door.

"Ahhhhh!" Amber screams in mortified terror. Rebecca furiously pushes her off the bed with the hammer still in her hand.

"PUT YOUR FUCKING CLOTHES ON AND TAKE YOUR SLUTTY ASS OUT OF MY HOUSE!!!" Rebecca bellows as veins pulsate on her neck and forehead. She throws Amber's clothes at her. Amber stands sobbing. Peter could feel his wife's steely eyes piercing his body as he sits on the bed. His head hangs down with ignominy.

Angelina races into the room.

"What happened?" she asks. She saw her mother standing in the middle; Amber scrambling to put on her clothes; and her eviscerated father sitting naked on her parents' bed. "Oh no." Angelina says regretfully as she turns away. Rebecca turns to her daughter.

"YOUR DAD'S CHEATING ON ME!"

Angelina intuitively responds with a wide-eyed look of shock. Angelina understands that it would hurt Rebecca if she found out that her daughter knew about the affair before she did.

"Why do you have to say it?" Peter asks with chagrinned defeat.

"What the fuck are you talking about? If you cared so much, why did you fuck the ho in the house?" She then scowls at the intern. "If you don't get those clothes on right now, I'm going to rip that clit off, stuff it down your throat, and run it out your ass!"

Amber's eyes are blood red now as tears flow in a downpour.

She turns back to her daughter.

"Take this cunt downstairs, and make sure her ass gets as far away from the house as possible."

"No problem," Angelina says. The two of them walk out of the room.

"You're an asshole," Rebecca snarls at her husband. Peter cannot muster the nerve to lift up his head and look at his wife.

"You're a fucking bastard!" Rebecca starts as tears begin to well in her eyes. "Denver told me! He saw you! I called my son a liar because I didn't want to believe it. My baby," Rebecca blubbers. She turns around at her son who is still standing by the doorway. "I'm sorry baby," she says with pained contrition. "I'm so sorry. You don't need to see this. Go downstairs."

Denver scurries downstairs. Rebecca slams the door and marches back to her unfaithful husband.

"YOU FUCKING DOG!!" Rebecca says as she hammers him across the face. Peter falls to the floor. His manhood now limp, she seizes it, squeezing on it fiercely as her long fingernails dig into him. Peter quakes with pain and humiliation.

"Good thing it's down. You need the blood back in your head," Rebecca hisses. "You damn fucker! I knew it! I saw you wiping your ring on the sheets." Rebecca remembers the scene from her dream and a passage from Denver's journal, hinting at how she is in the dark about the family's crisis. "How can you do this to me? How can you do this to your son? This is the second time he's seen you! He's in fucking therapy and you put him through this! Do you want to tear this family apart?" Rebecca says as she circles her husband.

"Your only son attempted suicide. SUICIDE PETER! He tried to tell me all of this; and, I didn't want to believe him. I snapped at him because I didn't want to hear the truth.

He was so distraught. My son almost died because of me."

She thinks about all the fraudulent prescriptions.

"No, he almost died because of me." Peter reflects restively as he sits with his back to the bed. His left leg is laid out in front of him with his right knee bent to his chest, as his arm rests limply on top of it.

"LOOK AT ME!" Rebecca screams at her husband. "I SAID, LOOK AT ME!"

"You don't want me to look at you," Peter whispers regretfully.

"Look at me," she says as she grits her teeth.

Peter slowly raises his head.

"Why?" Rebecca asks desperately.

Peter wipes his palms down his face.

"I don't know."

"Does she look better than me?"

"No."

"Because she has nice tits and a bouncy ass like I had when we got married? What is it?"

"Babe, it has nothing to do with that."

"Is she better than me?"

Peter looks up at his wife with furrowed brows and shakes his head "no."

"Just tell me Peter…I'm really hurting here."

"I'm hurting more than you."

"Oh, she doesn't know how to ride you?"

"Rebecca."

She moves in to her husband and starts pointing her finger into his face. "You don't fuck anybody else like that! You hear me! You don't fuck anybody like that!"

"I was thinking about you when I was fucking her like that."

Rebecca looks at her husband with wounded eyes, tears welled in her bottom lids.

"What would you do with her?"

"Rebecca you don't want to hear that."

"Yeah I do. Would you do everything you do with me, or you do more?"

"It's different; that's all I'm going to say. It was an escape. It's just going to make you more upset."

Rebecca's chest heaves in irate grief. She stares at her husband again.

"How long has this been going on?"

"It's been about two months."

"Two months!" Rebecca laughs in desperation. "I'm like a stranger to my own life. The wives are always the last ones to know right?"

"You knew when Denver told you. You've been giving me the cold shoulder."

"You knew when Denver told me?"

Peter nods his head.

"I still remember how I glowered at him that night. The scariest, loneliest night of his life. The first thing I should have done was rush over to his bedside and hug him, and let him know he should never feel alone again. If he didn't know it before, he has to know now—we love him. We'll always be there for him. I should have held him like I would never let him go.

What did I do? I just gave him this ice-cold stare. Almost like he should be sad that the medications and vodka weren't enough. He was probably hoping at that moment that he hadn't woken up. I'll never forgive myself for that. I didn't treat him like a son. In his darkest moment, I treated him like a traitor.

You wanted to ask me; but, you were too scared to find out. I knew I hit a low at that point. That kid idolizes me, and I failed him miserably..."

"You need to apologize to him."

"I will," Peter says as he gets up for the first time. He walks toward his wife. He is about to wrap his arm around her waist, but Rebecca moves away. "I'm sorry to you too. I love you Rebecca."

"And you're fucking some pussy from the office."

"I know this is all going to sound like bs to you; but, you don't know how tormented I've been. I strain to look at myself in the mirror. I'm not trying to make excuses, please believe me, but you know how I am —"

"I know."

"I've been controlling it these last few years, being able to put my energy into the research; but, it changed when she came around. It didn't start out like that. We were just working on projects and studies; and, she impressed me from the start. She's so smart, and dedicated… I fell. I'm sorry."

Rebecca sighs.

"It just had been so long Rebecca, and she was there… I'm not trying to excuse it, I'm just trying to explain, and make sense of everything myself. I never, for the life of me, ever thought that I'd be the one of the guys to do this. I'm so sorry."

"I didn't either."

Tears beat down Peter's face. He buries his head in his hands for a few moments. He manages to look up at his wife after collecting himself.

"I know it's going to be really hard for you to forgive me for this. I don't know if I could forgive myself. You know what; you don't even have to call me Peter. It can just be 'asshole,' 'bastard,' 'fucker,' whatever insult you want from now on. I deserve it.

I know we've lost something; but, I'll work the rest of my days to get it back."

Rebecca turns to her husband. Her eyes are irritated with hurt and consternation.

"Do you love her?"

"She's not you. You're stunning, wickedly funny, brilliant, caring and on top of all that you have vision. Plus, you won't hesitate to kick any one's ass, including mine."

Rebecca's manages a chuckle.

"She was a lover. You're a soul mate."

"No fucking."

"What?"

"We've only fucked like eight times in the last…10 months. That's it."

Peter shakes his head. "I've been trying to figure that out too."

"Nothing makes sense. Nothing is what it seems. Nothing is what it's supposed to be. It's like I'm falling down this hole and there's no bottom in sight."

"You'll always have me."

Rebecca looks up at her Peter.

"I don't think I have that anymore."

Peter closes his eyes trying to hold back tears.

Rebecca tosses and turns in her bed. Lily has been on the side where Peter usually sleeps. It is about 3:00 in the morning; and, she hadn't slept more than five minutes in the last four hours. She had to get up in an hour anyway; she figures she might as well stay up.

She picks up the phone. She dials Xavier. The phone rings about five times before he picks up.

"Hello?" he says, sounding aggravated.

"Hey Xavier. Sorry if this is a bad time."

"Who is this?"

"Rebecca!"

"Oh sorry. I just didn't expect to hear from you at this time. I know a lot has been going on," Rebecca hears sucking noises in the background. "Hey Bec, could I give you a call back later on this morning…"

Rebecca hangs up the phone as he's talking.

She calls Mimi. Her phone's busy.

She tries Alexander. His phone rings about three times and she gets his voicemail.

"Where's Peter when you need him?" She says to herself unconsciously.

Rebecca slithers out of bed and starts downstairs. Her heavy feet plod into the kitchen. She pours herself a glass of milk, and warms it in the microwave. Small sips warm her mouth as she looks desperately in the distance. Rebecca decides to pick up the phone.

"Hello," her mother says with a somnolent voice.

"Hi mom, it's Rebecca. I'm sorry if it's too early."

"No, you can call me anytime honey. Besides, it's barely after midnight here and I just got to sleep. What's wrong?"

Rebecca takes a deep breath before she starts.

"You were right."

"Well, you knew."

"Yeah I did."

"How did you find out?"

"I walked in on him."

"Oh, I'm familiar with the dramatic way."

Both of the women laugh.

"I'm sorry honey."

"You know, I never thought he'd be the guy to do it."

"I know; he's just such a fine man. He loves you so much. That's what makes it even more painful."

"It is. I don't know what went wrong. I mean, did I drive him to it?"

"It's never that easy hon."

"It's been like a monastery in this house. No, more like a creepy house of mirrors. Nothing is what it seems. The only thing that goes right is the wrong stuff. Denver was falling off the deep end…"

"What do you mean?"

"He wanted to end it."

"Did he attempt?"

"He did. He almost succeeded, landed in the hospital. If it weren't for Peter knowing CPR, and the great team of doctors and nurses at White Plains Hospital, you would have lost a grandson."

"I can't believe it. He always seems so well-adjusted."

"We always know how to cover things. Next time you see him, please act like you don't know. He'll be mortified by the sympathy. Only the family and the medical team know. We've been keeping it, and will continue to keep it, under wraps."

"You have my word Becky. I have a lot of reasons to love on him when I see him. I haven't seen both your kids in so long."

"I had been dealing with a lot, even before Denver's attempt. Sex was often the last thing on my mind. Hell, it often wasn't even on my mind at all. Like I said, it's been like a monastery in this house."

"That's no excuse."

"Of course not. I mean it's not like *I* haven't been tempted. But, men don't have willpower, they're all dogs—"

"Now, don't get jaded so quickly."

"If a guy like Peter can cheat, any guy will. Plus, statistics show that when they do it once, they'll do it again. Men are just bastards."

"He's not; and, I know another who wasn't."

Rebecca thinks for a moment.

"Dad."

"Yeah."

"I told you he was in my dream right?"

"Mmmm hmmm."

"He just appeared to me like an angel. He was so beautiful and so brilliant; he had this halo light illuminating the back of his head."

"That could've been him."

"I think the day he died was the worst day of my life."

"Was that in the dream?"

"Yeah it was… You shot him."

"I did?"

"Yeah, and you were turning the gun at me too. Aunt Rita told me about how dad died when I was 12. How he found you with one of your lovers, the ugly confrontation… Once I heard that, it was branded in my mind that you killed him. I know that's immature and horrible; but, I just wanted dad around so much with all of the crap we were going through. I believed if you weren't fooling around that wouldn't have happened. I know it was such a short time; but, it seems like the happiest days of my life were when he was alive. It's like a part of me died with him."

"You thought I killed you too."

"I'm so sorry mom. I didn't want to say it."

"Well, you've been keeping it in for almost 40 years; it's about time you did. Why didn't you tell me before? Now, I know why you hated me."

"I didn't hate you. I wasn't even really angry with you; I was just angry at how things were. I didn't understand why you couldn't keep a job; why you had to run around with men; why we were so poor—"

"And, why the only thing you ever relied on had to go away."

"I guess so."

"I know. I can't say it enough and I'll never make up for everything; but, I'm truly sorry Rebecca."

"I know mom; and, I accept it."

"Thank you."

"You know, so many things came to light during that dream. Things I had just buried, that I didn't want to touch. Now, I can look at them. The whole Jake issue too."

"How did that play out?"

"Well he comforted me right after dad died. And then we started to—"

"Have sex."

Rebecca sighs.

"Was I there?"

"Yeah you were right at the side, looking on stunned, but accepting it at the same time. I felt so hurt at how we were betraying you. I was just staring back at you crying, saying 'I'm so sorry.'"

"I know you've thought that I didn't love you. I just let him go on hurting you."

"I didn't understand why you never left him."

"Well, you said most of it at the funeral. I was weak. I felt like I needed him, that I couldn't survive without him. I was never the same after Charles died. It took me years to regain my sense of self-worth. That's how I was able to finally confront him about it, and all his other problems. I finally told him to get help."

"You did?"

"I never told you. I just couldn't bear to look you in the face and talk about it. I know I hadn't really shown you; but, I always loved you so much. I love all you kids; but, you've always been special to me. I still wonder how someone as screwed as I am could give birth to you."

"You're not screwed up mom; you're just trying to figure things out like the rest of us."

"Maybe. But you really are a precious part of my heart—you and your father. And, when I walked in on you and Jake, my heart was broken."

"That must have been just mortifying."

"I mean, I had mother's intuition that it had been going on; but, then it was right there. I told you I was familiar with the dramatic way."

"Yeah, you sure are."

"I felt the rage that I know you felt. I was so angry with both of you. I looked in your face and I saw my daughter and his mistress. I felt violated as a mother, and as a wife.

"At that time, I felt the best way I could deal with it was just not talking about it. That's why a lot of times I was cold to you. I said I'd rather ignore you than just blow up and vent all my anger and resentment. You don't know how it has haunted me. I know it wasn't your fault. He took advantage of you. But, it was so hard to understand that then."

"It's been torturing me too mom. I'm sorry."

"It wasn't your fault honey. I know exactly how you're feeling now. Jake didn't just cheat with you—he had so many women—but yours hurt me the most. I know Peter doesn't even seem like the same person anymore. Everything he does you'll be suspicious about; you'll look on the past and question everything he's done. If you get to the point where you actually have sex again, you'll just keep wondering if he's thinking about someone else."

"I don't want to live like that mom."

"You don't have to."

"How can't I? I don't believe in anything we had anymore."

"What you had is still there; you just need to work on it. He's still a great guy; he just has flaws. Jake wasn't the man Peter is; but, he wasn't a bad man either. We all have faults—some of us more than others—and I think you can only judge a man's goodness by how well he deals with them. Peter is not perfect. He never was. Hell, life isn't. You're getting that."

"I told you that you weren't screwed up."

Dawn laughs. "That's just age. It took me a while to get here. There's nothing that excuses adultery; but, there's always something that explains it. It might be worth trying to find that out."

"I don't know if I could get there."

"It seems impossible now; but, it can get better. I've been there. I won't tell you to stay or go; but, I know Peter loves you. All important relationships go through trials. Maybe you needed this."

"There were so many signs. I just didn't want to see them. I guess I needed a brick thrown at my head to finally get it."

Dawn chuckles. "I guess you did. You and Peter have something really good. There's some dirt on it, but it's still beautiful."

"Mom, I don't know if we had anything now."

"You may still have a story together. But, it's up to you if you want to write it."

"I've been feeling so alone. It's like everyone's let me down."

"That's what I felt too. But you know, God sets things up like that so you'll discover the strength He's given you. He's always there; you're never alone. I'm here too. Like I said, I'm only a phone call away."

"You could be closer than a phone call."

"You want to come out to Fresno? Well, I know you're so busy with everything…"

"Why don't you come out here? I'll fly you out."

Dawn is surprised. "OK, if you want to."

"I do. You haven't seen the kids in ages; they're so big now."

"I bet."

"Actually, they haven't seen any of the family in a long time. I know you haven't been in the New York area for years."

"I haven't; and, I miss it."

"I'm just starting to think about things… You need to hold on to what you have."

"You're learning."

"Finally. It's taken some time; but, it's coming. So, you check your schedule and you let me know later when's a good time to fly out."

"I will baby. Hey, I got some ideas about what we could do, and where we could go."

"What?"

And, Dawn begins to fill her daughter in.

XII

A young man is walking, and scrolling through his Facebook feed, as he nears the I See the Light Bangkok store. One post recounts the ฿5.8 million the Bangkok store grossed in its first 10 days of opening.

The man huffs and leaves his phone on the sidewalk. He enters the I See the Light store. He heads straight to the sunglass counter. He picks up a pair of golden and light blue shades. The man re-reads the words:

วิญญาณของคุณเป็นผู้มีอำนาจเท่านั้น

He approaches the cashier. He checks the timer on the device tucked into his knapsack. The store has 55 seconds.

The cashier smiles at the young man as she takes the shades. He avoids eye contact as he lays his knapsack on the counter.

Passers-by are enveloped in ash as they help survivors from the debris. Emergency vehicles arrive. First responders hastily make a path into the attack site as they push limbs and assorted body parts away.

Looks of fear, bemusement, and anger mark the faces of pedestrians. Survivors are furiously texting, tweeting, and posting on Facebook. Others are calling their loved ones through tears if their phones have not rung first.

Police emerge from the site with what is left of the knapsack and device. An officer relays a message on his walkie-talkie. The nearby BTS station is cordoned off, and commuters are turned away. A caravan of seven ambulances awaits to tend to survivors.

Rebecca steps off the train at Grand Central as she takes off her sunglasses. Her golden hair flails in the muggy, early August wind. Peter follows about a foot behind. He scurries to catch up with her. When he reaches his wife, he takes her face in her hands and plants a sweet kiss on his wife's lips. Rebecca stands passively. Peter gives a frustrated sigh.

"Give me a call when you get into the office. I love you," he says as he starts walking away.

"You're forgetting something."

"Oh."

Peter reluctantly pulls out a folded piece of paper from his pocket as he walks back to his wife. It is a table of all the places he was supposed to be for the day including addresses; times of arrival; times of departure; and names and numbers of the people with whom he was meeting.

"All the information is included here. I even put it in military time, down to the second so it would be easier for you."

"Thank you. You've always been meticulous," Rebecca says matter-of-factly without looking at her husband.

"How long do you want to keep doing this?"

"You should be happy this is all you're putting up with."

"Are you happy doing it?"

Rebecca glances at her husband for the first time since they got on the train.

"I've said time and time again, I'll endure this as long as it takes; but, you don't deserve this. Rebecca I love you enough to do whatever it takes to make you happy, even if that means you're not with me. Maybe we should just put an end to this. I'll leave; you can have the house…"

"So, you're just going to give up on your family like that and what? Start a life with Amber."

Peter has been seething throughout the trip. Now, he replies firmly.

"Rebecca, you know very well that she was transferred the morning after you found out.

I don't want to give up on this family; I want to salvage it. But, how are we benefiting the kids? They know exactly how bad things are. It stabs my heart every time I look at Denver's eyes. I can see the disappointment in his face. Angelina hates me too. I mean she can't even stand being in the house anymore; she spends every possible moment at school or with Chris now. We're keeping it together for what? For whom?

I have to live with this for the rest of my life, but my family doesn't."

"You should have thought about that before you started fucking that slut," Rebecca mutters under her breath.

"You're right; and, I can't take that back."

Rebecca looks back at her husband.

"You can't," she says coldly. "Look, I need to get to work. I'll see you later." Rebecca begins walking away. "What the fuck?!," Rebecca exclaims as she is looking at her phone.

"What?"

"There was a terrorist attack at the Bangkok I See the Light store. At least 50 people are dead."

"It's all this press. You need to get in touch with your Thai contacts and get up to the office."

"We need to beef up security at each location. No word on if this was a lone wolf or a coordinated attack. In any case, it can't happen again."

"This is unimaginable."

"Laura has already issued a statement. We have to get in touch with the PDs to ensure we have extra security. I won't have Darius pick me up. I'll take the chopper up."

"This is the priority. Whenever you can, if you can today, please keep me posted," Peter plaintively utters as he kisses his wife.

Rebecca manages to look back at him.

"Do we have more information about who was behind this?" Rebecca asks Minister Buapoke.

"It is still inconclusive; but, he appears to have acted alone. However, there has been an underground campaign of sorts on Facebook, WhatsApp, and all those platforms to foment feeling against Windows to the Soul. It's been going on now for about six weeks now. He may have not been involved with a terror group or traditionally radicalized; but, I am almost certain that that 'chatter,' if you will, at least gave him that extra push. Just like in Western countries, there has been anti-capitalist sentiment in this region. Anything that appears like a company is trying to take advantage—though Windows to the Soul is far from that—will stir some opposition. Especially among these younger people, 'imperialism,' as they see it, will no longer be brooked."

"I do understand the sentiment Ahmin. But, we have done so much to help Thailand. Is that not being covered?"

"It is Rebecca. But, you know how these kids get their news know. Just like in the States, they don't watch the broadcasts. It's what's posted on social media. And, they don't take the time to consider who is behind it. They're on it all day, their hands buried in their phones. It's like, how do you say, an 'echo chamber.' There's one idea; and, if all their friends are saying it, it must be true. There are no other perspectives."

"Yeah, sadly it's the same here. You took care of your funds right?"

"I sure did. They're stowed away in Panama. I won't even touch it till things simmer down a bit. Thanks again for your generosity."

"You've really looked out for us. We've ramped up security at all our U.S. stores, and those around the world. Are there still extra personnel at the Thai stores?"

"Definitely. We have assigned units for retail locations now, with special teams for I See the Light stores. Those who appear suspicious are not allowed entry. We are taking all precautions."

"How long can we maintain that?"

"We will do it for as long as is needed. You have my assurances. You want to check on Malaysia though, and confirm that the extra security is maintained there as well. I know you supported some contacts there as well; but, I can also make some overtures if you'd like (our governments are very close)."

"Thanks for the tips Ahmin; and, thanks again for all you are, and have been, doing. I'll check in with them by tomorrow morning, MYT. I'll be in touch by Friday."

Just as Rebecca is signing off, a group of four young men emerge from the Kelana Jaya station. One man advances ahead over the three, heading towards a police officer. The police officer pulls out his phone. A banking app is open.

The officer shows the man his phone. The verification of a 385,000RM transfer is clearly displayed. The officer nods his head, and allows the men in without even checking them.

Right on cue, he gets radioed. He tells the rest of the squad that he needs to leave immediately. He steals into a car and bolts away.

The Kuala Lumpur I See the Light store is engulfed in flames. Pedestrians frantically take cover as emergency responders stream in.

———oo◦❈◦oo———

Rebecca is reading about the Kuala Lumpur attack.

"At least 68 killed? What the fuck is going on? We have to close all the stores till further notice."

She is calling up Global Marketing Officer Daneca Hernandez.

"We're closing all the stores, worldwide, till further notice Daneca. They keep saying 'lone wolves'; but, this seems like a coordinated campaign. This is crazy as fuck. People are dying."

"It's catastrophic. We have to. I'm messaging now. We'll take it week by week."

"And, we need to follow-up with the Bangkok and Kuala Lumpur families. I'll get on with the Malay contacts as soon as we wrap up. That's what you have insurance for; but, we can't keep doing these payouts. That's another reason to close the stores now. We need to take as many precautions as possible. The other preemptives didn't work."

"Tragically they didn't. We'll just be concentrating on the website for now. We thought of planting flames, similar to our logo, on websites, like banner ads, but without the Windows to the Soul name. If someone clicks on it, they'll go to a page that recognizes the attacks, and commemorates the victims. There will be a small, subtle, nondescript link in the corner that points to the main site."

"That's perfect Daneca. Can we get that up today?"

"We can get that up before noon. We already ran it by IT. They've been working on it. I'll get in touch with the ad team now so the 'flames' can be up today too."

"I really appreciate all of you sticking through this. I hope you know how grateful I am."

"I do Rebecca—we all do. I just got the last confirmation for closure. Retail is officially offline."

"I'm happy we're stopping the bleeding."

"We're cauterizing as best as we can."

"I'll see you tomorrow Daneca. Thanks for everything."

"No, thank you Rebecca for persisting. We're getting through this."

"With you, and the rest of the team, we will. See you tomorrow."

"See you tomorrow."

Rebecca is getting another Skype call.

"When IT calls you, it has to be serious. We couldn't text or e-mail this?" Rebecca says with anxious humor.

"I wish we could sugarcoat it," CIO Rod Han says apprehensively.

"Just lay it on me Rod."

"The Windows to the Soul site has been hacked. At least 4.2 million credit-card numbers have been stolen."

"Murphy's Law…I thought we ramped up the firewall just last month. How did this happen?"

"We did. It appears they used some other 'backdoor' device. It may have even been booted from a USB, that allowed them to backend into the central servers. They were able to evade the security shields for the accounts too, including our two-step verification controls. This was quite sophisticated."

"Apparently. In any case, we have to start doing damage control—"

"A carefully worded statement was sent to PR about 40 minutes ago. Yep, it's already been tweeted."

Rebecca logs into her account. "Great more payouts…yeah, we'll cover the monitoring with Transunion…looks like there are more issues with the website."

She is scrolling through a flood of tweets referencing a DDoS attack.

"Rod, it looks like it was hit by one of those denial-of-service attacks…could you guys, and gals, check this?"

"I'm seeing them too. Already on it...This has Anonymous hallmarks."

The website features a picture of the sky with light streaming down. The caption reads, "We've been looking through your soul, and it's ugly as fuck."

"Maybe we can get that on the next pair of shades. At least I can use that as a bumper sticker."

"You can laugh at anything can't you?"

"On most days, yes."

"We should be able to get back up-and-running in about two, no more than four."

"That's two to four hours right?"

"Yeah, we know what to do; but, we have to be particularly deliberate. We have to transfer to the other cloud servers, while we reinforce our primary ones. We'll see if we can trace this too...We're on it."

"I trust that Rob. These are particularly expedient ways to immobilize an organization. The website is all we have now; and, those couple of hours will be especially hurtful. What can we do to prevent it from happening again?"

"After doing the server transfer, will expand the bandwidth provision, add filters to the router (so it can better screen for 'nefarious' packets)...there's a few things—a few effective things—we can do. All that will be done in less than 24 hours. Again, the site will be back up in no more than four."

"Could you give me an update in two?'

"Sure will. I'll let you know about the site status, and the precautionary measures taken to stop the DDoS from occurring again. We're becoming everyone's favorite target; but, we're up to the challenge."

"You still want to do this?"

"Damn right I do Rebecca. We got this."

"We got this. Thanks Rob."

"You know what, we'll be back online in two. I'll be in touch then."

"You can get back on Fortnite after. Thanks so much man."

Amber tentatively walked into the Westchester Neurological Sciences Center. She is wearing a modest black suit with blue stripes, with a form-fitting white scoop-neck shirt underneath. Dr. Lewis is tapping his feet, readying himself, at his desk.

"Thanks for coming by."

"Thanks for being willing to have another meeting. I really didn't want it to end like that. I'm still mortified honestly."

"Over a month later, it's still hard for me to come to terms with that night. A lot was going through my head; but, how you must have been feeling especially pained me. We should never have come home that night."

"Wives have a sixth sense. They know when things are going down, even if they can't quite articulate it."

"I respect you as a colleague; and, you deserved at least a conversation. You helped to save my son's life. If the medics didn't come so quickly, the CPR may have been in vain. At the very least, Denver could have suffered permanent brain damage. You'll always be precious to me for being there that night."

"I haven't forgotten that, nor could I ever forget it, myself. How has he been?"

"It's still a work in progress (we all are right?); but, he's managing things, and seeing things differently. I think he finally realizes that

Rebecca, Angelina, and I love him unconditionally. We weren't there as much as we should have been before; but, we're striving to do better now."

"I'm happy he's feeling that support. He's a wonderful kid, and so perceptive. He should never feel isolated."

"Again, thanks for being there.

I am also very aware of today's climate; and, I wanted to discuss things."

"You mean with Me Too/Time's Up? Oh, Peter, can I still call you that?"

"You can."

"No, I won't file a lawsuit."

"I value your word. It needs to be on paper though. There's a plum opening at NIH. You can sign it after we work out a position."

"You don't need to Peter. But, if it puts you at ease, I will."

"I'll put in six months salary as well, from my personal account. I don't want this being an issue a decade from now."

"I assure you it won't. I do have a request though."

Peter takes a labored sigh. "What's that Amber?"

"I don't want this to be our last meeting."

"Amber, we can't see each other anymore. I'll spend the rest of my life trying to save my marriage, or whatever is left of it. I love my wife."

"I don't mean the sex Peter. I l— I respected, and admired, you before then. Again, I hope one day I can do work half as good as yours. I still want to collaborate."

Peter throws his head back.

"You're one of the brightest minds in the field today. Anybody would be lucky to have you on his or her team."

"And, anybody should be honored to work alongside you," Amber says while looking longingly into Peter's eyes.

"We should get word on the grant in about five weeks. I think you would be a perfect fit for the dementia-myelination study. We can check in on Skype during the week, and we can meet—like this, in the office—as we review results. There will be conference opportunities too.

And, I will always be available to give you superlative recommendations. That will never change."

"I appreciate that Peter."

"You're still signing."

Amber smiles grudgingly. "I promise I will."

"How have you been?"

"You mean, since the 'incident'?"

"We can call it that."

"The transfer is working out. I've gotten used to the commute into the City every day (finally). I do miss the team here. But, I know it was for the best."

"It was," Peter repeats matter-of-factly as he looks resolutely at her.

"I have to say thank you."

"When we have the position assured, you'll get the agreement. After that's signed, the funds will be transferred."

"I mean that sincerely Peter. I had never felt so valued in my life. I felt like a person again."

"I wish it weren't so dramatic…I'd be lying if I said you didn't impact it either."

"I don't think I'll ever have that again."

"Don't sell yourself short. You deserve a lot more than to be someone's number two. That's all it would have ever been. And, again, we're not seeing each other anymore. That's over Amber."

"I realized that when I was ceremoniously escorted out by your daughter. Your wife's Bronx cheer was also heartwarming."

Peter manages a smile. "Again, I wished it weren't so dramatic."

"I'm not asking for that Peter. I just don't think I'll find anyone else."

"You won't if you keep pursuing guys who are unavailable. You're worth more than that. You deserve to be in a stable, loving relationship, and to have a family of your own."

"Why can't I believe that?"

"You've been hurt a lot, and somewhere along the line you were convinced of that. An older guy who's been married for almost 20 years, with two kids, shouldn't be your first choice."

"It was hardly right; but, I was okay with it."

"Ian was really sad to see you go. He still has a huge crush on you. He's a great-looking guy, Phi Beta Kappa…that's what you should be looking at. I'll give him your number. You're going out with him," Peter commanded, pointing his finger.

"OK."

"He's not Mr. Perfect. But, I think he might be what you need. No guy will fulfill all your needs. And, it's not fair, to yourself or any man, to expect that. Even if I had never met Rebecca, I could never do that for you."

"She still loves you?"

Peter gives Amber a puzzled glance. He is quite taken aback.

"She's hurt and disappointed. She might always be. But, yes she does. I know she still loves me."

"If the opportunity ever comes, please tell her I'm sorry."

"If it does, I will. She's angrier at me than she'll ever be at you. I brought you in the house; I said yes;…"

"I didn't make it easy."

"You're going out with Ian. You'll forget about me."

"That will never happen; but, I'll go out with him."

"Don't expect the world Amber. Just let someone love you."

"Thank you Peter."

Peter rose up from his chair, hugged Amber, and gave her a soft kiss on her cheek.

"I'll hold on to that."

The CEO's gaunt fingers race across the keyboard. She would take momentary breaks to bite her fingernails, which now resemble stumps. Rebecca also needs to readjust her pants every now and then since they now hang tenuously around her hips.

Rebecca throws away another cup of coffee, making a pile of five in the garbage can.

"That wasn't working."

She takes out four Vicodin pills. Rebecca pops the glass from an old mirror. She arranges the pills in the middle of the glass pane. She extracts a steak knife from her draw. Sharply, and strategically, she lays the steak knife atop the pills. Rebecca gives the steak knife two hard bangs. She separates the ashes into two short lines.

Rebecca snorts the first line. She waits for about 20 seconds. She dives down again.

"I have to start winding that in."

She sees Dafina's picture on her phone.

"Hey Daf."

"Hey mommy."

"How are you doing?"

"They just gave me some shots and took some blood."

"Oh, sorry baby."

"No, that's OK. At least I can get them."

"Your family would be so proud of you."

"They are mommy. I can't see them; but, they're always with me. I feel them."

"You do?"

"Yeah. I know with God's help, they brought you to me. You didn't come on your own."

Rebecca is pleasantly surprised by another one of Dafina's insights.

"No, I didn't."

"It's cool how you do your part and the Una – ve – ve—"

"The Universe."

"The Universe does the rest. Thanks. I prayed for a family, and you all came."

"You answered my prayers too Daf. Angelina and I are working on making this home."

Rebecca caught herself. This is the first time she had mentioned it.

"Thank you mommy!" Dafina squealed gleefully.

"Thank you angel."

"Mommy, I need to go with the nurse now. I'll talk to you later."

"OK Daf. Love you."

"I love you too."

Mimi prances into Rebecca's office as Rebecca hangs up the phone.

"Heyyy Rebecca."

"Heyyy Mimi. How are you doing?"

"Pretty good."

"I'm hanging in there. Getting back to some e-mails. The board and I are doing some wrangling with investors, trying to get them back on board."

"I know you will. When will the stores be back open?"

"September 18th," Rebecca says with a smile. "The 'flame' embeds Marketing thought of have been effective. It's been building web traffic, and helping to rehab our image. The website sales may help us to be in the black. There won't be sales growth; but, we'll be in the black."

"We got through this. Has there been a lot of fallout from the data breach?"

"About a quarter of those affected have taken advantage of the Transunion services. There have been about six lawsuits filed; but, it looks like those will be settled quickly."

"And, security will be strengthened at the stores?"

"That's really important. Aside from additional personnel, we'll have metal detectors, alongside alarms, to alert those who may be carrying weapons or devices. Additionally, we're coordinating with municipalities to add or expand stanchions outside of select stores (to guard against car attacks). We've become among the hardest soft targets it appears. We'll never let our guard down; but, we'll make sure our customers feel welcome."

"Their safety is our first priority."

"The Attacks underscored that even more. I still can't believe those happened."

"I can't either. I had this disembodied feeling as I saw the pictures on Facebook and Twitter, and on TV…it hurt that we can became 'those people' to so many."

"Actually, it still hurts. The focus is on keeping our customers safe and secure, and rebuilding our brand equity."

"The health and wellness screenings around the country, especially the focus on eye health should help the cause. And, we'll be re-opening here in the City?"

"That's looking like April 2021. And, we want that to be our flagship again.

As long as we don't have any more 'hiccups' we should be fine."

"It's been difficult avoiding those."

"It has. Hey, are you cold? I'm freezing in here."

"What do you mean? It's like 86 outside."

"I know, but I've been shivering all day."

"Those five cups of coffee didn't help?"

"Was it really that many?"

"Yeah, is everything cool?"

"I don't know; I've just felt so off these last weeks."

"I know how you feel."

"Really? What's up?"

"Everything's been so weird and uncertain. I mean look at here. Just a few months ago, it was bustling, all these cool people coming in and out and now it's—"

"Hey, don't worry about Windows to the Soul. As we were saying, things will be fine. You guys have been putting in so much extra work and keeping the faith. Don't lose it now. Your efforts will pay off big dividends. Believe me," Rebecca says with renewed vigor.

"I do."

"Good." Rebecca goes back to the keyboard. Mimi surveys Rebecca's desk and sees a picture of a striking African girl peeking out beside Rebecca's keyboard.

"Is this Dafina?" Mimi asks as she picks up the photo.

"Oh yeah. I've been meaning to show this to you. She's beautiful isn't she?" Rebecca replies as she's typing.

"She is."

"She's like the only highlight of the last few months. When I visit her, I just feel unconditional love."

"I know she has the same for you."

Rebecca takes her eyes off of the monitor for a moment and turns to Mimi.

"I do. That pictures a little old. If you can imagine it, she's even more adorable now. She's really come a long way since she got here from Tanzania a few months. She's a lot stronger; has gained some weight; and grown an inch or two. I have to take another picture of her."

"That's the power of love right there."

"You're so right. Unfortunately, she had to come halfway across the world to get the care she needed; but, we're all happy she's here. She's such an inspiration. I mean her mother died shortly after she gave birth to her; her dad died of AIDS; the disease has affected a lot of her family and friends; and she's battling it herself. Nevertheless, she maintains this ebullience and optimism. Daf is so bright and curious; every moment is full of wonder for her. You're just warmed by her spirituality. She's like the embodiment of everything Windows to the Soul stands for."

"It's like she's changed your life. It's amazing how children are sometimes the wisest teachers of all."

"She has taught me so much. You know her name Dafina means 'valuable' or 'precious.' And, she's been nothing less than a gift to me."

"You know, you should share this. You should write a column or something, like day-to-day accounts of your times with her, or like a children's book with your experiences together and how she's getting through the fight. So many people in Africa, here in America, and all around the world are being affected by this. I think it would serve as such a source of inspiration for so many people."

Rebecca sits more erect in her chair. "That didn't even cross my mind. That's a great idea."

Mimi becomes more excited. "And, all of the proceeds should go to fighting AIDS. You know with our resources, we can really do a lot for combating this crisis. You've got one of the leaders at home right?"

"I do. Angelina is so passionate about it. I'm so proud of her. She and her fellow UN Ambassadors fought so hard to get Dafina here. I know they'll do tremendous work when they get back to Africa in the winter."

"With you, her, and our resources working together, we can do some awesome stuff. And, we can get a lot of help from this too. What better way to show our commitment to better living and spirituality than something like this? It can't hurt our image."

"That's right. You know, whatever you've been smoking, I want to get my hands on some."

"I still need to keep that under wraps."

"Don't worry, I won't rat you out. You're just full of great ideas today."

"You know what, we shouldn't stop there. This could be a great springboard for kids' merchandise. A lot of our sales are skewing younger anyway—"

"That's true. Dafina loves the products and a lot of kids at Angelina's school still support us. It's died down with all the controversy; but, there would be a lot of posting on Instagram with the new designs."

"We can just have lines tailored to kids. We can even have baby clothes. I think Windows to the Soul needs to be more family-themed."

"These are the best ideas you've had in a long time."

"Thank you," Mimi says as she takes a nod. "I think this is one of the ways we can really get ourselves back on track."

"I think so too. I need to as well."

"Well, I'll let you get back to your e-mails. I'll see you later." Mimi skips out of Rebecca's office.

Rebecca's fingers resume their lightning speed on the keyboard. She suddenly stops and picks up the phone.

"Hi, could I speak to Dr. Chow? This is her client, Rebecca Lewis. Thanks."

"Hello?"

"Hi Dr. Chow."

"Hello! It's wonderful to hear from you."

"I bet you weren't expecting this."

Dr. Chow begins laughing. "I have to say I didn't. How have things been? Well I know they've been challenging as of late."

"They have; and, that's why I want to come see you. Let me start off by saying I'm sorry about how I stormed out last time. I was just being an idiot; and, I didn't want to admit to myself that I needed to work things out. But, I'm ready now."

"Well, I'm happy to hear that. When do you want to come in?"

"Actually, do you have any time today?"

"Today's a little busy; but, I can stay a bit later."

"I can be there by 7."

"OK, I'll see you then."

"Thanks so much Dr. Chow."

"Thank you. Take care."

Rebecca gets a call from counsel.

"A call from you or IT is rarely a positive thing."

"I can't say that this is positive."

"It's been all bad all the time Larry. I have to take this one too. What is it?"

"You have to testify in front of Congress next week, on August 7th. They want to investigate the supposed bribery that occurred with the openings of the Thailand and Malaysia stores. They're starting August recess on the 8th this year; and, they want to get you in before," Larry Berktram revealed.

"Are you serious? Haven't we all suffered enough? We endured two terrorist attacks; had over 100 of our customers killed (not to mention 50 more hurt); we had stores closed for weeks;…if we tried 'greasing any wheels' we obviously didn't add enough oil."

"We just need to say enough."

"Would we be able to run through this? I want a mock hearing, so I can be confidently fielding questions, and deflecting what they lob at me."

"That's part of the reason I called. Could we do some run-throughs on August 4th and 5th?"

"We have to. I'll be there. Could we talk around 6pm? I have to work on some things; but, I do need to fill you in on some details."

"Not a problem, I'll give you a call then."

"Thanks for being there Larry."

"You got a lot of support. I'm just one of the loyal soldiers. And, I'm happy to serve."

"You'll be in touch with Ed before the 4th? I effectively brokered this on my own. He had very little to do it. He gave a cursory look at the papers and basically told me where to sign."

"Where have we heard that before?"

They both laughed.

"I'm not that bad Larry. Is there any chance there will be indictments from this?"

"I have to review what you and Ed sent over (thanks for the zip files and the dummy e-mails…that helps to cover the paper trail); but, it doesn't smell like it. It should be like a Zuckerberg, we'll-drag-you-through-the-mud-for-a-day thing, and that should be it. The recent charitable donations, community events, and community outreach have helped too. I've been checking the feeds; and, there's been more 'they're helping a lot of people' and 'they helped me get care.' The goodwill is cropping back up."

"Thankfully. We've been going through our cash with all this. Those offshore accounts really started to kick in."

"Ha, let's be grateful that there was cash to burn through. I'll give you a call around 6pm."

"I'll talk to you then Larry. Thanks for being a good soldier, no for being a distinguished colonel."

"Happy to serve."

"Thanks."

"This is one of the days I'm happy I didn't call the driver in."

Rebecca has been going through scenarios, for next week's Congressional hearing, with Larry.

"You know I've been on 'hands-free'; I don't need any more legal problems."

"We don't. The sticking point is with the shell corporations."

"Can we credibly say that those were established to facilitate the transfers for the humanitarian donations, that was done to avoid red tape, and get it to those who needed it as quickly as possible. Can we say that we were just trying to expedite things—"

"We could. The transfers to the foreign ministers were done clandestinely enough. That hasn't been mentioned concretely. There's a specter, people are guessing; but, it hasn't been uncovered. We do want to hold off on further repatriation until this blows over."

"Of course. We've already made arrangements."

"And, the facilities in Asia are top-notch? They've been tending to survivors, we haven't had casualties…"

"No, we haven't. They give me updates every day. We replenish and send in reinforcements as soon as is needed. About eight to 12 families are being placed in permanent housing each day. It's a little bit of a slow start; but, we're picking up. We're making sure the shelters are manned and stocked for the individuals and families who are still waiting."

"And, we just have to emphasize the good work. We'll bring along testimonies from those on those ground. They're a few thousand miles away; but, those are the best 'character witnesses' we have.

We'll just lay off the transactions for now. I think we're fine. We'll drill into things a bit more with the run-throughs on the 4th and 5th."

"Sounds like a plan. I salute you Colonel Berktram."

"I salute you General Lewis. See you on the 4th."

"See you then."

"Wow, it seems like you had a breakthrough," Dr. Chow remarks as Rebecca reclines in the chair.

"I guess that's what it was. But there are some things I'm still trying to make sense of, especially the part with Denver and Angelina. It was so strange. I knew it was Denver sitting at the kitchen table; but, I didn't feel any kind of connection. There wasn't any familiarity there."

"Well, you probably feel like you don't really know him. He's your child and you love him; but, you don't know who he is."

"That's true; I feel that I'm just not a part of his life. And, when I tried to get closer to him, he just erected this glass wall around himself."

"It's a symbol of the emotional distance between you. You see him every day, and you're near each other; but, there's no real contact. You want to bridge that gap; but, you feel like he's not allowing it."

"Exactly. I really try Dr. Chow. We can talk about superficial things like how his game was and what he did in school; but, when I see something is bothering him, he doesn't want to share it with me. He's closer to his father; but, even then it's limited. Some kids in school beat him up and he didn't want to tell me. Out of desperation, I asked him some months back, 'Why don't you want to share your life with me?' And he says, 'You don't understand it.'

And, the unthinkable happened—he tried to end it."

"Denver tried to commit suicide?"

Rebecca nodded her head regretfully.

"That must have been absolutely devastating for you."

"You don't know Dr. Chow. I kept wondering to myself, 'How did this happen?'"

"How did he try?"

"He downed nearly a full bottle of vodka (he's about 118 pounds) from our cellar. We locked up all the alcohol now. And, he took 10 opioid pills. This was all at the house."

"How did he get the opioids?"

"*They were mine,*" Rebecca mouthed sheepishly.

"Did you have an accident? Why are you taking them?"

"I broke my wrist in the fall of 2017; and, my doctor prescribed Oxycodone. I liked the feeling; and, I felt it got through the day. I wanted to get my hands on more; but, I knew my injury wasn't serious nor was it safe to have other medications. I used alias to take out the other prescriptions. I was paying a pharmacist acquaintance of Peter's to write me additional prescriptions."

"Along with the Oxycodone, what other prescriptions were you on?"

"Vicodin and Percocet," Rebecca whispered with her head lowered.

"That's a lethal cocktail. He took all of them at the same time?"

Rebecca nodded her head contritely.

"He could easily have died. You could easily have died."

Rebecca looks back up. "I know."

"Are you still taking them?" Dr. Chow asks pointedly.

"They're also locked securely. Denver can never ac—"

"You need to stop."

"I'm not a junkie Dr. Chow. I'm not an addict."

"But, you feel like you need them."

"I—"

"You're high-performing, exceedingly functional, and consummately competent. But, you are an addict nonetheless."

"My performance has not been undermined."

"Your health has though. But, as a mom, I know what the worst thing is. Your son nearly died because of your pills, pills you didn't need."

Rebecca throws her head back.

"My dad was a functional alcoholic. Frighteningly, he was an accomplished pilot—never have an accident—but he was an alcoholic," Dr. Chow reflects.

"If I weren't popping pills, my kid wouldn't have attempted to take his own life."

"All addictions impact more than the addict. Why do you think you need them?"

"Dealing with breakneck changes at work, and the disconnection at home has been increasingly taxing. I can't make them go away; but, the pills helped to soften the pain, mask it. I found that vital."

"You can greatly alleviate the stress and anxiety. Completely eliminating it is unrealistic; but managing it is practical. Dr. Yellowleaf is among the best substance-abuse counselors in the City. You'll be seeing him and me from now on."

Dr. Chow texted Dr. Yellowleaf's number, e-mail, and office address.

"You'll start seeing him Wednesday, the 3rd."

"Maybe I'll finally 'get it' as Denver said I couldn't.:

"Maybe he meant something else by it."

"What do you mean?"

"Maybe he feels that you're not totally connected with life and its vitality as in feelings, emotions, and experiences. It may also mean identifying what is hard, and being pro-active about changing it—even when it may be uncomfortable…I know you want to do that now."

Rebecca is reminded of the passages she read in Denver's notebook.

"I guess I haven't been. He's so perceptive and intelligent. I think that heightened perception makes him feel even more when things aren't right. He's so sensitive; it's like he's carrying the world on his shoulders."

"Being very introverted and introspective, there is a lot of issues with which he's grappling and trying to work through. Even with his enormous intelligence, he's still a child and the cornerstone of stability in a child's life is his or her family. You're very busy with Windows to the Soul; Peter with his research; and Angelina is busy growing up and trying to save the world. Therefore, the family unit is more of a nebulous entity rather than something concrete. It's not tangible for him. Consequently, he feels alone."

"Angelina has grown up so much physically, emotionally and mentally. She'll be back in Africa in the winter. They'll go to Ghana, South Africa, Nigeria…"

"That's outstanding!"

"Yes it is. She just has this humanitarian spirit and drive. I'm so proud of her. But, then she appears like Janus in the dream, like two different girls."

"You feel like she's a different person now. You don't know her anymore."

"That's exactly how I felt a few months ago. I walk in on her phone-fucking, sorry, with a goodwill ambassador from her AIDS project who I found is her boyfriend—"

"How much of a shock was that?"

"It was an earth-shattering one. I just felt like I had lost it at that moment. This was my little girl, my little star student. Now the one I would go shopping and to the movies with is sucking cock. I'm sorry to make it so graphic but it just hit me like a Mack truck."

"That's understandable. And they're still seeing each other?"

Rebecca sighs.

"Yeah they are. I know it doesn't sound like the ideal situation; but, she's a mature girl and I know she needs someone older. They love each other; and, he's been a source of emotional support for her. Besides, I don't have to worry about paying for extra-curricular programs."

Dr. Chow laughs. "He's also standing in as a father figure in some ways."

"I know he is. And, I told her you can't build a healthy relationship on that; but, she insists that there's a lot more there. I knew the worst thing I could do was tell her that she couldn't see him. She'd find a way to do it anyhow and plus, I think there's a reason why they came into each other's lives. I need to let her learn the necessary lessons. After cautioning her, she's using protection and acting responsibly (I hope). And I remember in the dream, she was walking out the door; and, Chris was there to greet her. When they hugged each other, they became one. I'm wondering why I saw it like that."

"Well you said it; there's a reason why they came into each other's lives. You're giving them the space to figure that out."

"Maybe that's it."

"Peter was in the dream too right?"

"Yes, he was. It was strange. I walked into the bedroom and at first I saw my father lying in the bed. Then he became this kind of specter, flying away revealing Peter. And, Peter was there with the bed sheets in hand, wiping on his wedding ring. As he was cleaning, the ring would become tarnished."

"Infidelity."

"It was," Rebecca says sadly. "I walked in on him."

"Really?"

"Oh it was great. It should have been caught on tape."

"Did you just go crazy?"

"Yeah I did. I pushed her out of the bed, cursed at her… I totally went off on Peter. I think the worst thing about it is the kids saw some of it."

"That'll be traumatic for them."

"Yeah, I know and I would have done things differently; but, it was the heat of the moment and I couldn't hold back."

"It's difficult to in those kinds of situations. How long ago was this?"

"About two months ago, and the affair went on for about the same time."

"How bad has it been between you two?"

"Well we're still living together, that's a positive right?"

"How can you characterize it? Cold war?"

"I think that's the perfect way to say it. It's even hard for me to look at him. I've really been putting him through the ringer and he's been enduring it; but, I have the right to do that don't I?"

"Well you have the right to do anything, including the right to forgive."

"I know. My mom's been telling me that too and he's been really trying to make it up to me. I just cannot let go. I can't get over him hurting me like this."

"You can if you want to…You confirmed the affair after the backlash from the ad campaign, and the Southeast Asia scandals, right?"

"Yes, that's true."

"At that point, you must have felt everything was crashing down, since you identify so much with Windows to the Soul. He was the last thing you felt you could rely on, the rock. Unfortunately, that disintegrated as well. And, then the terrorist,attacks…Infidelity is painful for anyone; but, with all the crises, it's been especially painful for you."

"How do I get through it?"

"You know that you can't change the past; but, you can come to terms with it. You did that with your mother. You can do it with him too. You need to deal with those issues that are tearing you apart. Accept how Peter let you down; don't fight it. Accept your feelings about the sexual abuse. Accept how you have felt so alone so many times in your life.

That's what forgiveness really entails. Forgiveness is letting go of the pain. You don't forget what happened, nor should you; but, you take the past as a lesson, and look to the future. You realized that your mother was a tormented person, struggling with so many personal issues. You accepted that; and, that's how you forgave her. You have to do that with Peter. He's not perfect, no person is. You need to deal with your memory of Jake the same way. He was a flawed, complex man. If he had known better, he would have done better."

"It's going to be difficult; but, I have to."

"That's the right mindset; and, I'll help you with that. But most importantly, you have to forgive yourself. Forgive yourself for the feelings you had when you found out about the affair; for what you felt during the sexual abuse; for being distant from your kids; and everything else. You have to forgive yourself for being a human being."

"I do. You know I've really tried to be a good person, and to do what's right. But recently, it's like I've been getting it from all sides. I know God is there and I believe in Him, but I've been wondering why He's letting me go through this."

"I can't speak for Him; but, I can try to make an educated guess at best. Perhaps your belief is not as pure as you think."

"What? No Dr. Chow, I believe in Him very strongly, that's why I even have Windows to the Soul."

"I know, but God doesn't work for us; he's not an arbitrary leader. I believe everything we experience in our lives is a product of our deeds, spanning the whole of our existence. It's not a question of what He lets happen; it's about what has to happen based upon the destiny you've created. Perhaps you weren't leading your life the way you should have been; you lost your connection with Him. These happened to bring you on the right path."

"To bring me back to the Source."

"To bring you back to the Source. Exactly. I've had some very trying times in my life as well (we can talk about those later). After each crisis, I realized that I had grown so much and there was, at the very least, one great jewel that I could take away from it. I think you've already had some."

"Well the first thing that comes to my mind is this beautiful girl I've been blessed to have in my life, Dafina. She came here from Tanzania recently to get treatment for AIDS; and, I've fallen in love with her. She also has with me. Despite everything she's been through, she's the personification of optimism, goodness and true spirituality. We were talking about belief in God; well, hers is incredible."

"That truly is a jewel. Has she been improving?"

"She has been tremendously. She's gotten so much better."

"How long will she be here?"

"Initially, she was only supposed to be here till September; but, we've been able to keep her almost two months longer. I promised her that I'd keep her here as long as I can. I got a new Porsche and Corvette early in the year; but, I'm selling them. I wanted to put the money into Windows to the Soul; but, a lot of it will go for her medical care."

"That's heroic."

"I don't know if I'd call it that."

"Well, what else would you call it? I think it's fair to say she would have been dead by now if she hadn't had you to provide for her. Does she have family in Tanzania?"

"Her mother died of AIDS when she was very little. Her father died of AIDS. The disease has also afflicted many of her family members. Her family really has been ravaged by sickness and poverty. Now, we're the only family she has."

"You should adopt her."

"Wow. I mean I love her Dr. Chow, and I do feel like she's mine; but, I don't think I can take another child on. I'm not doing too well with two."

"Well, like all children, she'll be a challenge. But, you'll rise to the occasion. You can make time for her."

"I know this is so selfish; but, I can't take another child dying. She has a terminal disease; she may not be around that long. I'm already attached to her; but, I don't want to be even more so. I've been through that enough. I can't go through it again."

"Her condition is critical; but, the prognosis for AIDS patients gets better all the time. You know many patients are living for years now. Even if she doesn't have a lot of time left, you give her the love you feel everyday she's here. That will last her more than a lifetime. I think she's come to teach you how to live in the moment. Take that lesson."

—◦◦◦❯◉❮◦◦◦—

It is three minutes to 1am as Rebecca crawls into bed. She props her pillows against the headboard and lays her back against them. Her eyes close and she begins her now nightly meditation.

After collecting her thoughts, she sets her pillows down and slithers under the covers. She feels the urge to get up. Rebecca rises out of bed and starts walking down to the second floor.

The door of one of the bedrooms is open. Peter is sitting on the bed, writing. Rebecca knocks on the door.

"Hey."

"Could I come in?"

"Of course." Peter moves his books to the side to make room for his wife. Rebecca sits on the bed.

"What's going on?"

"You know Dafina, the girl Angelina and I have been visiting all the time?"

"Yes. I still haven't met her."

"You know how I've just fallen in love with her right?"

"Yes, I do. I know she's an adorable girl."

"Well, I want us to adopt her."

Peter looks at his books in reflection for a moment.

"She's a wonderful girl Rebecca; but, I don't know if we can handle that. Dafina is a child with special needs. She needs as much of our time as possible; and, with our schedules, I don't think we can provide adequately for her."

"I know, I was thinking the same thing; but, I see her almost every day anyway. We're paying most of her hospital bills; and, she calls me mom now. We can do this if we want to.

Besides, maybe she can teach us how to be parents again, and force us to be a family."

Peter bends his head back in deep thought.

"Well, from my years in medicine, I've seen miracles happen when people are surrounded by love. I know with you and Angelina's devotion, she's already done so much better...The prognosis for AIDS patients has drastically improved.

I guess we can. But, we're going to have to make a lot of changes."

"I know and that's another thing I wanted to talk to you about. Dafina is a brilliant girl, in all senses of the word; and, she deserves to be part of a wonderful family. Before we bring her in I want to make sure we work on us."

"I know things have been less than perfect these last several months."

"It goes back further than that Pete. Ever since I began Windows to the Soul, I've just drowned myself in my work. Around the same time, you were making great strides, and our home was left behind. Denver's trapped in his own frightened world. We almost lost him Peter."

"I remember that every day. I had never been so grateful for the CPR training."

"Thank you for saving our son."

"He's our child. I would never have let him go."

Rebecca takes a deep breath.

"And, Angelina's in search of love and affection, looking like a slut half the time... I mean we're losing them. We need to get our family back."

"I had no idea how badly Denver was doing. I was so dismayed when I found out that Angelina was having sex. I just keep asking myself, 'What happened?' It's as much my fault as it is yours.

Can we talk about the opioids? There's no way we're bringing another kid in if we don't handle this."

"You know I started with Dr. Yellowleaf Peter. I'm getting a handle on this."

"I don't see it here, and I've never seen it here; but, I don't know what you're doing in the office. How do I know you're not snorting lines there?"

"Peter!"

"I mean it. How did it get to that point?"

"I realized how much I relied on them after the wrist accident. They really got me through the day. The terrorist attacks riled me."

"They got me too."

"Over 100 people died at my stores. My stores!"

Peter closed his eyes.

"I have to deal with that for the rest of my life."

Rebecca continues before Peter could start.

"But, I promised myself I wouldn't become an addict."

"You were on three of the most addictive medications. Versace shoes or no Versace shoes…you're still an addict."

Rebecca uncharacteristically has no salvo.

"How long should it take the adoption to go through?"

"With all the support we've been giving Daf, things can be expedited. It can be finalized in four months."

"By December?"

"Yeah."

"So, we got four months to kick this."

Rebecca nods her head.

"You've been dealing with it. We've been surviving it. But, Dafina doesn't need any more. It's not fair to her."

"You're right Pete. December 3rd, I'm clean."

"We're drawing a line in the sand?"

"And, there's no negotiation."

Rebecca comes by Peter and opens the calendar to December 3, 2019 on her phone. She enters "CLEAN!!!!!!!!!" with a two-week reminder.

"Done."

"It's set."

She throws out two of the prescriptions from her bag. She leaves the Vicodin canister.

"I'm leaving this one; but, I won't get through the whole thing."

"You and I will tell Dr. Yellowleaf. That's a promise?"

"It's a promise."

Rebecca comes closer to her husband.

"It's not just my mess or the kids Peter. It's us too.

The affair blindsided me; but, that was just the culmination of this downward spiral. Meeting with Dr. Chow yesterday, I've really started to reflect on things… I think I need to tell you this."

"Tell me what?"

"I know I've told you how Jake hit us, was a drunk and abused my mother but he also molested me."

"He did what?"

"Yes, for six years. I've never really come to terms with it. I told myself early on that I'm not going to give myself totally to you because intimacy has been so hard. When I got so busy with Windows to the Soul, I used that as an excuse not to be as close. It was like a relief to me. I didn't want to feel like I wasn't in control, like that girl over 20 years ago."

"I had no idea."

"I didn't tell you because I wasn't comfortable with it, but I'm ready to deal with it now. The abuse wasn't the only source of pain; I got pregnant with him too—"

"Really?"

"I ended up losing the baby though. He beat me one night."

"Wow. I'm so sorry. And then you had the miscarriage with Anthony…"

"Right. And, because I haven't dealt with all of that, my relationship with Denver and Angelina has suffered…I've just been keeping everything—and everyone—at a distance. I think taking Dafina into our family will help me, force me, to deal."

"I think you call this an epiphany."

"It's been a long time coming. I've really started to think about things. I need to purify. She can't come into this."

Peter starts stroking his wife's arm.

"She won't. I promise."

Rebecca sits on the bed.

"We have to work on this too," Rebecca says as she moves her hands back and forth between the two of them. "I know you've been trying so hard; but, I haven't given you a centimeter."

"You have every reason not to."

"No, if I want a marriage I have to. I have to do it for us. Now, there's someone else to do it for. She may never experience that for herself; but, we can give her the next best thing." Rebecca takes a deep breath and turns her body toward her husband. "I just want to make a brand new start.

I forgive you."

Peter immediately embraces his wife. Tears wash both of their faces as they are warmed by each other's arms.

"Thank you," he whispers in her ear.

Rebecca rests her head on her husband's shoulder for a moment. She then turns her lips toward her husband's ear.

"Peter," she whispers.

"Yes."

"I want to feel again."

Peter releases his wife, holds her by the arms and looks starkly into her eyes. He stands up. He swoops his wife from the bed, carries her across his arms and walks up to their bedroom.

Peter and Rebecca could not wait for the bed. Rebecca backs the door shut. Peter's lips attack hers. Their tongues engage in a furious, passionate rhythm. He could feel Rebecca's heart beating ardently through her chest, hungering for the love that she had denied herself as he whips her nightgown over her head. The lace drops helplessly to the floor. Her chest is heaving. Ringlets of sweat stream down her body, feeling the passion that seemed impossible just hours before.

Their tongues unlock; but, they want more, crave more. His long tool thrusts toward the caverns of his wife's mouth, plumbing deeper and deeper each time, as if he could touch the surface of her soul.

Peter frees her mouth and moves toward her neck. Rebecca can feel his body pulsating as she rubs against his growing hardness. She closes her eyes and thrusts her head back while sensual, wet kisses move frantically down her neck, and strong hands firmly take her from behind.

He lays his wife down on the bed. His mouth besieges her breasts as their hardening orbs slide against his insatiable tongue. Firm, sweaty fingers race across her long torso, waiting to capture the throbbing beneath. She feels his finger probing her, piercing her increasing passion.

Peter slides his tongue up and down between her chest and begins to glide down her body. Rebecca bends toward him, letting him graze the insides of her folds and begin consuming her. Peter tastes, eats and savors her hardness as her rousing wetness moistens his lips. Rebecca arches, riding his tongue as it slides against her erect tool, throbbing in ecstasy. He probes her depths furiously as hot, desiring waves besiege his mouth.

She breaks from his grasp and lowers her wet body to the bed.

"I want you," she says breathlessly.

He takes her by her torso and turns her around, laying her flat on the bed. He straddles her as he takes his pulsating tool to the foot of her neck, slides it down the small of her back, and between her cheeks. Rebecca groans in anticipation as she kneels on the bed. She throws her arms back, wrapping them firmly around Peter. He pulls her in. She moves into him and he moves into her as she grows wetter and tighter—wanting him, needing him.

She escapes from his grasp for a moment and lies longingly on the bed. Rebecca pulls her husband towards her. Their bodies rock furiously as one, hungry to feel each other—merge with each other—again. Their spirits strain to burst through their passionate, sweaty bodies, to recapture that which they had lost. She could feel him, getting harder, beating within as his thighs rub against her body. Her tidal waves hasten his thrusts. He goes deeper each moment. He goes faster with each second. They are engaged in a lustful, titillating mambo choreographed by their union.

Peter releases his tool from the deluge. His wife—with heavy breaths—slithers toward him, eager to show him the depths of her love. She mounts on the stallion, riding it with ardent furor, coming down on him in rapturous abandon. Peter grunts in ardor as she pounds down deeper and deeper, flooding his shaft with fluid ecstasy. She could feel her husband bursting inside of her. Drops are coming from the floodgates.

Harder she came on him.

Deeper.

Harder.

Deeper.

Her husband roars in tempestuous surrender.

"Come on baby," she whispers seductively as she continues to give to him, feed him.

She owned him.

And, he owned her.

They are reaching climax, waiting to marvel at the love that consumed them, overwhelmed them.

He comes.

His power fills her, his devotion inundates her as in that moment she realizes that nobody could love her like this man could. Rebecca collapses atop her husband. Their warm bodies glisten as they bask in the light of what they had.

"It's my turn," Rebecca says to her husband with her eyes still lit by amorous fire.

She slides her tongue from her husband's neck down to the tip of her husband's shaft. As she seized her husband's pouch, she slithered and glided tantalizingly up and down her husband's full manhood. Rebecca relished her husband's anticipant throbbing pelting the back of her throat.

Dr. Lewis is heading into New York-Presbyterian Komansky Children's Hospital. He left the office an hour early.

"Hello Dr. Lewis. You're here for Dafina?"

"Hi Beth. Sure am. 605 right?"

"Yes," Beth nods as she hands Peter a "visitor" sticker.

"Thanks so much."

Peter mentally rehearses what he will say to Dafina when he meets her. Thrombectomies, neuroendoscopies, NIH presentations, proposing to Rebecca…those were nothing compared to this.

"Why am I feeling so nervous? It's just my daughter," he thinks as the elevator arrives at the sixth floor.

"And, why is this elevator taking so long to open?"

Room 605 is straight ahead.

Dafina is sitting up eagerly in her bed. She is scrolling through Angelina's Instagram posts from the UN Ambassadors event. Dafina is writing some new words and phrases in her trusted notebook—featuring a picture of the *Black Panther* cast, with an image of Dafina and Angelina doing the "Wakanda forever salute" superimposed, on the cover—as Peter walks into the hospital room.

"Mommy's husband!"

She catches the small smirk from Dr. Lewis.

"Sorry, Dr. Lewis." She did not feel comfortable calling a White man she had never met "daddy."

"The first one was fine. I've been getting used to that the last several years. Thanks for remembering I'm a doctor."

The joke registered on a subconscious level for Dafina.

"I've been waiting to meet you!" she exclaims with a bright smile.

"I have been too. I just wanted it to be the right time."

"It's always the right time Dr. Lewis."

"I got a little something for you."

Peter unveiled a plush, golden teddy bear. He almost forgot the doll. She is a rich mahogany with striking chestnut eyes, and Esperanza Spalding hair. Dafina is enthralled with all 18 inches of her.

"Thank you for the teddy. She's gorgeous. Did Mommy pick this out?"

"It's a custom doll. FAO (a huge toy store) showed me a design. I made a couple of changes, including the hair."

He and Dafina winked at each other.

"I did this one sort of on my own."

"These are the best gifts Dr. Lewis. Better than Christmas."

"You don't know how much that means. Do you like it here?"

"I do. Mommy and Angelina are wonderful. And, the doctors and nurses take such good care of me.

I can't wait to be in a home though."

"I've been in hospitals for about 40 years. You never get used to them."

Dafina nods knowingly.

"Do you have any family back in Tanzania?"

"My mom told me my dad was shot when I was two (my mom said); but, I believe he died of AIDS. My mom died of AIDS tol. I have a brother and sister. I hope they're OK. I miss them. They're healthy though."

"I hope you can see them soon too. Have you lost a lot of your family to AIDS?"

"My mom, my dad, cousins, older brother…yes, a lot. Even before my mom died—"

"How long ago was that?"

Dafina turns her head up, searching through her mind.

"Two years I think."

"And, you're eight right?"

"I turned nine last week," she says pointing proudly at the birthday cap on the counter.

"Happy belated birthday. Sorry I missed that."

"That's OK. I'm still getting gifts anyway," Dafina said sweetly.

"I think I got a late birthday gift myself."

"When is your birthday?"

"July 26th."

"I'll remember next time."

"How many of your friends were like you, having lost so many loved ones to AIDS?"

"All my friends had lost at least one person—mom, dad, brother. Some lost mul..mul…"

"Multiple," Peter finishes, shaking his head.

"Multiple. Thank you Dr. Lewis."

"I've never experienced that kind of loss. How do you and your friends do it?"

"So many people are going through it; so, you aren't by yourself. It's weird. Even before my mom died, I felt like an orphan."

"Yes, sadly, that's the right word."

"I knew she was going, and most of my family was gone. I wanted to be OK with not having her. It wasn't that bad though. Again, all my friends saw people dying.

God always takes care of us. He brought me here."

"That belief is what has gotten you through?"

"That is all I have."

"I know Mommy and Angelina are working hard to have you stay here. They're doing all that they can. You couldn't have two better people fighting for you."

"I know Dr. Lewis. I have people who love me. I can't feel alone."

"I wish I had your strength."

"It doesn't come from me Dr. Lewis."

Peter wonders if he can handle getting any more lessons from a nine-year-old. He checks his phone.

"Wow, I have to head back up."

He beams at Dafina as he takes his attaché.

"You didn't make my day; you made my year. Thank you."

"You slayed my life!" Dafina rejoices with impish amusement.

Peter smiles with surprised amusement.

"I saw it on Snapchat. I don't really know what it means; but, I figured I could use it now."

"It completely worked."

He gave Dafina a kiss on her forehead.

"I'll see you again soon."

"6:30 sharp."

"I told you I never have a problem getting up," Xavier says slyly.

"And, I told myself I'd stop walking into things."

"I totally teed that one up."

"I know."

"You wanna lay it on me?"

"It's really no big deal, I just wanted to get it out of the way, before the day started…you're now President of Windows to the Soul."

Xavier could not blink.

"You're not serious Becky."

"I'm actually more serious than I've been in a long time. I have to step away for a little bit; and, you'll be overseeing day-to-day operations. I'm still holding on to the CEO mantle—for now. If I'm harpooned on the 7th, this may be all yours. It's a PR, mental-health, and operational move. I also needed to leave things with someone who will manage with accountability."

"Thank you."

"You'll have 19% of shares on June 4th. I'm still majority shareholder."

"As it should be.

Look, we're friends. Are you certain you want to do this? Are you certain you need to do this?"

"Yes, to both. The contract is right here. I just wanted to make sure you'd accept."

"I accept. And, I promise you won't regret this."

"I know. That's why I made the decision. You'll be reintroduced to the Board on the 13th. You want to give them an overview of where you want Windows to go."

"I got some ideas; but, I'll have more by then."

"Alexander and Mimi are getting promoted to new executive positions. Daneca will be replacing you."

"She'll make a great COO. I had been thinking about expanding more into sports apparel and equipment. There will be significant overhead; but, I had been researching improving designs for helmets, and goggles for the U.S. National Team. We can work on structures that are more aero-dynamic and—"

"Glide more easily through the water. We would be working on the lens angle and materials. That could work."

"They could be nine-figure deals, and can give us a lot of exposure."

"The Insight line has the most advanced technology. That would be a good place to start. You're talking with R&D?"

"They had designs for the prototype. But, of course, I wanted to confirm it with you first."

"It has a lot of potential. We'll work on getting some early designs in for trials. If they're effective, we'll be front and center for the Championships. And, we'll be ready for training camp for the 2021 season. This would be better than the Superbowl ad."

"I'm thinking that too. So, I'll be able to afford one of those soon."

Xavier points at a penthouse overlooking Central Park.

"Yeah, 19%. Again, it's all about accountability."

"It's always been with me. Will it be like a 'Comey' thing?"

"You're talking about the Congressional hearing? Oh lordy no."

Xavier chuckles.

"They won't be preempting any shows. And, I don't think it's being streamed on Facebook. Now that you say it though, we should stream it on the website. Seeing a CEO implode on Capitol Hill is a main event."

"I honestly think you'll be fine. There isn't anything you haven't gotten through."

"I'm really tired of dodging bullets man."

"At least you're able to dodge them. This is just another test. You'll get you're A."

"I'd even be satisfied with an A- for this one."

Xavier smirks.

"No matter what happens, we got the Board meeting at 9am on the 13th; and, a new President will be unveiled."

"I'm ready. When will you get to DC?"

"I'll be there tomorrow night, on the 6th. I touch down at Reagan at 7pm. I would have left tonight; but, I have an appointment."

"It starts at 10am."

"Yeah, that's the schedule. Something tells me they won't be as punctual as you though. When's the last time a balanced budget passed?"

"Exactly. I wish I could text you insults—"

"That I could lob at Congressional leaders? They check devices; but, I got a few in arsenal. You know I got a two-minute fuse as it is."

"It's a thirty-second fuse on the best days."

They both enjoys belly laughs.

"Thanks for being there man."

"Thanks for this incredible opportunity. We got this."

"We got this."

XIV

Rebecca gets patted down before she is allowed to head toward the metal detectors.

I'm coming to testify…I'm not even going to think about a joke for that one.

She takes off her ivory jacket, and slightly zips down her sky-blue dress. She rolls up her three-quarter sleeves, trying to breathe before she enters the Chamber.

Rebecca raises her arms in the detector. She gives the guards a polite smile as she collects her possessions.

"It'll be nothing," a male guard whispers.

Rebecca checks her phone. She has 12 minutes before she needs to be in the Chamber.

"Sir, where is the ladies' room?"

"Just walk straight down the hall, make a left. It'll be the third door on your right."

"Thanks so much sir."

Rebecca walks stoically down the Capitol hallway. She quickly darts into the third door on the left, as if she is already trying to evade capture.

"I might as well practice the escape plan now."

Rebecca hops into a stall. She yanks at the door to ensure that it is securely locked.

Rebecca reaches into her purse, and extracts a pill vial full of white powder. She pops the vial open, and taps several ounces into the palm of her left hand. Rebecca snorts the ounces into her left nostril. She begins to tap some more into her right hand.

"It's bad enough that they think you committed bribery. Do you need to be a druggie too?" Rebecca asks with self-deprecating despair.

The CEO rubs her hands to disperse the powder, and then wipes them down with a wad of toilet paper. She looks at the repository bin in the stall.

"You're strong enough to be grilled in Congress. Are you strong enough to get rid of this?"

Strikingly diaphanous images of Angelina, Denver, and Dafina flicker through her mind. The image of Dafina was rivetingly ethereal. Two images of crowds at I See the Light stores emerge. Within seconds, they are engulfed in flames. The images pixelate and dissolve. The sound of Peter's stern, but comforting, voice plaintively asking "that's a promise?" reverberated through her head.

Rebecca closes her eyes, throws her head back, and lets out a deep sigh.

"You weren't before. Now, you have to be."

She drops the vial into the repository bin.

"Wouldn't thank make a great story? I hope they see this... 'Snorting and shooting up in Congress.' That may be the real reason the government shutdown dragged so long. Maybe TMZ can get wind of this."

Rebecca remembers to wipe her nose—just in case there are traces of her, she vows, last momentary lapse—which remain. She finally emerges from the stall.

A woman, about 26-years-old, with a chartreuse and lilac-striped hijab, walked into the bathroom. She spots Rebecca.

"Rebecca Lewis! Windows to the Soul!"

Rebecca smiles back. *Now I'm really happy I wiped my nose,* she thinks to herself.

Rebecca moves toward the hand drivers.

"Right, you're testifying today."

"I hope so," Rebecca mutters with some apprehensive resignation.

"I can only imagine it would be a tad nerve-wracking," the woman says as she moves her thumb toward her index finger, and closes her right eye.

"A tad," Rebecca echoes as she replicates the motion.

"I thought the ad campaign was ill-conceived myself, and the humanitarian work in the Southeast Asia was somewhat opportunistic, self-serving."

Rebecca manages a humble and chastened smile.

"It seems like the hearing is getting underway early. Tribunals in the ladies' room…who says they aren't attacking the deficit? The taxpayers will thank you."

The woman laughs and shrugs her shoulders.

"I do appreciate your candor. Please know that we've learned from the ad campaign. And, we won't make another mistake like that again."

"Oh, I know. I still wear your stuff."

The woman takes out a pair of onyx shades from her handbag.

"I was going to say, you don't need to worry. I think you're a symbol for a lot of women. I really appreciate the diversity at your company too."

"Thanks for that."

"Even if you pulled some strings, you helped a lot of people. And, being scared doesn't get you anywhere."

"Sometimes, anger can be just as unproductive," Rebecca concurs.

"These say, 'Fear will get you up, but only courage will get you through.'"

"I feel like I'm on "Meet the Press" now."

The two women laugh again.

"Thanks for throwing my words back at me, and reminding me of them. That's true; and, I'll keep that in mind through the next hours. Thanks for the pep talk."

"I think I have one."

The young woman starts.

"The measure of a woman is not the number of times she stumbled, but the number of times she got back up."

"I actually like that. Do I need to give you royalties?"

"Could I get some swag for now though, maybe some free shades?"

Rebecca immediate gives hers to the woman.

"Come with me into the Chamber, and watch, at least, for a little while. DM me on Twitter. Give me your contact info, and we'll send you a case. Let me know how I did okay, and what more Windows to the Soul can do. Again, it's different now."

The young woman beamed.

"We gotta hurry up, or I'll be held in contempt."

The women hustle into the Chamber. Rebecca's new friend takes her place near the back. Rebecca moves toward the chair behind "Mrs. Lewis." Larry, Ed, and Ira are sitting beside her. Peter got in about a half hour ago, and is now sitting behind his wife.

"Good morning Mrs. Lewis."

"Good morning Senator."

Rebecca begins with her statement.

"Windows to the Soul was founded in 2008, the year of the historic downturn. The intent was, and continues to be, to create fashionable eyewear and accessories that do more than brighten up any outfit, or even grant a new perspective on even the most challenging day. The drive is to help the public, average people, to integrate spirituality, practically and fashionably, into their everyday. Through words of insight and versatile designs, individuals could gain some of the direction and focus they need to power through their day, take full advantage of moments, and surmount obstacles.

However, those words are more than PR or catchy slogans. It powers every facet of our operations, and motivates our neighborhood outreach. Our production is 90% sustainable, the highest level of any eyewear company currently. We will attain 95% sustainability by 2024. Fifteen percent of our net income is donated to charities including those providing medical support, educational assistance, and environmental protection, here in the States and internationally. We conduct at least 30 health and wellness screenings, with a focus on eye health, around the country, to ensure we do our part in helping all Americans get the medical support they need, regardless of socioeconomic status and level of advantage. Additionally, we have awarded over $8 million in scholarships to deserving high-school and college students; and, we will increase scholarships by 4% per year through 2022. The growth rate will be increased to at least 7% thereafter. With developing alliances, we'll soon be creating products that meet specialized eyewear needs. We began with a concentration on the eyes; but, now, our focus is on the whole community.

We have been spreading our international reach, particularly in the last 18 months, making efforts to be among the first organizations present during times of need and tragedy. With our growing presence in Southeast Asia, we were ready and willing to intervene when the disastrous typhoon struck. We helped in establishing mobile clinics, marshaling relief workers, and getting survivors into permanent housing. We are also playing an integral role in rebuilding battered communities. The expeditiousness of these efforts, coupled with our efficiency in establishing market share in the region, has raised suspicion. Accusations of bribery, money laundering, and other acts have been made, despite the thousands we have helped, and continue to help, at this very moment. These accusations are untrue, categorically untrue, and insult the integrity of every man and woman in our organization, along with that of our devoted, tireless partners on the ground. All we have strived to do is assist. That our dedicated intentions are now being questioned is at the very least disillusioning. Nevertheless, we will stay true to our mission of helping the world see the light, and continue our humanitarian efforts.

I, and the whole Windows to the Soul team, are grateful for this invitation to Capitol Hill; and, the opportunity to dispel any notions of graft and impropriety."

Rebecca now scans all the leaders in the Chamber.

"Our company has fostered too much goodwill and spent too many years building the trust of our customers and our partners to squander it through illegal acts and underhanded dealings with foreign governments. Such acts are against the law, and, just as importantly to us, they are against our values.

Today, we strive to clear the air and put a definitive end to these rumors. Thank you."

Rebecca is feeling more confident. Her hands are still shaking subtly (they have since she has reduced the number of pills she takes each day). She rests her hands strategically in her lap.

The senator from Missouri starts.

"Malay Skies, an organization registered to Windows to the Soul, LLC began operating just three days after Typhoon Pakpao struck. The company had no sales, and the products or services are still unknown. However, the equivalent of $3 million passed through the account, directly to the Thai government, four days after the hurricane hit. What is the nature of Malay Skies?"

"Senator, we, like all of you, were seeing the mounting death toll. We knew certain areas, especially rural regions, with little infrastructure, were particularly in need; and, we had to act quickly. Whether it was distributing food, disseminating medical supplies, or expanding shelters, time was of the essence; and, the Thai people could not wait. We wanted to avoid red tape and ensure that funds were received expeditiously. Malay Skies was established to facilitate finds transfer, and distribution to local charities that were working tirelessly on the ground."

"To whom did those funds go?"

"The roughly three million went to the Ministry of Public Health and the Ministry of Social Development, and were distributed afterwards. It bears mentioning 3,200 families were placed in permanent housing; 50 mobile clinics were established; and 400 more relief workers were hired within a week of those funds being distributed."

The senator from Washington begins.

"There have been tight repatriation controls in Southeast Asia. There are often 'probationary' periods, lasting years, which limit funds released. You seem to have skirted all of them. What was behind that?"

"Thank you for the question. I would like to underscore that there has only been one transfer, which was scheduled months before Typhoon Pakpao struck. Conditions were set not only regarding the time of transfers, but also the minimum amount required for transfers to be initiated, along with the limits, the maximum amounts, for transfers. The Thai stores had near record revenues during those first few weeks; so, transfer requirements were met and the 'ceilings' for transfer amounts were being approached. The Thai government did not relax repatriation policies for Windows to the Soul. They actually drove quite a hard bargain. The repatriation was made on account of promises for ongoing community development, namely schools and hospitals in under-resourced and under-served areas. Some of these projects are underway now; and, the rest will be underway as infrastructure is resuscitated.

Moreover, a sizable portion of that transfer—and again, only one— was ploughed back into relief and humanitarian efforts in the country. As with Malay Skies, this was also an effort to help in directing funds, and ensuring they went where they were needed most. I would like to underscore, again, that no graft occurred. Measures were taken to ensure efficient distribution of funds."

The senator from Massachusetts begins.

"There have been questions about the spike in charitable contributions and outreach, as you call it, with Windows to the Soul as of late. Your organization has been accused of trying to distract from the bribery accusations, and these are surface efforts. How do you ensure the accountability of these campaigns?"

"Thanks for that question as well Senator. There has been a curious confluence of events in the last 18 months or so. Amid these disasters overseas, and also at home, Windows to the Soul was experiencing strong growth—the strongest growth in the company's history. Sales had grown over 30%, on average, annually over the past five years. And, with some key media deals, we were poised for more expansion. Simply, we had the cash to finally get involved as much as we had always wanted to. As sad as we were about the effects of disasters and the wreckage left in their aftermath, we were grateful for the opportunity to make a difference.

And, just as we hold our operations to the highest levels of accountability, we do the same for our charitable efforts. We are in constant contact with local partners to ensure needs are being served. We also have a number of stringent metrics—across distribution, supplies and material received, and money spent—upon which staff is judged, at the end of efforts. The first priority is helping those in need; and, the second priority is recognizing staff that met, and exceeded, established goals. Promotions in our organization are also based on the quality of humanitarian work. Eighty-five percent of communities in which we have invested are at least 75% rebuilt; we have helped over 15,000 individuals and families gain vital eye care; and, we have aided in protecting over 160 sites across 15 countries. We have held ourselves accountable; and, we are proud of our record."

The senator from Oklahoma starts.

"Windows to the Soul is just the latest company to violate the public's trust, and privacy, with the recent hacking. Why did this happen? Despite everything, you all seem to be having a banner year; so, you have the funds. Why weren't better precautions taken?"

"Thanks for the question Senator. The hack pained us as much as it did our customers Senator. Frankly, it surprised us too, as we thought the measures we had been taking were sufficient. We had the firewalls, we had the multiple levels of verification, we had fortified the servers… we thought we did all we need to do. Then, the hack happens. The IT team is more cognizant of the changes than I am; but, we added filters to the servers to check nefarious traffic, expanded our array of alternate servers, narrowed authorizations for the site, and taken other effective measures in the aftermath to prevent this kind of insidious, backdoor attack from happening again. Cybersecurity is not a one-off. Just as government, and government officials, have to stay vigilant regarding threats each day, private organizations, like Windows to the Soul, must keep close watch daily, and with every moment. We have a superb team; and, they are even more watchful now. We have redoubled our efforts."

The senator from Georgia starts.

"Your company has put on a face for years, saying you're here to 'enlighten' humanity, 'bring people to the light,' and other hoo-ha. The ad campaign shows the public welfare was the last thing you care about it. Hell, the hacking shows you don't even take your customers' confidentiality seriously. With that record, why should we believe there wasn't chicanery in Southeast Asia? Why should we believe you 'fortified' your IT against another attack? Simply, why should we believe you? There's a whole lot of fluff here. Your words seem just as cheap as your shades."

"There was a lot there Senator. Thanks for making your thoughts known. First of all, let me address the impugning of our shades…our sunglasses have been recognized as 'highest quality' three years in a row by The Vision Council. If our words are as good as the quality of our shades, we're actually in fine shape sir. I would even say, confidently, that our words are better than the quality of our shades; and, that's saying a lot."

A few senators smirk.

"Now, to more pressing matters. Our record is the best testimony to our ideals and values. As was already stated, the organizations were established in Malaysia and Thailand to facilitate the distribution of funds, and to ensure resources reach those, who were in dire need, quickly. Just this week, we have already granted $75,000 to a number of deserving charities; and, it's only Wednesday. I have to say, we never claimed to 'enlighten' people or 'bring them to the light,' as you put it. We only strive, and have always strived, to help people connect to their spirituality in a practical; stylish; and, ideally, inspirational, way each day. From the feedback we get from customers every day, the way our designs have been embraced, and how passionate our customers are about helping us in our humanitarian work and serving the cause, we've done that. I am trying to dispel the doubts; but, if you have questions about me, you could look at our record, and how we have responded to our customers. Again, we're all very proud, and will remain proud, of that."

The senator from Utah starts.

"That abysmal ad campaign, where you used footage from wildfires, September 11th, what have you. How much money did you all make from that?"

"Senator, I think if we could calculate how much money we generated from an ad campaign they'd be charging companies even more."

Muffled laughs emerge from the panel.

"Actually, if I may, the better question may be, 'How much did we *lose* from the campaign?' I can't tell you that definitely either; but, I am certain it was millions. However, the loss to the bottom line is not what hurt. It was the trust our customers lost in us. We're just now rebuilding that.

It's been a difficult, but instructive, year. Our customers' well-being is paramount; and, faithfully honoring the memories and legacies of their loved ones is instrumental to that. We lost sight of that principle with the ad campaign. We will forever regret it. And, we will never dishonor our customers again."

The senator from Massachusetts begins.

"There's been a lot of uncertainty with coverage; and, many young families, especially in my state, are grappling with losing vision plans and eye-care coverage. Could we coordinate?"

"Thank you Senator. We have a number of partners in Massachusetts. We'll follow up with your office, and see what could be arranged."

"Her shades won't be the only freebies. They'll all be calling me tomorrow," Rebecca thought. *"That's cool; we'll make sure we get some kickbacks and tax breaks out of them then. And, they better keep it on the dl."*

The senator from Pennsylvania begins.

"My office will be following up with Windows to the Soul as well Mrs. Lewis. Let me ask, 'What is the biggest regret you have from the last two years?'"

"The ad campaign; the hacking; and, the dishonoring of our customers—and the rancor, resentment, and violence that sewed—all have to be up there. But, as proud as we are of the work we're doing, everyday we consider what we didn't accomplish. We think about the individuals and families across the country and internationally that we still haven't helped, those who still need our services. Right now, we're pushing our eyeware designs, in particular, toward better fulfilling medical needs. We want to be more than the ones who gave you the coolest shades you've ever worn in your life. We, literally, also want to be the ones who enhanced your vision. Until we reach everyone, across the globe who needs our services, we'll always have regrets."

Fifteen more senators await to ask Rebecca questions. She is actually looking forward to it.

—∘∘◦❧◦∘∘—

"You came off really well," Xavier said with relief.

"No, I think *we* came off really well."

"It almost became an infomercial after a while."

"There were some softballs there for sure. I think they just started to shift to how much money they could get out of us."

"How many have been calling us?"

"Ha, we've gotten inquiries from 25 states so far. The team told me some of them started calling as I was still answering questions. You'll be fielding some of those requests later this week. Daneca will help."

"Do you really need me to be president?"

Rebecca chuckles.

"It's all about delegation man. But, we're getting something, or a lot, out of these. We're not signing any checks until we get ironclad assurances of kickbacks and some tax breaks. And, they better be undercover. You scratch my back, I scratch yours. But, I'll ride you."

"That's the way you've always liked it."

The current Windows to the Soul CEO is shaking her head.

"Hey, I'm 19% remember? I can say crap like that."

"You actually *always* said crap like that."

The two are about two feet from the Board room.

"Let's do this," Rebecca says with anticipation as she gives Xavier a motivational squeeze on his shoulder.

"Good morning everyone."

"You survived," a board woman jokes.

"I did. Our stock rose 25% at close."

"What are we doing about the state requests?"

"We're making sure we get ours. I was just telling Xavier that we won't write out any checks until we get assurances, ironclad, of kickbacks and tax breaks. They wanted to rake us through the coals. We're still not getting burned. But, we'll make sure we keep details of the deals under wraps. We don't need to destroy any of the goodwill we've been working so hard to rebuild.

I've done more than enough talking these last several days. It's time you hear from our new president, Xavier Marx.

"New president?" The Board asks with some doubtful curiosity.

"Yes, new president. I need to step back a little bit. My hands will still be firmly at the wheel; and, we'll be keeping the momentum going. Now, I have a more than a worthy co-captain."

"Do we really need to make this change? You got through the hearing, by many accounts, with flying colors. The controversies have died down. We need someone experienced at the helm."

"Personally, I need to Richard. But, I did not make this decision without a lot of thought and care. Again, I'm still firmly here; and, Xavier is more than experienced. He has been with us for 12 years, since we were in our virtual office. He has been at the forefront of all our key initiatives and expansions."

Xavier gets in.

"I've served as COO for nine years. We've never posted a loss. This would have been a disastrous year for us. But, even with all the 'scandals,' we'll bring in more than $200 million with a margin of just under 32%. That has to do with the vision Rebecca has always set, and the skilled team she has assembled. I'm a key part of that."

"Have you ever run a sales division?"

"I authorize all product expansions that are proposed, and coordinate with Marketing and Sales in monitoring performance and setting strategy. Rebecca and I have final say on all product decisions. It's been that way for nine years."

"What is the highest number of staff you have ever supervised?"

"As COO, again what I've been doing for almost a decade, 128 employees are under my control. Are there any other interview questions?"

"What is your experience with budgeting and forecasting, and how precise have your projections been?"

"Rebecca, I, and the finance team have always worked hand-in-hand on creating projections, since my term began. I have also played an integral role in control activities, specifically assessing by how much we have underestimated or overestimated expense items, and by how much we have surpassed, or failed, to meet projected revenue. Variances, since my term began, have averaged 4%."

"Where do you plan to take the company's market focus? Do you want to continue to focus on younger, upper-middle-income consumers, or were you considering pivoting to a more urban customer base?"

"Well, that's an obvious question. Being that I'm Black, urban is the only way to go. And, to make sure we 'blackify' Windows to the Soul, we'll make sure all our models come in only the brightest colors. I declare today—75% of our models will be screaming yellow exclusively. Oh, and for Christmas, we'll release special edition models that have 'nigga' on the side. Oh, and we'll have a few that have 'OG' on the side too. It'll be 100% negro up in here…we'll start production tomorrow."

The Board is aghast.

"And, you believed all that because I'm Black (and Black people usually say crap like that). No, we'll continue pursuing a diversified market of up-and-coming, and upper-income clients. Next."

"How would you define the Windows to the Soul customer? Do you think you understand them, relate to them?"

"Being that I created over 65% of the Windows to the Soul designs during our first two years, and those designs continue to be some of our best-selling, yes, I have an intimate understanding of our customers. The Windows to the Soul customer is forward-looking, stylish, and spiritual, wanting to be connected to that which is beyond himself or herself while still having feet firmly on the ground. Our customers are also decidedly unpretentious, but undeniably chic; so, our subtle, unobtrusive, but standout, designs are ideal fits. I am one of those millions of customers. Before I authorize an idea, I ask myself, 'Would I wear that?'"

"How will you lead? How will you get others to follow you?"

"Again, 128 people are under my supervision. I do that each day. What I will continue to do is emphasize our values of foresight, creativity, and quality. And, I'll add one more to that—sustainability. Our manufacturing will be 100% sustainable no later than 2027. However, we're on track to meet that standard significantly before. I'll continue to remind the team that we have experienced extraordinary growth, and weathered some tumultuous storms, because we have created a product that defines a state of mind, and, idealistically, will help customers, reach a new state of being. The staff come here every day knowing that they are helping to add a higher-minded and haute couture splash of the spiritual to customers' daily lives.

Plus, it's nice riding a winning horse. We'll be the biggest eyewear brand by 2026."

"The company is facing a lot of challenges, and there are a lot of changes in the eyewear industry. How will you ensure the company adequately responds?"

"What we have to ensure is that we stay on the pulse, stay cognizant of our customers' needs. Perhaps, even more importantly, we have to anticipate our market's future needs and preferences, even before they realize them. The focus on leading-edge designs will continue to enable us to respond to the market demand in a differentiated way. Along with continuing to provide refined, statement designs, we have to maintain our low expense growth, which we have over the last five years, so we have the margins, which yields the cash, that is required to pivot quickly, be nimble, and respond optimally, especially relative to other leading providers."

"And, to piggyback on that, how do you plan to consistently stay engaged with the target customers, and our key markets?"

"We'll use many of the traditional methods including surveys and focus groups; but, our chief intent on social media will be more focused, namely getting feedback from customers on color, shape, design, context (where do they wear models?), and other issues. We'll give customers incentives for offering feedback (which must be redeemed within a week). Whether it's taking a selfie with a favorite design or highlighting a design that always gives you confidence, or sharing personal stories about 'adventures' while wearing Windows to the Soul gear—or anything us. We'll always keep the channels of communication open. Through the triumphs, and the travails, our customers have never been shy about letting us know they're feelings; and, we've always been responsive."

"You're saying all the right things Xavier. Nevertheless, branding is important; and, maintaining the face of our company is a requirement that can't be compromised?"

The board member turns.

"Rebecca, how public will he be?"

Rebecca is taken aback by the question, actually nearly all the questions. For the first time in nearly a decade, she is seeing how her Board truly is.

"As public as I've been—"

"Is there an issue with the presentation?" Xavier asks Lisa boldly.

"I just wonder if it accords with the brand."

Xavier beats Rebecca to the punch.

"Please elaborate. How might I not accord with the brand?"

"Well, we're really expanding the customer base now; and, we don't want to alienate key customers. We don't want them to think that Windows to the Soul has become—"

"Oh, let me finish it for you—an 'urban' brand. That would be the only reason why a young, Black guy would be promoted to president."

The Board becomes obstreperous.

"Why does it always come down to that?"

"It does because you all—can I say that?—you all always make it about that. Would you have doubts about someone else?"

"This is a major decision; and, we have to do our due diligence. We have to ask questions."

"Of course you do, and of course you should. Ask about strategy, numbers, what I'm bringing. Inquiring about how I may damage the brand is somewhat insulting."

"Let's start doing that then," Rebecca inserts plaintively.

"Fine, what are some of your plans."

"We'll expand our prescription eyewear offerings 24% by the end of the second quarter next year. We'll be offering customized eyewear with leading-edge, and some of the most durable, designs. Windows to the Soul will be among the fourth largest prescription eyewear providers by June 2021, and will catapult over current leaders soon after. Additionally, we'll be expanding out wearables segment, namely our watches, by 13% within the first quarter. R&D is refining the retinal scans for security controls and optimization. We'll have the enhanced sunglass designs available in a week, and can make substantial sales during the rest of the summer season. And, Rebecca and I were just discussing this a few days ago. Extending our athletic alliances can really help us diversify, and, most importantly, fortify the bottom line. We're working on improved helmet designs, that are more aero-dynamic and improve peripheral vision, for the NFL. We're also working on new designs for goggles for the swim team—a more fluid structure, if you will—that helps water glide more quickly and easily off, and can aid in giving swimmers better focus. Designs are still being refined; but, these are potentially high, nine-figure deals. With our growth now, we're on track to cross the billion-dollar threshold by 2023.

Aside from eventually making us the premier eyewear brand, we'll have the cash to fund our humanitarian projects. I'm not just taking about out overseas projects. We'll likely have requests from all 50 states by the end of this meeting."

The Board members chuckled.

"Actually, I think we've already gotten that," Rebecca adds. "We may have gotten about $200 million in kickbacks too. Please tell me all the phones were checked."

The board members nod.

"We had a path before," Rebecca said. "Now, we're charting a course."

"The work from R&D sounds promising. Thanks for the overview Xavier. I hope there weren't any misunderstandings."

"Oh, not at all. I hope you also know where I stand now."

"Oh, we do," Lisa says with some trepidation.

"Do you want me to fire the Board," Rebecca scribbles on the notepad.

"No need," Xavier writes in response. "They just needed to know I wasn't a coon."

Hello. I'm Rebecca Lewis, the CEO of Windows to the Soul. The last time I came to you like this, I was apologizing for missteps, and dishonoring you, our loyal customers, and, in many ways, Windows to the Soul's values.

Now, I'm coming to you asking for your cooperation. You have supported us throughout these years, through the triumphs and challenges, because you all believe, as we do, that everyone of us should be able to see the light. We ask you in helping us fulfill that, yes, vision. Forty-four cents of every Windows to the Soul sale, from February 8th through March 18th will go toward funding life-changing laser retinopathy treatments for needy children. We aim to cover 2,500 surgeries."

"That's nearly $28 million. Hi, I'm Xavier Marx, the President of Windows to the Soul. It's a tall order; but, there is no challenge that this community has not been able to meet. And, we know when it comes to someone in need, we're all even more motivated. Please log on to the website now, or go to your nearest I See the Light store, to help the cause. You can even buy shades for families, with a few words of encouragement added, as a customized gift. From now till March 18th, know that every sale will not only be helping you see the light; it'll help you serve as a guiding light to someone else."

"We're doing this together. We got this because we got you. Thanks for being the world's greatest customers. And, now we can help some deserving children get the world's greatest gift. Thank you."

Angelina is seeing the ad before she watches the Ariana Grande video on YouTube.

"There have been a lot of celebrities on Instagram with their I See the Light shades and gear. Have you been seeing a spike in sales?"

"We're on track to reach $28 million. The campaign has been running for a week and we're 40% there. Xavier's and Daneca's idea about 'classing-up' the bargain shades has really been a boon. Over 40% of sales have been coming from the under $60 models."

"And, everybody's excited about this. The picture book with Dafina will be helping the retinopathy effort too right?"

"Yeah, 100% of proceeds from that will go towards the surgeries."

"She was so excited about helping out. I'm happy Random House was able to rush it out in time for the drive."

"Me too. Do you need more volunteers for the Jackson Heights event?"

"We needed about 30 more, and the confirmations are coming in on Facebook. We should have all of them in by 8pm tonight. All the volunteers will be bringing a book, and participating in the dramatic readings. We're still working on creating a production the kids can put on too. They're coming up with some good ideas. We'll have the script before two weeks, and start rehearsals."

"And, the volunteers will be serving as reading tutors at the schools too, right?"

"Yeah, about 60% will be helping out weekly, and the rest will be there twice monthly. Everybody wants to pitch in. I'm happy we're doing more stuff in the City now."

"We need to. We can do the Jackson Heights event again around Christmastime. We should plan something similar for the Bronx. Let's see if we can get local bands for both."

"That's a great idea. We can have a live soundtrack for the kids' productions."

"And, live house music the whole night. I wish I had that when I was a kid."

"When's the new opening for the opioid treatment center on Staten Island?"

"The authorizations are coming in now. We're on track for May 14th. We wanted to make sure we were up-and-running when the college kids get out."

"Yeah, since it's by the Ferry, it'll be conveniently located for anyone in the City too. I definitely want to be there with you at the opening."

"I wouldn't do it, and couldn't have done it, without all your legwork."

"So, are we still confirming all the travel dates for the summer."

"That's a go too. We'll be in Nigeria from July 2nd to July 13th, Kenya from July 14th to July 22nd, South Africa from July 23rd to August 2nd, and Tanzania from August 3rd to August 12th."

"And, we're getting Dafina's sister and brother!" Angelina exclaims clapping her hands.

"Dad and Denver are so excited about the trip."

"I know. It'll be a service trip for all of us. Your dad has wanted to get more into relief work. This will be an excellent introduction.

And, we get new members of the family. We're just adopting now. My 47-year-old ass is not popping out any more kids. I'm still wondering how I got this."

Angelina cocks her head to the side with raised eyebrows as Rebecca cradles her belly. She is eight months pregnant.

The two women pull into the drive way.

"Damn, I have to post for the column. I'll be including a few excerpts from the picture book.

Rebecca hurries, gingerly, to the couch and picks up her laptop.

"Hi everyone," she says, hardly making contact. She starts typing feverishly.

Rebecca has been writing the "Coming into Focus" column since November of 2019, in which she documents her experiences with Dafina. The column is carried weekly, in print and online, in over 40 periodicals across the country. There are an estimated eight million readers. She and Dafina are Instagram stars as well. Their joint column has over three million followers.

"Hey Dafina, could you check Mommy's post?"

Dafina skips over.

"You should add a line about the new HIV drug that'll be released in September. You want that to be on the radar. I saw the doctor from the study on the news yesterday. It looks like it'll be a real gamechanger."

"Thanks so much for reminding me. I made the note on my phone, but I didn't check it before I started. Thanks so much baby."

"I didn't even know you all got back," Peter says with a warm smile.

"Hey love."

Peter wraps his right arm around her shoulders and caresses her full belly with his left. At her foot lies the manuscript for the next children's book she is writing with Dafina. Rebecca and Peter are discussing writing a memoir about their relationship, and weathering marital storms.

The unexpectedly balmy February air lures the family outside. Rebecca's brothers and their kids soon become rapt in a football game. Rebecca, Angelina, Dawn, and some of the other relatives sit at the table under the sprawling tree, engaging in colorful conversation. Denver sits on the patio with one of his older cousins. The two young men begin an impassioned conversation about politics. Denver begins writing furiously in his notebook as he nods his head. They may be able to solve the world's problems within the afternoon.

The laughs of Greg, Tom, and Michael ring through the backyard. Rebecca and Peter bring out some more sandwiches and burgers for the group outside.

"Hey guys, I never thought I'd see the day Rebecca would put on some weight," Greg says to his two brothers. They laugh in unison.

"I'm still waiting to see the day you'll lose some," Rebecca retorts back. The other two brothers let out an "ooooo." Greg gives her a playful punch on the shoulder. Dawn catches it as she walks toward the kitchen.

"Don't do that Greg; she's eight months!" Dawn exclaims out of motherly instinct.

"It's OK. We're just playing around," Rebecca says trying to calm mother.

"So, when's the family leaving for Africa again?"

"The first week of July. Oh mom, the Seavers, the Dixons, and the Robinsons will be over so we have to go shopping tomorrow."

"Sure."

Peter brings his wife's attention to the TV. "Let's see if they talk about you guys."

"So Ken, what's your pick for the company to watch?"

"I have to say Windows to the Soul. The major faux pas with the ad campaign and the relief effort seems like ages ago; and the no frills, sincere ad featuring CEO Rebecca Lewis and President Xavier Marx has being doing wonders. It looks like they'll reach their $28 million goal before mid-March, and enjoy a late boost for first-quarter sales. There's also been a lot of buzz about the new kids' lines they've recently unveiled and 'Greener Pastures' has really been picking up steam with its organic materials and eco-friendly production process. Plus, they're unveiling enhanced equipment and eyewear for the NFL and U.S. swim team. Rebecca has come out saying she's committed to fully embracing all the company stands for, and has seemingly been through this tremendous personal metamorphosis.

On top of all that she's expecting a child; adopted a little African girl who's suffering from AIDS; and has gotten more involved in charity work—including the fight against AIDS, education, disaster-relief, and a whole host of efforts—all toward living more in line with the Windows to the Soul principles. It's really resonating with the public. With all of that going on, she's going to be working a little bit more behind the scenes; Marx has been doing a great job marshalling the troops, and he's been bringing some top people in."

"They've done some major overhauling too right?"

"Definitely. They've done some supply-chain shuffling, which has really allowed them to cut costs; pulled back on some expansion plans; and redesigned their engineering methods, helping the bottom line stay in the black. Plus, they have some really sexy designs coming out that my wife and her friends are excited about; so, that's a good sign."

The panelists chuckle.

"2021 has started off strongly. The surgery drive has really boosted sales, as mentioned. $600 million is well within reach by the end of the year. Those Congressional hearings are also a distant memory. They went without incident. Actually, she started looking way better after that. They're definitely back on track."

"When does it look like they'll crack a billion?"

"Guidance is saying 2025, but they can do it in 2024. They're really feeling the momentum now. The market's back on their side."

Peter kisses his wife on the cheek. Dafina runs into the house. She plants affectionate kisses on her mother and father. A Windows to the Soul scarf graces her head. She squeezes beside Peter and Rebecca.

"You like your scarf?"

"No, I *love* it."

Dafina goes to her mother, and nestles up to her.

"Let me read what it says!"

"Please do," Rebecca says.

She unties her scarf, lays it out on her lap and prepares for her recital.

"The journey begins where the wandering ends."

"That was beautiful."

9 781949 723946